Julian, valet and occasional bodyguard to a literal fairy tale prince, wants nothing more than to keep her job. However, that entails keeping anyone from finding out that she's female.

Prince Alberic, tall, blond, gorgeous, and more than a little sadistic, is not the only one of very few people aware of Julian's secret, but he fully intends to take advantage of it by making her his secret mistress—whether Julian wants to be one or not.

Ordered by his father the King, Prince Alberic and Julian take off for Lyoness and a Unicorn hunt to win a princess bride. However, not only are there two princesses instead of one—Rose Red and Snow White—there really is a unicorn, and that unicorn intends to claim both princesses for his own.

To make things more interesting, there is one more contender for the hands of the two princesses and their kingdom: a Black Sorcerer with a penchant for unleashing Monsters, and a deadly obsession.

And adding more to the mix—Julian...

SPLINTERED MIRROR
Copyright © 2025 Morgan Hawke
ISBN: 978-1-4874-4285-9
Cover art by Martine Jardin

Published by Extasy Books Inc

Look for us online at:
www.extasybooks.com

SPLINTERED MIRROR

BY

MORGAN HAWKE

Splintered Mirror
A Sordid Fairy Tale

Once upon a time, an amazingly beautiful prince named Alberic lived in the enchanted land of Nod. The prince had long golden hair, emerald-green eyes, and a face women swooned over. Unfortunately, this very same prince was also sarcastic, sadistic, and demonically temperamental. Supposedly, he wasn't actually a demon, but I had my doubts — as did anyone else who happened to cross his path.

My name is Julian, I was his valet.

Prologue

In a Fairy-Tale Kingdom

It all began with my brother Julian. He was adorable and sweet to a fault. He had big blue eyes surrounded by long girlish lashes and raven's wing black curls that flew with the slightest breeze. He would smile with his candy-pink, Cupid's bow lips, and utterly adorable dimples would indent both chubby cheeks.

I looked just like him, except for the dimples. I had them; I didn't show them nearly as much. I was far too busy to smile.

Julian was my twin, younger by only two hours. Standing side by side, we appeared to be identical. The only real difference between us was that he was a boy, and I was...not. Our names were practically identical, too, Julian and Julianna. To make things even more confusing, we both answer to the name Julian.

Everyone loved my brother because he was kind, helpful, and a pushover. If someone needed something done, they went to find Julian and sobbed out their pitiful plight.

Farmer Jenkins came by practically daily. "Oh! My back hurts so badly, but I need my stables swept out!"

Julian would pout sweetly and occasionally shed a tear. "Oh, I'm so sorry to hear that." Then his smile would appear, escorted by his dimples. "I'll take care of that for you!"

However, as soon as the man's back was turned, Julian ran and got me. "Julian! I need a hand with something!"

I never refused him. I just couldn't. Julian meant well, but he was a total klutz. It took him hours to sweep one small pile of straw across the hearth and forget about shoveling out a stable before nightfall.

I hated to see him cry, partly because people would come out of the woodwork to see what was wrong and then immediately glare at me. However, the main reason was that his weeping would make me weep without fail.

Mother said it was because twins were connected that way.

I didn't know if that was true, but his moods affected me strongly. If he was happy, so was I. If he was miserable, I was too. In short, I was quite literally at the mercy of his tears and smiles, so I did whatever he asked just to keep my own eyes from tearing up.

Anyway, when I walked in to do his work, no one ever said anything. They rarely said thank you when I finished, either. I did the job as fast as possible and got the hell out. If they did address me, it was pretty much a guarantee that they wanted something else done.

That's when I flashed my dimples. "Don't you think you got enough free labor for today?"

Their cheeks would slacken in shock, and then they would scowl. "Oh, it's you. I thought you were sweet Julian."

I would grin even wider, but my dimples would disappear. You see, my dimples only appear when I'm happy. "Nope, sorry to disappoint you, but you got sour Julian. I'll be going now." I didn't believe in sticking around where I wasn't wanted.

I suppose it really wasn't their fault for thinking I was Julian. Being twins, there wasn't much to tell us apart. It didn't help that Mom and Pop dressed us alike, too. We wore identical blue wool frock coats over brown wool waistcoats

2

and breeches with matching white shirts. Our neckerchiefs were bow-tied around our collars exactly the same way. The same cobbler made our brown calfskin knee boots. Last but not least, Mom refused to cut our hair, so we wore the same long curling ponytail tied with identical blue bows.

Despite the fact that no girl or matron I knew wore breeches, I didn't see any problem wearing the same clothes as my brother. It made perfect sense to me. It was cheaper to dress me like my brother rather than make all the petticoats and fripperies that went into girl's clothes. They were more durable, too.

Truthfully, dresses were completely impractical with all the farm work I did: sweeping this, shoveling that, hauling odds and ends from here to there. Then there was milking cows, grooming horses, finding lost calves and lambs that had run into the woods, and getting cats down from trees. By the time I reached fourteen, I was so used to running around in breeches that I wouldn't have known what to do with a dress if I'd had one.

However, that was the winter that Pop decided to take the whole family to Kingsborough for the Winter Festival.

In the misty dregs of a frosty dawn, my twin brother and I were set on the back of our parents' rickety farm wagon, right next to the quilts my mother planned to sell. We'd been scrubbed pink, and our black hair brushed and tied within an inch of our lives. It was a special occasion, so Mom had actually heated the pressing iron and smoothed our white shirts and neckerchiefs to pristine crispness.

At exactly the same height and slender build, wearing identical winter-felted, slate-blue frockcoats and our Sunday-best breeches, we were a matching pair.

Passing by the back of the wagon, Pop shook his head and smiled. "Two peas in a pod."

Mom, however, stopped and stared hard at me, then

3

furrowed her brow and tilted her head, clearly troubled by something.

I frowned at her. "Is something wrong?"

She nibbled on her bottom lip, then smiled and patted my knee. "Nothing that can't wait until we get back." She moved past and climbed up on the wooden seat next to Pop.

My brother leaned close to me and smiled slyly. "Ha! You forgot something, didn't you?"

I whacked the back of his head with my open palm. "I'm not the one who forgets things!"

"Hey!" He curled his hands into fists.

I folded my arms across my chest and curled my lip. "If you try it, you know I'll beat you."

Mom turned around and glared at us both. "No fighting in your good clothes!"

My brother and I winced and answered in nearly identical voices. "Yes, Mom!" My brother's voice had started to crack on the occasional word.

Pop clucked to the brown dray horses and the wagon rolled down the road with the two of us kicking our freshly polished boot heels off the open tailgate. The wagon rumbled at a slow plod through farmlands, woodlands, and past small towns. We reached Kingsborough just as the city gates opened.

After stopping at a modest livery to stable the horses and stow the wagon, we all strolled into the market common, along with fully half the kingdom's population.

The Kingsborough Winter Festival was the year's biggest shopping event. People from all over the kingdom crammed in to wander among the thousands of cobbled crafters' booths. Many stopped to gawk at pageant plays under tents. Many more got blistering drunk among family members they hadn't seen in a year, and everyone danced their toes to bloody ribbons in the square at least once.

4

In the midst of the hustle and bustle of the holiday crowd, I was separated from my parents and my brother. It was not a big deal. I knew where to find the inn where Pop had left the wagon. Worse came to worse, if they left without me, I knew the way home. Granted, it would mean almost a four-hour walk, but I'd walked further.

Now, if Julian had gotten separated, that would have been a real cause for alarm. Julian had a notoriously bad sense of direction. He was forever getting lost in the middle of open fields.

Completely unruffled by the fact that I was alone in a monstrous crowd full of total strangers I wandered about looking to my heart's content. In the middle of the town common, I stopped at a tailor's booth to stare at a wine-red, velvet frock coat trimmed in a black braid with gold buttons. It was a very fine coat with wide lapels and broad cuffs embroidered in black silk—something a true gentleman would wear. I'd never seen anything more lovely in my life. I covered my mouth with my sleeve to hide the fact that I was drooling.

Suddenly, I was surrounded by a gaggle of cooing and rather busty girls. Between them, I swear the ruffle, bustle, and ribbon quota was off the scale. Rather like a herd of geese, they all called out the same word over and over. "Julian! Julian! Julian!"

I turned and smiled, flashing my dimples. "Yes?" I had no idea who any of them were, so I bowed politely. "Can I help you?"

The tallest girl shook her head majestically, tossing her honey-brown curls in the process. "Oh, you bad boy!" She delivered a magnificent pout. "Don't you remember me, Julian?"

Oh... I felt my dimples fade from my cheeks. "Sorry, I'm Julianna. Julian is my twin."

The entire group of girls went round-eyed and slack jawed. "You're a *girl*?"

I nodded. "Julian went that way." I pointed off toward the north. "He's with our parents shopping."

The tall girl narrowed her black eyes at me. "You don't look like a girl."

I frowned. Where the heck did that come from? I folded my arms across my conspicuously flat chest. "Well, I *am* a girl."

The tall girl set her hands on her hips and loomed over me. "If you're a girl, then why are you dressed like that?"

I leaned back, away from the cloud of over-sweet perfume that was threatening to choke me. "Because these are the clothes my parents gave me. Why else?"

She shook her head. "Girls do *not* wear pants."

I ground my teeth. "Well, I *am* a girl, and I *am* wearing pants." I grabbed the sides of my breeches and tugged on them. "See? Pants."

The gathering of girls flapped their aprons and squawked loudly in agitation. What could my parents possibly be thinking, dressing a girl like a boy?

I turned my back to look once again at the wine-red coat and tried to ignore them. So, I wore pants. What was the big deal?

I was grabbed by the shoulder of my coat and jerked back around.

The tall girl lifted her chin and smiled, showing an awful lot of teeth. "I say we check to see if you really are a girl."

The entire circle of girls smiled with her. Despite all the ruffles and bows, they strongly reminded me of a pack of feral dogs that had just cornered something fun to eat.

I felt my stomach fall into my bowels. I had no idea what they were planning, but I knew damned well I wasn't going to like it.

The entire pack attacked me in one snarling mass, tugging

and pulling at my coat and yanking at my breeches.

I fought back, kicking and screaming, but there were just too many hands. "Get off me!"

"Excuse me."

Every hand released me at once.

I fell and landed hard on my butt in the dust. "Ow!" My gaze locked on the backside of a pair of mirror gloss black boots. Only inches from my nose was a pair of sharply pointed silver spurs. I lunged to my feet.

The most beautiful boy I had ever seen turned to stare at me. His features were more delicate than a porcelain doll's with eyes as green as grass. His slightly frowning lips were shiny and pale pink like wet rose petals. His waist-length golden hair was drawn back and tied negligently with a black velvet bow, the tail trailing over the shoulder of his gold velvet frock coat. Gold buttons marched down the front of the coat and along the edges of the huge bell sleeves. The coat's cream satin broad lapels, bell sleeves, and flounced skirts were heavily embroidered in silver thread. His bow-tied velvet sash was as black as pitch.

I'd never seen anyone like him. He looked like an angel.

The angelic boy's dark brows lowered over his grass-green eyes, and his frown deepened. "You don't have time to play around with them."

My mouth fell open. "What?" Was that supposed to make sense?

The girls just stood there in a half circle, stiff as boards with their eyes wide and their faces white.

He pulled the wide strap of his white leather shoulder bag from over his head "You're supposed to carry my bag." He tossed it at me, practically slamming it into my stomach and gave me the most beautiful and chilling smile I'd ever seen. "Make like a horse, peon."

In that instant I knew that he might look like an angel, but

7

clearly, he was the farthest thing from it. Out of sheer habit from years of doing this, that, and the other thing for just about everyone, I pulled the strap over my shoulder and settled the huge bag against my butt. "What's a peon?"

The evil angel smirked. "Anyone that isn't the prince."

The prince? The prince? This was the king's son? My jaw tried to hit the ground.

He grabbed the strap crossing my chest and towed me after him and away from the stunned pack of girls. There was a riding crop at the small of his back tucked into his black sash. "You may address me as your highness, not your majesty, that's my father, or simply, prince. Got it, peon?"

I was still too stunned to think, never mind speak.

He glanced over his shoulder at me. "Close your mouth or I'll put something in it."

God, what a brat! I curled my lip. "Yeah? Like what?"

"My boot, for one." He gave me a chilling smile, his eyes narrowing. "Though I suppose I could find a pony bridle that would fit you."

I shivered hard. There was no doubt in my mind that he'd actually put a bridle on me if it suited him. I raised both my hands. "No, thank you!"

He nodded firmly and dragged me off to a nearby bookseller's booth where he promptly pointed at the largest and most expensive book they had on sale. "Wrap that up and charge it to the king."

The crafter stuttered in gratitude then hurriedly wrapped the book up in brown paper and string. He then hefted the huge book with both hands and held it out.

The prince gave me a pointed look.

I took the book from the crafter and tucked it into the white leather bag.

The prince nodded and went on to the next crafter, then the next, then the next, selecting item after item, and charging it all to the king.

The bag on my shoulder got heavier and heavier. When not one more thing could be crammed into it, I resorted to carrying packages in my arms. When not one more thing could be crammed into my arms, pockets, or coat, I stopped in my tracks. "With all due respect, prince, I can't carry one more thing."

The prince turned from the leather crafter's table and smiled. "Sure you can." He lifted what appeared to be a very delicate and very ornate pony bridle. The crossbar to the bit was wrapped in leather. He turned back to the crafter. "Wrap the reins and bridle but give me the bit."

I took one unsteady step back from the smiling prince. "You wouldn't...?"

The prince took the paper parcel of wrapped leather and tucked it into his coat, then turned to face me, hefting the silver embossed bit. "What was I saying about that open mouth of yours?"

I took another step back, teetering dangerously under all the heavy parcels I held. "You must be joking! You...you couldn't be that cruel!"

He reached out to grab the strap of his white bag that crossed my chest, effectively holding me in place—and keeping me from tipping over.

"I never say what I don't mean." He crammed the bit into my mouth. "And yes, I am that cruel." He pointed a finger at my face. "Don't you dare spit that out, or...?" He reached behind him and pulled out the riding crop. "I'll have to punish you." He grinned.

Unable to say a damned thing in my own defense, I moaned around the bit and gave him my best pitiful look.

"Pouting doesn't work on me." He swung the whip behind me and swatted the bag against my rump, making a sharp smacking sound. "Giddy-up!"

I jumped away from his whip and very nearly tipped over.

He grabbed the bag's strap, keeping me upright, and snorted. "You're rather clumsy, aren't you?"

I growled around the bit and leveled a hot, angry stare at him.

The prince swung the crop, again smacking the bag on my rump loudly. "Move it, peon!"

I flinched at the loud sound and tipped a little too far to one side.

The prince tisked in annoyance and grabbed the shoulder strap, keeping me upright. "Don't fall down! I don't want you damaging my goods." He turned sharply. "We're going this way." He tugged the bag strap, towing me right through the thickest crowds, swinging his crop left and right. "Out of my way!"

People dodged out of his way.

The sun had already begun to set, and the crowd we were walking through was getting decidedly drunk. In fact, we walked through several fights in progress, but not one of them took a swing at the prince. They parted, bowed, and once we'd passed, dove back into their fights.

It was the most bizarre thing I'd ever seen.

At the very edge of the festival site, the prince dragged me toward an ornate white coach embellished with gold vines and drawn by six white horses. "I'm back!"

The coachman shoved a small bottle back into his caped greatcoat's breast pocket and clambered down from his seat. Practically tripping over himself, he got the coach door open, and the steps lowered from inside the door just in time to let the prince climb in without pause.

I was dragged into the coach after the prince and shoved into the seat next to him. I stared in shock at him. What was I doing in his coach?

The prince lifted a delicate brow. "You didn't think *I* was going to carry all that stuff into the castle, did you?"

I rolled my eyes. It figured. I turned and tried to talk around the bit in my mouth. "Ken I tek dis outta my mouf now?"

The prince leaned over to grab a walking stick jammed between the seat and the coach's sidewall. "No."

I stared. He had to be kidding! "Bu ahm droolin'!" I *was* drooling too, all over the place. The shoulder of my coat was wet from wiping off my chin. I couldn't use my handkerchief; my hands were full.

He smiled. "I know." He raised the stick and banged on the roof.

The coach lurched forward.

I was slammed back into my seat and suddenly grateful that I was sitting next to the prince rather than across from him. Otherwise, I would have been thrown to the floor.

The trip to the castle was swift and bumpy, but the coach's seat was amazingly comfortable. It also was my first chance to sit since the wagon ride up. I would have passed out in sheer bliss if it weren't for all the packages I held and the bit in my mouth.

The coach lurched to a halt.

I was snapped out of my half-doze by a hand on my coat collar dragging me out of my seat. I don't know how I did it, but I got out of the coach without dropping a thing.

Standing under the covered drive next to the prince, I looked over at the entry alcove and stared at the monstrous staircase leading up into the palace with utter horror. There were more stairs than I could count. Technically, I couldn't count beyond my fingers and toes, but that staircase would take the fingers and toes of at least a dozen people to count.

The prince tugged at his lapels, shrugging his coat back into place. "Dinner better be ready when I get there. I'm starved."

My stomach chose that moment to growl loudly. I hadn't eaten a thing since my bread and cheese at lunch.

The prince snorted, then rolled his eyes dramatically. "All right, fine. I'll see if I can find a doggie bowl or something and feed you too."

Suddenly, that staircase didn't look so bad. I had no idea what a doggie bowl was, but if there was going to be food at the end of that staircase then I was more than happy to climb it.

The prince grabbed onto the bag strap and towed me into the alcove at the foot of the stairs. He jerked hard, turning me to the left to face a broad oak door. He reached up to grasp the curved brass lever handle and tilted his head toward the staircase. "I don't do stairs." He pulled the door open revealing what looked like a cast iron cage with gold flourishes and brass fittings.

I blinked. I had no idea what I was looking at.

The prince turned to me. "And if you know what's good for you, you will never ever make me wait by taking the stairs yourself."

I turned to stare at him. What the hell was he talking about?

The prince slid the gate to the left, opening it then hauled me into the cast iron cage with him. He turned around to grab the gate and slid it closed. He grabbed the handle of a crank on the right wall. "Up is up, down is down. The numbers tell you what floor."

I just stared. Was that supposed to make sense? I spoke slowly around the bit still clenched in my teeth. "What's a number?"

The prince rolled his eyes and cracked a sour smile. "Let me guess, you can't read *or* write?" He pulled the crank down. The entire room shuddered and began to fall very, very slowly.

My heart tried to leap out of my throat, and my knees

12

quaked under me. Wide-eyed, I turned to the prince, hoping he'd know what to do.

With his right hand on his hip, he tapped his foot impatiently while pouting at the gate. "This stupid thing is so slow!" He glanced at me and his eyes widened slightly. He snorted, and a slight smile appeared. "You've never been on an elevator, have you?"

If he was referring to the falling room we were in, then hell no I hadn't. I shook my head, side to side.

A smirk curled his perfect lips. "Scared you stiff, didn't it?"

My teeth clenched on the leather wrapping the pony bit. *Bastard...* It had, but I would be damned before I admitted it. I lifted my head and sniffed in disdain.

His brow lifted, and he snorted, but his smirk stayed firmly in place. "I suppose it's only fair to warn you that it gets scarier from here on. You'll probably pee your pants."

I planted my feet firmly and glared at him full in the eyes. *We'll just see about that.*

The elevator dinged. The prince shoved the lever back to the middle position and stepped forward to grab the gate and slide it open. He looked over at me. "Come on, peon."

I followed him out of the...elevator and down an arching mortared stone hallway past door after door until we reached one of battered oak doors that had a small window with bars.

The prince lifted his foot and slammed it flat against the door hard, the heel making a loud thunk against the wood, then again, and again. He dropped his foot, crossed his arms, and lifted his chin, clearly waiting. "Whatever you do, don't look away from him."

I glanced over at him. *Look away from who?*

The door opened with an ominous creek, and a huge, broad-shouldered man looked out. His face bore hideous scars that looked as though a bear had raked his face from his right eyebrow all the way across and down to the left side of his neck. However, under those scars, he had an incredibly handsome face with high cheekbones, a strong jaw, and perfectly shaped petal pink lips. He also had the palest blue eyes I'd ever seen and lustrous black hair that fell in waves down his back. He eyed the prince, then me.

I couldn't have looked away if I'd tried.

"Captain..." The prince jabbed his thumb toward me. "I need you to hand out this stuff to whoever needs it."

The door opened wider, and the man stepped back.

The prince strode in. "Come on, peon."

I walked into a large room with a huge wooden trestle table. Blown glass oil lamps sat on either end, shedding light on several large, unrolled maps.

The prince stopped before the table and peered at the maps, then glanced over at me. "Drop the bags, peon."

I started setting the stuff down on the bench closest to me.

The prince turned to the huge man. "As you can see, I got a new toy."

My head shot up to look over at him. He was not referring to me...?

The prince smirked at me. "This one seems to be pretty durable."

I blinked. Was that a compliment?

The man's lips curled up into a breathtaking smile, revealing perfectly even, snowy white teeth. It was damned near blinding.

The prince grabbed me by the lapel and dragged me next to him. "This is..." He pulled the bit from my teeth. "Name."

I licked my stretched lips. "Julian."

The prince lifted his brow. "Last name...?"

"Ashcroft."

He nodded. "Julian Ashcroft, I'd like you to meet Reinhardt, captain of the palace guards."

I bowed to the captain. "Pleased to meet you, sir."

14

The prince grabbed my collar and jerked me back upright from my bow. "Reinhardt, before you distribute the goods, I want you to find Mr. and Mrs. Ashcroft and buy Julian from them."

I stiffened. "What?" I grabbed for the hand holding my collar. "No! You can't do that!" *My parents need me! My brother needs me!*

"I am the prince." He hissed in my ear. "I can do anything I please, and it pleases me to keep my new toy." The prince's gaze narrowed on the captain of the palace guards. "Make sure that the sale is legally binding. I want utter and unquestionable ownership. Do not fail me."

The captain bowed. "Yes, my prince." He turned to me. "Where are your parents staying?"

That pushy brat...! I spoke through clenched teeth. "I'm not telling you!"

The prince promptly twisted my arm behind me and wrapped his other arm around my throat. "Oh, yes you will."

Pain stabbed deep in my twisted shoulder. I winced, but I wasn't about to cry out. I sucked in a deep breath past the arm strangling my windpipe. "No, I won't!" I twisted to glare over my shoulder at the prince. "Buying people is wrong!"

The prince's jaw tightened, but he stopped wrenching my arm up, though he didn't release it or my throat. "How is it wrong to make your parents suffer less? Are you saying your parents don't need the money? Are you really that selfish?"

I froze. My parents *were* poor. They *did* need the money. They always needed money.

His breath brushed against my ear. "You will have new clothes, good food, and an education in addition to a position that doesn't involve grubbing in the dirt. If your parents truly care for you, they'll want you to have those things."

My anger drained away, replaced by a fist of despair trying to crush my heart. Would my parents really be better off with the money rather than me? Would going back home really be selfish? Perhaps, but something in the blackest pit of my heart told me that staying would be just as selfish.

You see, I *wanted* to stay. It wasn't because I liked him, because I honestly wasn't sure if I did. It was the simple fact that no one had ever wanted *me* before, and certainly not enough to buy me from my parents. Julian was the one everyone liked. I was merely his sour shadow and the one that did all the chores.

The prince's arm lowered from around my throat to around my chest. He released my wrist, letting my arm fall to my side, and closed his other arm around me in what appeared to be a hug. His voice dropped to a whisper. "Don't you want to make your parents happy that one of their children will never starve, that one of their children will actually have a future?"

I nodded. I did want to make them happy, but... "If I tell you, I want to go, too. I want to see them."

The captain nodded. "To say goodbye." His voice was deep, yet barely more than a whisper.

"To..." I couldn't say it. The weight around my heart was crushing the breath from me. "Yeah."

"Done." The prince released me.

Oh God... I collapsed on the floor. *What have I done?*

The tall, scarred, yet still handsome captain of the palace guards leaned down to grasp my hand and tugged, encouraging me to stand. Before I realized it, I was trotting down the corridor in his wake. Only moments later, I was led out into the night-dark castle yard. Dozens of torches lit the broad, noisy, and crowded expanse to nearly daylight, but I saw nothing. We stopped before an incredibly tall black horse and I was lifted into the saddle. The captain mounted behind me.

The horse cantered out of the yard, across the drawbridge,

16

and into the town. A dozen mounted soldiers followed in our wake.

My eyes burned so badly that I could barely see to point out the hostel.

A soldier dismounted and went inside. Only moments later my parents followed the soldier back out.

The captain dismounted from behind me and walked over to speak quietly to my father.

I nearly fell off the horse in my haste to rush to my mother's arms. I knew I was doing the right thing, but I still felt awful.

Buried in my mother's skirts, I was hustled into the inn and up the staircase. My brother Julian stood at the top of the stairs.

I was shoved into the small room. The door closed on me, leaving me alone. I pressed my ear to the door but heard only the barest of whispers and hasty footsteps going down the staircase. I turned to face the room, my eyes barely noticing the narrow bed with the trundle cot beside it. The fire set behind the grate was small, but the warmth was welcome.

My mother entered the room and started tugging on my clothes, undressing me. She had me undressed to only my shirt before it occurred to me that I needed to remain dressed to go back to the castle. "Mom, I'm supposed to go back."

"It's all right Julianna." She pulled back the covers on the cot and encouraged me to lie down among the blankets. "Everything is all right now." She pressed a mug of lukewarm soup into my hand. "Drink this. We'll worry about such things in the morning."

I drank my soup. I was too hungry to pass up food of any kind. Exhaustion weighed my eyes heavily. I gave her back the mug and fell back onto the bed. My head touched the feather pillow, and I fell asleep.

I was shaken from sleep in the chill hours before dawn and urged to dress. Mother was already dressed and wearing her traveling shawl. She wrapped a brown cloak around my shoulders and pulled the hood up over my head. "It's cold." With ungodly haste, she hustled me down the back stairs and out into the yard where my father waited with the horses already harnessed to the wagon.

Julian was nowhere to be seen.

Mother lifted me into the back and urged me to sit among a few paper-wrapped parcels, then rushed to hop on the driver's bench with my father.

Father snapped the reins on the horses and the wagon lurched forward.

I twisted around to look at them. "Wait! Where's Julian?"

My father didn't turn around. "Don't worry about Julian. Your brother is fulfilling his duty to his family."

Fulfilling his duty? I frowned. "Did someone take him on as an apprentice?"

My parents looked at each other.

My mother turned to face me with a smile. "Yes! Yes indeed, that's exactly what happened. I'm sure his new master will let him visit as soon as he's settled in."

I turned around to stare at the passing trees and nibbled on my bottom lip. Julian being apprenticed was indeed a very fine thing, except for the fact that he couldn't actually do anything. I'd done everything for him. Hopefully, his sweetness would win his master over enough that he wouldn't be beaten too badly when his lack of skill was uncovered.

Then something else occurred to me. I turned around. "Pop, wasn't I supposed to go back to the castle with the captain? Didn't the prince buy me?"

Both my parents stiffened.

Mother turned around to face me with a smile. "Your father was able to talk him out of it."

I blinked in astonishment. Pop did...? *My* clumsy, simple-minded Pop talked him out of it? Apparently, my father was far more clever than I'd thought. Not only that, but it seemed that my parents loved me more than gold. I'd had no idea that they loved me that much.

The pain that had been lurking around my heart suddenly burst and tears spilled down my cheeks. I turned so I could wrap my arms around my mother's waist. Tears choked my throat, but I got the words out. "I love you. I love you both so much."

Pop hunched on the bench.

The rest of the ride home was very quiet.

The following day was pretty much normal, except for the fact that Julian wasn't there. I awoke, dressed, grabbed a hunk of bread and cheese for breakfast, and went out to do my chores, as well as Julian's share, but that was normal too. I'd always done Julian's share.

My day progressed like any other, and yet I found myself listening for the cheerful voice of my sweet and foolish twin. I tried to be happy for him. Honestly, I did, but I couldn't help wishing that he was there, with me.

The only thing to cheer my day was when the local farmers found out that sweet Julian was no longer available for…favors. Their crestfallen and in some cases, horrified expressions are memories I still cherish to this day.

That night pain erupted deep in my belly. When I rose in the morning, I discovered blood on my thighs. I stared at my scarlet-stained sheets in astonishment. My woman's blood had finally come. I didn't panic, Mom had told me what to expect the year before. I snuck downstairs to her bedside and whispered the…situation in her ear.

She sighed and set her hand on her brow. "It's about time."

Without going into any details, Mother helped me deal with the problem, then handed me a handful of clothes wrapped in a green wool shawl. "You'll be wearing this from now on."

I untied the shawl and discovered a green wool skirt with matching bodice, several lacy chemises, a couple of ruffled petticoats, some lace and ruffled knickers, stockings, and an ash-boned, corselet. I stared at them in shock. "What's all this?"

Mother crossed her arms. "What you should have been wearing all along."

I looked up at her. "I can't do chores wearing…this!"

Mother snorted and unbuttoned the neck to my nightshirt. "Skirts never stopped me." She tugged the nightshirt up and off of me. "More importantly, you can't catch a husband in breeches!" She tugged the frilly under-things free of the pile.

My mouth fell open. "A husband…?"

Mother handed me the pantalettes. "You can't expect your father and I to support you all of your life. You need a house and family of your own."

"But I don't want a husband!" I put the pantalettes on.

Mother tossed the chemise over my head and smiled grimly. "You will change your mind, believe me." She leaned close to lace the rib-cinching corselet over the chemise. "Don't ever think that women don't have appetites to equal a man's.

Appetites? I stared at her in complete bafflement. At the dinner table, Julian always ate about double what I did.

Helpless against her sheer determination, I was wrestled into the stockings, the petticoats, the skirt, and laced into the matching bodice before I knew what hit me. Leather slippers were set on my feet, and then she quite literally shoved me down the attic stairs.

At the breakfast table, my father's eyes widened and his

mouth fell open, along with the three farmhands that helped work our fields.

My mother wiped her hands on her apron. "No more working in the fields, the barn, or the stable. It's time she learned the duties of a proper wife."

Pop shrugged. "Well, Julian *is* a girl."

Mom curled her lip at the farmhands, and it wasn't a smile. "That's right. You'll have to do your own chores from now on, boys."

I spent my day doing women's work and developed a whole new level of respect for them. It took a lot of muscle to scrub clothes clean and extreme attention to detail to cook food properly and bake bread among the coals in the oven set into the hearth. What made it all worth it was seeing my mother smiling while working at her side.

The lunch was just about ready to be set out on the plank table when Mom set a mug of tea in my hand. "I can see why everyone was so disappointed when you put on that dress."

I looked up at her. "Hm?"

She patted my shoulder. "You're a hard worker, my girl. There won't be a man in the village that won't be willing to pay a nice fat bride price to have you for a wife."

I stared at her. "But I don't want to be a wife!"

She shook her head and smiled. "Just wait. Once you meet the right boy, you'll change your mind."

As far as I was concerned, she was out of her mind.

Only minutes later, Pop and our three farmhands trooped in, pulling their boots off by the door. The hands dropped onto the benches lining the table with decided slouches. Their brows were furrowed and not one smiled.

Pop walked over to Mom with a pair of wicker baskets overflowing with paper-wrapped goods. Apparently, he'd gone into the village and done some shopping. He leaned close and whispered in her ear.

Despite my straining, I couldn't hear what he said.

Whatever it was, it made Mom happy. She smiled and patted him on the cheek, then snatched the basket from his hand. "Boys, you'll need to unload the wagon as soon as you're finished eating."

The farmhands slouched lower and eyed me resentfully.

I blinked at them as innocently as I knew how. Gee, did they really miss me doing all those menial tasks that badly?

The hand sitting next to me leaned close. "Are you sure you wouldn't rather put on some pants and get some sun on your cheeks?"

I turned to him with the sweetest smile I could manage, dimples and all. "Why? Is there something you want me to do for you?"

Mom whirled, quick as an adder, and smacked the table with her long-handled wooden spoon. The thwack rattled every dish on the table. "No! No man's chores, is that understood?"

Everyone pulled their hands back behind them and leaned away from the table wide-eyed. "Yes, ma'am!" they chorused.

Mom nodded. "Good."

That afternoon, after spreading the sheets out on the line to dry, I walked to the back door and heard my parents arguing in the kitchen.

My father's voice was husky and trembling. "What are we going to do when they find out? We could be executed!"

Mom sighed. "Husband, no one is going to execute anyone. We've done nothing wrong. We fulfilled the contract. They wanted Julian, they got Julian."

I stiffened. They were talking about my twin! Was he in

trouble already?"

"But what if they notice the...difference?"

Mom snorted. "What if they do? Even if the neighbors will tell them, there was only one boy by the name of Julian from this family."

I frowned. Something wasn't right about this conversation.

My mother suddenly called out. "Julianna!"

I jerked where I stood. *Crap!* I took a breath, turned my face away from the door, and called out. "Yeah, Mom? I rounded the corner to step into the kitchen, kicking off the wooden clogs covering my leather shoes. "The laundry is all on the line."

Mom looked at me suspiciously, then reached to the side to snag a good-sized wicker basket and shoved it into my hands. "Go out to the far meadow and pick some flowers."

I stared at her wide-eyed. "Flowers?"

She nodded firmly. "Something with a strong scent, like wild roses. I want to see if we can make the tallow candles smell sweeter when they're burned." She turned me around and shoved me toward the door. "Fill the basket."

I heaved a sigh and stepped back into my clogs. "Flowers... All righty then." All that just to keep me from hearing what kind of trouble my brother had gotten himself into? I seriously considered just ducking around the corner and waiting for them to start talking again.

Mom stepped outside the door and smiled at me. "Consider it a treat for all the hard work you've done." She didn't go back inside.

Damn it. I smiled hugely. "Thanks, Mom." With my shawl tied around my hips and the basket on my arm, I turned and clomped out of the backyard, heading for the meadow on the edge of the woods.

What kind of trouble could Julian be in? Had Julian's new master found out just how lazy Julian was? I loved my brother, don't get me wrong, but considering all the work I did for him — and I did it *all*, I was under no illusions.

I shook my head and stomped across the wooden stile bridging the fence dividing the cow pasture from the meadow by the woods. If Julian was in trouble with his master for being his lazy self, there wasn't anything I could do about it. I couldn't serve his apprenticeship for him even if I wanted to.

It had only been two days, but God, I missed him.

I heaved a sigh and wandered through the tall grass, sniffing the flowers for good strong scents. The sun was warm, the breeze was cool, the swallows were warbling, and the flowers plentiful. It was a very nice spring afternoon. So nice, in fact, that I almost missed the shadow standing at the edge of the tree line. A larger, bulkier shadow behind it told me that there was a horse standing back there, too.

Rather than stare stupidly at what might be an extremely dangerous person or, worse, a monster, I kept a smile firmly on my lips and let my gaze slide right past, pretending I hadn't seen anything. I used my small knife to cut a few flowers close to me and stuffed them in my basket. As casually as I could, I turned away and started heading back toward the gate, cutting the occasional flower as I went.

A youthful and achingly familiar voice called out. "Julian?"

I froze. *That sounds like...* I turned around.

Standing at the very edge of the trees in a pool of sunlight with his hands clasped before him was a youth with long black hair. His white neckcloth was sloppily knotted and looked a bit ragged at the ends, but his bottle-green coat was clearly of excellent quality. It was my brother.

The flower basket fell from my nerveless fingers. "Julian?"

He gave me a trembling smile. "Could you come here for a minute?"

I lifted my skirts and ran through the tall grasses straight for him. "Julian...!" At the last second, I threw out my arms and leapt onto him, bowling us both over into the grass. "Julian!" I sat up, straddling his stomach, and grabbed onto the shoulders of his coat. "Where have you been? How have you been? Mom said you'd been apprenticed. What are you doing here? Are you in some kind of trouble? Gods, you didn't run away from your master did you?"

Julian lifted his hands and chuckled. "Um, about that..."

"You *did* run away!"

"Well, not exactly..." He pushed at my shoulders, "Could you um, get off me? You're heavy."

I rolled my eyes. "It's not my fault I've got more muscle than you." I got up off him and stepped back. "Well? Either you did run away, or you didn't. Which is it?"

"He didn't run away. *You* did." The voice was youthful, annoyed, and very familiar.

The hair on the back of my neck lifted. I turned sharply to look at the patch of woods behind my brother.

From the trees stepped the prince. His midnight blue velvet frock coat and pants blended a little too well with the shadows, but there was no mistaking the long golden curls hanging loose about the pale and cherubic face. His lips curved in a smile, but his eyes narrowed. With a sharp slash, he pointed his riding crop at my brother. "Did you honestly think I wouldn't know an impostor?"

My brother leapt to his feet to cower behind me. "I'm sorry! I'm sorry! Don't hurt me!"

I folded my arms across my nonexistent chest and lifted my chin, but I didn't take my eyes off the prince. "Brother, what are you doing with the prince?"

My brother waved his hands. "It wasn't *my* idea...!"

The prince rolled his eyes and tisked in open disgust. "Ah, the parents." He shook his head. "I should have realized." He

25

abruptly pointed his whip at my brother. "You—" He then pointed at me. "—And, you. Switch clothes."

My brother started unbuttoning his coat with extreme speed.

I gaped at him. "What for?"

The prince folded his arms across his chest. "Isn't it obvious? You're coming with me, and that useless impostor is staying here."

My mouth fell open in sheer astonishment. "I can't do that!"

His gaze narrowed and his lips curled into a vicious smile. "Oh, so you don't mind if I have your parents arrested for attempting to cheat one of the royal family? That's punishable by beheading if I'm not mistaken."

I glared at the prince, but my knees were wobbling with fright. "You wouldn't...!"

The prince glared right back. "I purchased *you*, not that!" He pointed his whip at my brother. "I *will* have what is mine!" He slapped the whip against his gloved palm. It made a loud snap.

My brother grabbed me from behind, wrapping his arms around my waist. His whisper was high-pitched with open terror. "Please, Julian, switch with me! Please! Please! *Please!* He's crazy and scary! I can't deal with him! Please do it for me! I swear I'll never ask for another thing, ever!"

I wilted where I stood. I knew exactly how scary the prince was, and truthfully, Julian really was no match for him. I pulled the cap from my head and tugged the apron from around my waist. "Fine."

Julian burst into happy tears. "Thank you! Thank you!"

"Whatever..." I shoved him off me to unhook the front of my gown then pulled off the top, exposing the corset over my chemise. I turned my back to my brother. "You need to help me out of this."

The prince took three steps to me and grabbed my arm. "You're *my* servant. I'll get you out of that." He jerked on my arm to turn me away from him.

I turned my head to look back at him and lifted a brow. "Do you even know how to unlace one of these?"

He smiled. "Of course." He then pulled a knife from his boot.

I jerked forward in alarm. "Whoa! Hey!"

The prince grabbed the shoulder strap of my corset. "Hold still!" He slid the blade down the laces—slicing them apart in one breath. The corset fell to the grass. He sneered. "I don't even know why you're wearing one of those. You don't have any kind of a figure to squeeze."

"Shut up! I'll get one eventually."

The prince growled at my back. "Not if I have anything to say about it--and that's shut up, *your highness*, peon."

I rolled my eyes. "Fine then, shut up, *Your Highness*." A harsh tug at my waist warned me that the hooks on my skirt had been released. The skirt billowed to the ground. The bum roll at my hips fell atop the skirt then my petticoats billowed off me.

Suddenly I was naked but for my stockings, knee garters, and chemise, which was just barely long enough to cover my bum and privates.

My brother wordlessly handed me his white silk shirt.

I pulled it on over my chemise then pulled on my brother's knee breeches and tucked the shirt in. I normally wore short pants under my breeches, but right then I didn't have any. Women didn't wear short pants under their clothes. I didn't ask for my brother's as it was most likely the only thing he'd be wearing home. There was no way in hell he'd fit into my dress--not without the corset anyway.

In less time than I'd thought, I was fully dressed in my brother's clothes: shirt, pants, waistcoat, neckcloth, stockings, boots, and frock coat.

My brother, however, stood shivering in only his short pants and stockings.

The prince frowned but nodded. "Good enough." He grabbed me by the coat collar. "Let's go, peon." With a hard tug, the prince towed me into the trees.

My brother waved and smiled happily. "Do your best!" However, I couldn't help but feel that my brother was really saying, "Better *you* than me." I could actually *feel* just how happy he really was to be left behind.

Despite the fact that the prince would not be a kind master, I had no illusions. I was going into a situation where I'd have to hide my gender probably for the rest of my life, and I found myself smiling uncontrollably. For once, someone actually preferred *me* to my brother.

His hand unrelenting on my coat collar, the prince dragged me over to a pair of ponies. One was snowy white with a thick cottony mane and tail wearing a red velvet saddle blanket with an ornate black and gold saddle. The bridle gleamed with gold buckles and ornaments. Obviously, the prince's mount.

Next to the white pony stood a pitch-black pony with a mane and tail just as fluffy. It wore a simple brown leather bridle and saddle and had a mean look in his eye.

The prince shoved me toward the black pony. "Hurry up and get on. I have to get back before the captain comes looking for me."

I ripped up a hunk of grass and walked over to unknot the black pony's reins from the tree branch. "They send out the captain of the guard to find you?" I dodged the pony's kick without thought. "I know you're the heir, but isn't that a bit much?"

The prince unknotted his own pony's reins and sighed heavily. "My father could care less about my personal safety."

28

He set his foot in the stirrup and swung up into the saddle. "But for some reason, the captain seems to have made it his personal mission to keep track of my whereabouts."

The black pony turned his head to snap at me.

I shoved my handful of grass into the pony's mouth.

The pony snorted but started chewing on the grass.

I took that moment to set my foot in the stirrup and swung up into the pony's saddle.

The prince frowned at me.

I tilted my head to the side. "What?"

The prince snorted and smiled. "Nothing. Let's go." He shoved his riding crop in the back of his sash, leaned forward, and clapped his heels against his pony's sides. His mount set out at a canter.

With an affronted squeal, my mount rushed after him.

I ducked low to the saddle to keep from being swept from the saddle by the tree's branches.

We broke from the trees and came out in a grassy field. After that was a half-tilled field, and after that was an apple orchard. It seemed that instead of taking the road, the prince intended to go cross country, cutting through fields and pastures.

I didn't mind. It was a gorgeous early spring day. The sun was warm and the breeze cool, perfect for a ride. However, most of the ride was at a trot. Ponies, being small, simply can't hold a canter for long stretches. Trotting meant a lot of posting up and down in the saddle, which is not comfortable on the butt or the knees, let me tell you. Even worse, I hadn't ridden in a while.

I was *so* going to pay for this ride later.

Far quicker than I expected, the town and battlements of Kingsborough came into view. However, rather than head for the town's main gate, the prince led me back into the trees to a tall, aged brick wall. We rode along the wall for quite a stretch until we came to a tall wooden door heavily braced with iron bands that were set deep into the wall.

The prince pulled out a huge iron key and shoved it into the lock. A loud squeak announced the turning of the tumblers. He backed his pony up. "Get the door, peon."

I nudged my pony over to the door and pulled the heavy iron handle, towing it open.

The prince trotted through the open doorway.

I followed after to find the castle standing stark and close only a hundred yards or so away. We had apparently entered a back garden. However, from the looks of the overgrown hedges, waist-high grass, and tangled rose thickets it had been abandoned a long time ago.

Well, mostly abandoned.

"Welcome back, Your Highness." The voice was deep, rumbling, and familiar.

On my immediate right, the tall, dark, scarred, and armored captain of the guard stood in a glaring match with the prince. Both of them wore scowls and had their arms crossed. Even so, the prince was clearly on the losing end of their battle. Despite the fact that the prince was mounted and the captain standing on the ground, the extremely tall captain towered over him.

As quietly as I could, I pulled the door closed. Unfortunately, the door took that moment to squeak horrifically loud.

The captain turned his narrow-eyed glare on me.

I flinched but forced a smile on my lips. "Uh, good afternoon, Captain."

The captain's eyes widened, and his jaw went slack.

Huh? That was an odd reaction. I blinked. "What...?"

The prince snorted and smiled. "As you can see, I went out to fix *your* mistake."

The captain frowned and took three long strides to me.

Sheer terror froze me in the saddle.

His huge hand closed on my jaw, lifting my chin. He peered hard at my face.

I couldn't help but tremble in his grip, but I didn't dare look away.

"Good lord, there really are two of them." He stepped back, letting me go.

The prince sighed. "I told you there was a twin." He pointed a finger at me. "*That's* the right one!"

The captain rolled his eyes. "Fine, fine... As if I could tell the difference after only one meeting."

The prince folded his arms together and curled his lip. "I knew instantly."

The captain turned and held out his hand to the prince. "The key, Your Highness."

The prince blinked innocently at the tall, imposing captain. "What key?"

The captain lifted a black brow. "I *was* standing right next to the door when you unlocked it, Your Highness."

The prince scowled but handed over the key. He abruptly frowned. "How did you know I'd come through *this* gate?"

The captain smiled, though it was faint. "Simple logic." From somewhere under his cape, he pulled out a large iron ring crammed with keys. "You were missing. This key was missing." He began to work the key back onto the ring. "Ergo you'd return through the gate the key belonged to."

The prince pouted ferociously. "Why can't you be as stupid as the rest of the castle staff?"

The captain hid the ring of keys back under his cape and rolled his eyes. "It's a curse I must bear."

My eyes widened. The scariest and most stoic man I had ever met had just made a *joke*.

The captain narrowed his eyes at me. "And might I suggest a visit to Magister Theodoric's laboratory for a full check-up?"

I frowned. "What for?"

The prince abruptly grinned. "Oh, good idea." He turned his narrowed green gaze and chilling smile on me. "New pets do need to be properly cleaned and checked for parasites."

My mouth fell open. "What...?" I clenched my teeth in annoyance. "I do not have...whatever it was you just said." I had no clue what a para-sight was, but I definitely didn't have any. "And since when am I a *pet*?"

"Since the moment your father signed your papers making you my property, peon." The prince lifted his chin and urged his pony into a brisk walk onto a faint path through the overgrown garden. "And when you're done, I'll set up an appropriate punishment for leaving me without my permission."

I urged my pony to follow after him. "Punishment! I didn't even know about the switch! My parents didn't tell me anything." I turned away and lowered my voice. "I just figured you didn't want me anymore."

The prince turned in the saddle to frown at me. A long moment of silence fell between us, then... "Would you rather I punished your parents...?"

He *could* and I strongly suspected that he wouldn't hesitate either. I waved my hands in alarm. "No! No! It's okay!" I turned away with a scowl. "I'll take their punishment."

The prince nodded. "Now *that's* the peon I know and—" He closed his mouth with a snap.

I rolled my eyes. "I have a name, you know." I *had* told it to him.

The prince blinked with contrived innocence. "You do?"

I glared at him. "It's Julian."

"Julian..." He rolled the name around in his mouth as though tasting it. "Juuulian..." He shook his head. "I prefer peon."

I slapped my palm to my brow. "I agreed to switch with

32

my brother, why?"

The prince spoke very dryly. "Because that lazy good-for-nothing wouldn't have survived much longer in my company." He shook his head. "He was always crying and shivering in the corner."

"That lazy good-for-nothing is my brother!" I spurred my pony to ride at the prince's side and glared at him directly. "*What* did you do to him?"

The prince smiled at me. "Don't worry, it's nothing I won't do to you, too."

My eyes widened then I scowled. "Was that supposed to make me feel *better*?"

The prince pressed a gloved finger to his bottom lip and looked upward. "No, I don't think so."

I rolled my eyes. "Why must you be so mean?"

He pursed his lips and tilted his head as though in thought, but a smile curved his lips. "Entertainment value, I suppose."

Somehow, I had no difficulty believing him whatsoever.

The prince nudged his pony ahead of mine and lifted his hand. "Now, for your orders, peon." He turned in the saddle to point at me. "My orders always come first, is that understood?"

I tilted my head to the side. "Even before the king's?"

He narrowed his eyes and snarled. "*I* bought you. You are *mine*, not his!"

I blinked. There was real anger in his words. I had a strong suspicion that there was something deeper behind it; something...painful and lonely. I couldn't help but respond to it. I nodded my head and smiled. "Your orders come first. I am yours, and yours only."

His eyes widened and the anger in his expression bled away. He dropped his head and turned away. "You are not to leave my side without my express permission."

I rolled my eyes. "Well, obviously I can't sleep in the same

33

room you do."

"I've cleaned out one of my closets for you."

A closet. I looked to the side and smiled sourly. "Gee, how generous."

He nodded. "It was. I had to have a wardrobe brought in for the clothes your brother displaced." He lifted his hand again. "Also, you are not to accept anything; food, drink, clothes, trinkets...anything at all from any hand but mine."

I tilted my head to the side. That was a bit odd, but... "Okay."

He turned a scowl on me. "It's to keep you from being poisoned or cursed, idiot."

I stiffened. "Poisoned...? *Cursed...?*"

The prince heaved a sigh. "I'm the heir, remember? The fastest way to manipulate me is to threaten my toys."

I frowned. "So now I'm a *toy?*"

The prince rolled his eyes. "You always were a toy." He turned to me and smirked openly. "Why do you think no one said anything when I bought you?" He waved a hand. "They hope you'll prove enough of a distraction to keep me out of trouble."

I ground my teeth in annoyance. "I'll do my best."

The prince turned a glare on me. "You'll do my bidding!"

I rolled my eyes. "Yes, Your Majesty."

He snorted. "It's *your highness*, until I replace my father anyway. Oh, and one more thing." He turned in the saddle to grab the reins of my pony, bringing us side by side and knee to knee. He brought his face close to mine and spoke in a fierce whisper. "No one is to know *what* you are. That's *my* secret to share--not yours."

I frowned. "It's not like I can hide what I am—"a girl."— forever."

"You *will* hide it until *I* deem it time to reveal it. Is that understood?"

34

I leaned away from his vehement glare. "Uh, sure, but it's going to show after a while."

The prince looked away and released my pony's bridle. "There are ways to hide anything." He turned sharply to face me. "As long as you don't do anything stupid or *girly*."

I snorted. "I've never done anything girly in my life!"

His golden brow lifted, and a smile curved his lips. "Oh? That wasn't you picking flowers in a dress?"

I ground my teeth. "That was Mother's idea, not mine."

He lifted his chin and snorted. "My point is, *you* are a *boy* until I say you can be a girl, got it?"

I rolled my eyes once again. "Yes, Your Highness." Truthfully, it wasn't that big of a deal. I had far more experience playing a boy than a girl anyway. How difficult could it be to just *stay* one? Really?

Once Upon a Time

"Fetch, peon." With a sweet smile that made him look angelic and years younger than thirteen, Prince Alberic, the only heir to the Kingdom of Nod's throne, tossed yet another tin soldier over the cracked rim of the disused fountain.

The toy disappeared into the fountain's murky water with a soft *kerplunk*.

Royal heir or not, I glared at the thirteen-year-old brat from my superior position of fourteen years old, and two and a half inches taller. "Aren't you a little old to be playing this game?"

Just then, an autumn breeze chose that moment to whisk through the trees, sweeping red-gold leaves from their nearly naked limbs and then across me.

Despite my best efforts, I shivered hard. Even though my blue frock coat and matching knee breeches were fairly heavy wool, and the knee-length black waistcoat was, too, I was *freezing*. This was due to the fact that I was standing waist-deep in the fountain's icy water. I was pathetically grateful that the fountain itself wasn't actually spouting water like it was supposed to, or I would have been completely soaked. "And it's *not* summer, in case you haven't noticed?"

"So?" The prince thumbed back a long golden lock escaping the black velvet bow that bound the rest of his incredibly long hair to the back of his neck. The green-eyed, blond, royal pain in my ass was exquisitely dressed in a green velvet frock coat heavily embroidered with silver. A fortune in lace was around his throat held by an emerald brooch worth an entire small kingdom.

We were in one of the palace's overgrown and lesser-used gardens. One of the few places we could play without the near-constant stares of the maids, or footmen. Not that the prince cared. He was used to it. It was me that couldn't handle being watched so closely, or rather, their looks of pity. After all, I was there for a reason; to keep the royal brat from playing with *them*.

Alberic pointed at the water, his angelic smile fading into his more customary demonic smirk. "Fetch!"

Soaked and annoyed beyond all endurance, I dug around in the water until I found the soldier, then threw it at his head. I missed, of course, which annoyed me even more, so I shouted at the top of my lungs, "I quit! Go find another playmate to torture!"

The Prince stared at me wide-eyed, his petal-pink lips slightly parted. "Quit?" He leapt to his feet and pointed at me with a scowl on his cherubic face. "You can't quit! I *bought* you!"

I dragged myself out of the fountain and wrung out my long black ponytail. "I can, too, quit!" I flipped my wet ponytail to my back and sneered in his face. "You may have paid my parents for me, but I'm not a contracted apprentice. Anything else is slavery, and slavery is still illegal in this kingdom."

Alberic scowled. "Damn it, I should have never let you sit in on my kingdom law classes…"

"Well, it's too late now." I smiled with pure malice and wrung out the hem of my coat next to his highly polished shoes, making a nice little puddle. Shoes I had spent hours polishing, so no, I was *not* about to soak them in rancid water. "In fact…" I set my fisted hands on my wet hips. "I'm going home right now!" I turned on my heel and squelched toward the garden gate that opened into the woods.

Alberic chased after me. "No! I'm the prince, and I say you can't quit!"

I took off running. "I *quit!* I *quit!* I *quit!*"

He charged after me. "You're *not!* You're *not!* You're *not!*"

"Am *too!* Am *too!* Am *too!*"

The gate was locked, of course, but the maple tree right next to it overhung the wall. However, since I was taller, I could reach the lowest branch where it wasn't quite low enough for my prince to grab, and he knew it. Even better, he wasn't anywhere near as good at climbing trees as I was.

"You...! Get your butt back here, peon!"

"Make me!" I jumped to grab onto the maple's branch and swung myself up. Constantly carrying things around for the prince hither, thither, and yon had put some serious strength in my arms. I moved across the branches to the other side of the wall, then dropped out of the tree to land on my hands and knees by the gate.

Alberic grabbed onto the cast iron bars and screamed at me, "I will have you dragged back and whipped for this!"

I stuck my tongue out. "Gotta catch me first!" I bolted into the woods. It briefly occurred to me that my prince probably *would* have the palace guard drag me back, and he did like using that riding crop of his, but right then I just didn't care. I was making a point.

The walk home through the woods got dark fast. Being autumn, night came early. However, the moon was very full and bright, and most of the leaves had already fallen from the trees, so I had no trouble seeing at all. My hands chilled, as did my wet feet, but I had pockets to tuck my hands into, and my wool frock coat was more than enough to keep most of the rest of me warm. Wool stays warm even when wet. However, my wool breeches only went to the knee, so my shins tried to go numb on me, but the brisk walk and the heat of my anger helped.

By the time I got to my parents' thatch-roofed farmhouse, I was bone tired and seriously questioning the wisdom of a trek home rather than simply escaping to the castle's maze of attics. It was easily possible to hide there for a few days, and best of all, the prince had never been able to find me there. Far too late to do anything about my rash decision and shaking with exhaustion, I lifted the wooden latch to the back door and opened it.

Strangely, it was dark inside, and no one was there.

Just to make things even odder, the big heavy oak table had been shoved to the far-left side, almost against the water pump's sink. Dishes and spoons were scattered across the table, along with spilled stew. Mom's prized glass oil lamp sat right on the edge. Other than the hearth fire, it was the only light in the room. None of the mirrored wall candles were lit. The four chairs were scattered around the room, and one of them was shattered almost to splinters.

Had my parents gotten into one of their fights? Frowning, I headed straight for the river-stone fireplace to warm my hands by the fire. I didn't hear any shouting, so hopefully, the fight was over. "Mom? Dad? Julian?"

Julian, my twin, was younger by only two hours. Standing side by side, we appeared to be identical. The only real difference was that one of us was a boy, and the other was not. Our names were practically identical, too, Julian and Julianna. To make things even more confusing, we both answer to the name Julian.

Not a sound answered me. The house was dead quiet, except for the crackling fire.

Where was everybody? Had my parents gone out to the barn for their shouting match? They would if the fight was about money or Dad's occasional gambling. But then, where

39

was my twin? He hated fights, so he wouldn't have followed them to the barn...?

Something splattered under my shoe.

I looked down and discovered that I had stepped into a puddle, a thick *red* puddle. A thick red puddle that was seeping from pieces of...something heaped in the deep shadow at the side of the fireplace. It looked like someone had butchered a hog right there in the kitchen. That was seriously odd, because Dad butchered the hogs out in the shed, and it was in so many pieces...

I squinted at it, wondering why it looked so messy. That's when I realized that it hadn't been butchered, it had been ripped apart. A bit of white caught my eye, white that was slowly turning red. It looked like a...sleeve.

I jerked back sharply. That *wasn't* a hog. Hogs didn't wear clothes.

I stared, frozen in total shock, my mind completely unable to accept what I was seeing. Icy panic began to spill into my veins, but I couldn't tear my eyes away. My throat closed so tight that my voice came out in barely a whisper. "Mom? Dad? Julian?"

Something large and heavy moved behind me.

I whirled to look.

Something huge was coming down the ladder from the loft, something big and...furry. Rounded ears lifted at the top of its round furry head, and it pointed its short muzzle at me. It looked like...a bear.

Only, bears didn't normally wear clothing, although what it wore was torn almost to pieces. Bears didn't have hands either, but this one did, tipped with long black claws that curved. The way it stepped down the stairs was definitely not bear-like. Its eyes suddenly glowed green. The mouth opened, showing long jagged teeth, and a bass growl rolled from its massive chest.

That definitely wasn't a man, but it definitely wasn't a bear either. It was a *monster*.

My mouth opened, but I didn't scream. I *couldn't* scream. My throat had closed far too tightly.

Suddenly, the latch to the door lifted, and the door flew open, slamming against the wall. Prince Alberic, still in his green and silver suit, but also wearing a dark cloak that was much too big for him, marched into my parent's house and bellowed out, "Turn over, Julian, at once!"

I turned to stare at my prince wide-eyed.

Spotting me by the hearth, my prince scowled ferociously at me. "You are in *so* much trouble, peon."

I was in *trouble*? I almost laughed.

The thing on the stairs roared and came crashing down into the main room, aiming straight for my prince.

I bolted across the room, not thinking, only reacting. There was no time for thought, only the desperate need to act. I plowed into Alberic, knocking him bodily to the floor and away from those reaching claws.

Alberic grunted under me and winced. "Ow..."

"Joo lee aaahn..." The voice was deep and rumbled so loud that the floor actually vibrated. It was also very, *very* close.

I looked over my shoulder.

The monster stood over us, its clawed hands dripping red. It also reeked hideously. Worst of all, it stood between us and the door. There was absolutely no way past it.

Eyes wide and panting harshly with fear, I flipped over onto my butt and scrabbled frantically backward, shoving Alberic back against the wall.

Alberic sat behind me and stared with his eyes just as wide as mine. He leaned forward to breathe nervously in my ear. "What is *that*?"

My throat was still too tight to speak, but I got a whisper out. "Monster."

The monster took in a deep growling breath, and then let out with that deep thundering voice. "Jooo lee ahn…"

I blinked. Was it saying my name?

"What?" Alberic growled. "Oh, hell no," he muttered, then abruptly stood up and pointed his finger at the monster. "*My peon! Back off!*"

For a moment, I thought he'd actually snapped.

Suddenly, a blue-white light burst around him and engulfed us both in blinding brilliance. The light seared my eyes, so I threw up an arm to cover them.

The monster howled and thundered off.

The light suddenly went out.

I dropped my arm from my eyes in time to have Alberic collapse on top of me, out cold. His weight knocked the breath out of me, and I sat there stunned and gasping for what felt like an eternity but couldn't have been more than a few heartbeats. When I finally caught my breath, I realized two things.

The monster had fled to the far side of the room, its face covered by both hairy arms.

The doorway was clear.

In a near-blind panic, I grabbed my unconscious prince under the arms and dragged him toward the door as fast as I could do it. In my haste, I slammed my side into the kitchen table, knocking Mother's glass oil lamp off it to shatter on the floor. Oil spilled across the floor and ignited.

I didn't stop to look. I was too busy dragging Alberic out the door.

I made it to Mother's herb garden, where I was forced to stop for breath and to get a better grip on my prince. He weighed a freaking ton. However, the only real thought going through my mind was that we needed help. That…*thing* was fast, and it would definitely catch us once it got out that door.

The road.

I needed to get to the road, and hopefully, someone would be on it…preferably someone with a fast horse.

Ducking down, I heaved Alberic over my shoulder and stood up, lifting him up like a sack of flour — a very heavy sack of flour. Hunched under him, my legs shaking from the strain, I scrambled around the house to the open gate at the road.

A deafening roar of blazing heat hit my side, knocking me over. It spilled us both on the packed dirt of the road, right into the path of several horsemen in black cloaks.

Dimly, I realized it was a troop of palace guards led by Reinhardt, captain of the palace guards. The captain's black horse danced back, snorting. Captain Reinhardt reined his horse back and leaned over the saddle. "Julian? Prince!"

I pointed at the house, and suddenly, my voice came back loud and clear. "Monster!" That was when I realized that the thatch-roofed cottage I had been born in had become a raging inferno.

The captain frowned. "What?"

Inside the house, the monster roared. It crashed through the front door howling and streaming flames right in front of the palace guards.

All of the horses screamed in fright and went mad, bucking and rearing. The men shouted. I was deafened by the explosion of too many muskets going off, far too close.

I threw myself on top of Alberic.

The monster roared thunderously and ran off into the fields.

The captain pointed at two of his men and shouted. "You two, get these two back to the palace!" He drew his saber and waved it toward the monster. "The rest of you, after it! Don't let it get away!" He slammed his heels into his horse's sides and charged into the fields after the monster.

His men followed in a wave of shouting and pounding hooves.

I vaguely felt someone lift me from the ground, but I refused to let go of Alberic's coat. The world receded into gray fog.

I awoke to find myself slumped against the wall in the prince's bedchamber. Directly across the room from me, the prince, in his ruffled nightshirt, lay tucked under the silk coverlet of his velvet-draped bed. He lay very, *very* still.

On the opposite side of the bed, Theo, the royal alchemist and physician, had his palm on the prince's brow.

I rose to my feet on shaking legs. Dully, I noticed that my coat was muddy and that there were suspicious-looking red stains on my knees and stockings. My shoes were gone. Worst of all, I stank of smoke and something else, something foul. I almost retched.

It wasn't a dream. It had all happened. The monster, the dead…somebody in my house, the fire… Somehow, we had gotten away. Somehow, we had both survived. The relief was so profound I was attacked by a wave of dizziness and almost fell to the floor. I put a hand on the wall to steady myself.

I focused on my prince and Theo. My teeth chattered so strongly I could barely speak. "Will he live?"

Theo snorted. "He's merely asleep." He rose from the chair by the prince's bed and towered over me. "Now, as for you…"

I shook my head. "I'm not hurt." Despite the fact that I couldn't stop shaking, and the bruises I could feel starting to introduce themselves, I wasn't actually injured.

Theo took hold of my arm and hauled me away from my prince's side. "I'll be the judge of that."

Before I could think to protest, the royal alchemist had

pulled the clothes from my body and uncovered my deepest secret, the one shared by only my prince and me.

I stared at him, completely nude and utterly unconcerned by that fact. I should have cared, but my exposure was nothing compared to what I had seen in my parents' house, and what it meant. Half-mad with the terror beginning to freeze my blood, I grabbed his sleeve. "My family…?"

Theo looked at me, and his stern expression melted. He closed his eyes and shook his head, solemnly.

I refused to acknowledge what I saw in his face. "My family? My parents, my brother…?"

Theo sighed and opened his eyes to look at me. "They're…gone."

Gone? My throat tightened my voice to a whisper. "Wh—where?" Despite what I had seen, I wanted to believe that they had all just run away and hadn't been found yet.

Theo heaved another sigh. "The beast…" He shook his head sharply. "They've all gone to a better place, Julian."

Better place meant… I just stared, my heart beginning to freeze solid in my chest. "A-all of them? My brother, too?"

Theo held my gaze. "I'm sorry, Julian."

I didn't cry. I *couldn't* cry. This was much, *much* too big for tears. Instead, I could feel the ice around my heart closing in to crush it. I suddenly heard the wind howling in my ears. Theo's face started to go very far away.

A sharp shake brought me back. "Julian!"

I blinked up at Theo, completely and utterly numb. "Yes?"

"Prince Alberic will want you when he awakens." Theo shoved some of the prince's old clothes into my arms, then pushed me into my prince's bathing chamber. The wall candles were lit, and the huge marble bath was full and steaming. "Hurry up and bathe." He left, closing the bath chamber's door behind him.

I bathed and bathed, scrubbing every inch of myself with

soap and a cloth until I was red and raw. I had to get the dirt off, the stains off, and the smell off. When the water had gone too cold to stand anymore, I drained the tub and scrubbed it, too, leaving no trace of my bath behind. Only then did I dress.

When I came out of the bath chamber, Theo was gone and so were my ruined clothes.

I sat on the chair by the window beside my sleeping prince. He was hurt because of me and my family. I couldn't accept that they were gone. That everyone I loved... That everyone that loved me... That I was alone. I just...*couldn't*.

I never noticed when I fell asleep, but I suddenly woke with my head pillowed on my prince's coverlet. I sat up to find my prince staring at me while gripping my hand hard enough to bruise my fingers. That was when I remembered the strange blue-white light that had come from him. I blinked at him in awe. "You saved me."

He blinked, then scowled. "Don't be stupid."

I clenched my fingers around his. "You *did*. That light you made drove the m-monster off."

His scowl deepened and he looked away, his cheeks turning pink. "Like I'm going to let a stupid peasant kill *my* peon?"

I licked my dry lips. "It was a m-monster."

He shook his head hard. "Whatever." He glanced at me. "Don't mention it." He abruptly turned a hard glare on me. "I mean it, that's an order! Don't ever mention that I did...*that*."

I nodded sharply. "Okay! I won't mention it!" However, I wasn't quite sure if he meant the light he'd made or the fact that he'd saved my life. I decided not to mention either, just to be safe.

He looked away briefly, then turned back to me and shouted, "Don't you *ever* put yourself in danger like that again! Do you hear me? You don't get to die until *I* say you can die! Got it?" He squeezed my hand even harder, glaring

46

at me with narrowed eyes. "And you're *not* quitting."

I stared at his blushing face, then down at my fingers, going numb from his grip on my hand. At that moment, I suddenly realized that there really was a human heart within my beautiful but vicious prince and that someone still alive cared for me, even if it was only a little. That's when the tears came...in torrents. "Okay, I w-won't qu-quit."

He nodded. "Good." He rolled his eyes. "And stop crying, idiot."

I snapped awake in my narrow bed, gasping for breath with tears running down my face. I hadn't had that dream in years.

My family had died that night, all of them. Captain Reinhardt wouldn't tell me exactly what had happened to them, only that yes, the monster had killed them.

I could pretty much guess anyway.

He did reassure me that they had found the monster that killed my family and destroyed it. He also told me that there had been attacks on several farms that night by the same kind of monster. Half a dozen families had been murdered in addition to mine, but nobody had any idea why.

I wasn't allowed to go to my family's funeral.

The prince and I were practically locked in the castle for two whole months. When Captain Reinhardt finally let us go outside, it was only on the castle grounds and under close guard. That was when the daily weapons and fighting instruction started: guns, knives, swords, hand-to-hand combat. Captain Reinhardt showed no mercy. It was like he took it personally.

I sat up and scrubbed at my cheeks, looking around my

room while my breathing went back to normal. The small, rounded door by the fireplace opened to the hallway, but the one on my right side across from the bed opened directly into Alberic's room. My room had once been a closet for my prince's clothes. Even so, it was far bigger than the attic space I'd shared with my brother. The small glassed-in narrow-slit window right next to my bed showed signs of gray dawn.

It was time to begin my day.

I shoved my way out from under my covers and pulled off my nightshirt to begin the process of binding my breasts and then dressing in male attire. I was my prince's valet, and I had much to do before he awoke.

One

While standing in his extravagant white and gold bedchamber, my prince spoke in a voice that was dangerously low, almost a growl. "So, have you taken a lover yet, Julian?"

Standing toe to toe in the midst of tying my prince's lace-trimmed neckcloth into a florid bow, I froze. "What?" I steadied my hands to finish the bow. Once upon a time, I had been a full two and a half inches taller. Sadly, that time had long since passed. I risked an upward glance to gauge his expression. *What the hell is he going on about?*

The morning sunlight falling from the row of tall dormer windows directly behind him gave his hip-length blond hair a lovely metallic gold sheen, but his emerald-green eyes were narrowed under lowered golden brows. A small smile played at the corner of his perfectly sculpted lips.

I couldn't quite repress my shiver. My fairy tale prince was obviously in one of his more dangerously playful moods.

"A lover." My prince waved one hand in a lazy circle. "Someone you have sex with. Have you taken one yet?"

I blew out a sigh and rolled my eyes. "No, of course not!" I was, after all, under my prince's orders not to reveal my...secret.

Alberic snorted. "Oh, come on, Julian!" He folded his arms across his rather broad chest. You wouldn't think a man as slender in build as he would have such a broad chest, but my prince was a lot more athletic than he liked to let on. He was almost solid whip-cord muscle; a fact he liked to hide under frivolous clothes. The toe of his spit-polished black riding boot tapped. "You're how old now, and you're telling me that you're still a virgin?"

"I'm nineteen, and yes, I am." I turned away and walked over to the ornately carved mirrored vanity, wracking my brain for what he could possibly be trying to get at. "Is there something wrong with that?"

He snorted. "I lost my virginity at sixteen."

With my back to him, I curled my lips in disgust. "I know. I was there under the bed where you told me to hide when it happened." It was the most embarrassing moment of my life, too. Who knew that a woman could be so *loud*?

I collected his knee-length gold brocaded waistcoat from the back of the chair and then turned to face him. "I can't do *that*, remember? Not without revealing the truth about what I am." I lifted the waistcoat so he could put his arms into the long vest.

Alberic turned his back to me and shrugged into the offered waistcoat. "Actually, you could... As long as you didn't get undressed all the way. Say, merely dropping your pants?"

"That wouldn't work." I obligingly straightened his voluminous shirt sleeves, lifted his heavy blond mane from inside the back of his vest, and straightened the black velvet bow that held back his obscenely long golden hair. "Certain things would still be plainly visible."

Alberic turned back around to face me, one brow lifted. "One doesn't need to drop one's pants *that* far down for anal sex." He lifted his gloved hand and casually thumbed an errant strand of my long black hair behind my ear.

I held his gaze steadily. "I have no interest in...*that*."

"Is that so?" He turned away. "Theo says you've gathered

quite a bit of interest among the courtiers — the *male* courtiers, and more than a few of their valets."

Interest? I hadn't thought anyone had noticed me beyond the fact that I was the drab valet to the temperamental heir to the crown. Theo, on the other hand, or rather Magister Alistair Theodoric, court alchemist and royal physician, was the only other living person who knew about my...unusual situation. Could *he* have said something to someone?

Doubtful. Highly doubtful. He favored the prince far too much.

My prince turned back to me with narrowed eyes. "Are you *sure* your...situation hasn't been compromised?"

I reached up to fasten the prince's gold waistcoat buttons from top to bottom, carefully avoiding his sharp gaze. "I sincerely doubt Theo has said anything to anyone."

He leaned close, his breath ghosting across the top of my hair. "I'm sure he hasn't, which is why I'm asking if you've taken a lover."

My fingers shook, but I continued with my prince's buttons. "I already told you, no, I have not taken any lovers."

Very casually, Alberic lifted his hands into my line of sight and tugged on his black calfskin gloves, stretching his fingers out very like a cat flexing its claws. "If you want sex, I'd be happy to fuck you, Julian, or should I say, Juli*anna*?"

I swallowed hard. "No thank you." He had more than enough paramours already. I had no intention of being yet another notch on his proverbial bedpost.

"I think you missed my point." His voice was light and his smile sweet, but his green eyes were narrowed to slits. That was bad. It meant he was planning something, or worse, he'd already set a plan into motion.

Even as a shiver slithered down my spine, I felt a spark of annoyance. "Then what, exactly *is* your point?"

A smirk curved his lips. "You're a female, and females

51

have *needs*."

I felt the blood leave my face. Yes, I was a female, and yes, I occasionally had…needs, but I also had a hand that I was perfectly happy to use. "I am fully in control of my *needs*, thank you very much."

Alberic moved toward the windows and stopped at the side of his blue velvet-draped canopied bed. "I'm not so sure about that." He lifted a discarded neck cloth from the leopard skin draped across the coverlet of his bed and looked over at me. "Your bedroom is only one thin door away from mine, you know."

I winced. In other words, he'd heard me dealing with my…needs. Apparently keeping my face in the pillow hadn't been quite enough. "Are you sure I wasn't just using the chamber pot?" Which was a painfully embarrassing thought in its own right.

Alberic snorted. "You never use your chamber pot. You use the pull-chain toilet in my bath, and I have never heard you moan like *that* in there."

My face burning, I looked away.

Alberic snorted. "Julian, do you honestly think I don't know what a woman sounds like when she's being pleasured?"

I barely contained my flinch. Of course he knew. Despite the fact that most people were utterly terrified of the painfully beautiful and gleefully brutal prince, and with good reason, Alberic was also known for being…*creative* in bed.

I lifted his long black dressing gown from the end of his bed with the intent to hang it in the huge wardrobe that occupied the entire back wall, just to give my shaking hands something to do. "What I do in my own bedchamber at night has nothing to do with you."

"Oh, but I think it does."

"What?" I practically threw his dressing gown into the

wardrobe and turned to stare at him. "In what way?" I waved my hand at nothing in particular. "It's *my* body! I can do with it what I like!"

"*Whose* body?" He twisted the silk neckcloth around both hands, pulling it taut between them, and then he smiled. "Did you forget that I *own* you?"

I stiffened. I hadn't forgotten. There was no way in hell I would ever forget how he'd bought me from my parents. Sheer bravado had me straighten my shoulders and lift my chin. "What exactly is that supposed to mean?"

He pursed his lips and let the neckcloth slide through his fingers. "It means that it's time we added a few new games to our…arrangement."

"Games?" That was bad. That was *really* bad. His games were always painful—for me. "What kind of games?"

Alberic rolled his eyes dramatically. "Don't be dense. I'm a male; you're a female. What games do you *think* I'm referring to?"

My jaw went slack with horror. "You don't mean s-s-s-…" I couldn't even say it.

Alberic's smile broadened to show his teeth. All things considered; one would expect they'd be serrated. Nope. They were perfectly even and snowy white. "Yes, sex."

Two

Of all the nightmare scenarios I thought might come about upon being the prince's valet, being seen as a bedpartner had *not* been one of them. I shook my head, thoroughly confused. "But I'm not your type!" The prince's taste ran toward women who were, and I quote, 'full in the bosom, narrow in the waist, delicate of demeanor, and pretty in the face.'

I wasn't any of those things. "I don't even *look* female!" Well, my black, wavy hair was long enough to brush my waist, but that was only because my prince refused to let me cut it.

Alberic snorted. "So you don't have breasts..."

"I do so—!" I slapped both hands over my mouth and turned away from him. God, sometimes I was a real idiot! He did *not* need to know that I had a full complement of female curves hiding under my tight waistcoat and very full-skirted frock coat. I turned around and threw out both my hands. "Look, I don't have any feminine graces at all. I don't sing, or dance, or wear fancy dresses. I have no clue how to use cosmetics..." I struggled for something more to add. "There is not a damned thing delicate about me at all!"

Alberic snorted, but there was a smile playing at the corner of his lips. "You do take punishment rather well."

"*What?*" Anger sparked and burned in the back of my skull. "Forget it! No way in hell! I have no intention of being one of your...paramours! Unlike you, I am not a deviant, thank you very much!" I already had more than my share of bondage, domination, and humiliation, just catering to his whims on a daily basis.

"Julian, don't get above yourself." Alberic tossed the neckcloth he'd been toying with on the bed and set his hands on his hips. "My paramours are of *noble* birth. You are a lowly peon. You don't deserve my more specialized forms of play. No whips for you."

I curled my lip in a sour smile. "Thank you. I think."

A spectacular smile graced his lips, and his green eyes practically gleamed. "You are, after all, still a tender virgin."

My blood turned to ice water. *Oh shit... Damn, maybe I should have claimed at least one lover?*

Alberic raked his fingers through the tail of his long golden mane. "Very well, then..." He lifted a finger. "Our first order of business is contraception."

I tilted my head in mystification. "Contra-what?"

"Contraception. I can't have you getting pregnant. That would ruin everything." Alberic strode past me, heading for the door. "Come along, Julian, you have an appointment with Theo." He opened the bedchamber door and stepped through into the hallway beyond.

I was rooted to the spot. *Pregnant?* He was actually *serious* about doing...*that* with me? I looked over at the window. Perhaps I could sneak out and hide in another kingdom?

Alberic ducked back into the chamber and grabbed the bow of my neckcloth. "Now, Julian." Hauling me after him by my neckcloth, he towed me through the doorway and down the hall.

I grabbed onto my prince's wrist with both hands and dug my boot heels into the carpet, trying to slow him down. "Why this? Why *me*?"

Alberic kept walking, dragging me along behind him.

"Because I want to. Why else do I ever do anything?"

He had a point. I tugged harder, not that it did a damned bit of good. Alberic was unnaturally strong. I could have just punched him—I'd actually paid attention to our Oriental hand-to-hand fighting instructor—but I wasn't sure I wanted to take that chance. As I said before, my prince was *creative*...even more so when it came to revenge. "But I'm not feminine in any way!"

Alberic stopped at the end of the hall before the palace elevator. He slammed open the wrought iron folding gate. "But you *are* female."

"So what?" I threw myself back, using all of my weight in hopes of breaking his grip on the bow of my neckcloth. "Like that's ever mattered to you before?"

He grunted but kept a firm hold on my neckcloth and lifted an elegant brow. "True, I have been remiss. My apologies." He shoved me bodily into the elevator car.

I slammed against the back wall, my butt impacting with the iron bars of the back gate. "Ow!" That was going to leave a nice bruise. I hissed in pain and rubbed my butt. "Damn it..."

My prince rolled the elevator gate closed and grabbed the brass lever on the left wall. "Oh, quit whining." He shoved the lever up. "I've done worse to you."

An electrical buzz sounded, and the car began to rise.

I suppose one could consider being rolled down the three-story master staircase in a rug worse, or being shoved off a horse when riding pillion or stabbed during sword and knife practice, or even kicked just for the hell of it. Then there was the time he hung me sideways from a tree to make a swing... I straightened against the back gate and eased away from him. "Can't you find someone else to play with? There are plenty of females a lot more attractive than me."

Alberic turned to face me. His brow lifted and the corner

of his mouth tilted down. "I assure you that I only play with *extremely* attractive females."

"Huh?" It almost sounded as though he'd given me some sort of back-handed compliment.

Alberic turned and stalked toward me. "Would you like to know your most attractive feature?" He smiled, and it was heart-stopping in its cruelty.

I cowered back in the corner. "Um, not really."

He reached out and cupped my jaw in his black-gloved hand. "What I find most attractive about you…" He tilted my chin up, forcibly raising my face to meet his heated green gaze. "Beyond your ocean blue eyes and blue-black hair, is that you are utterly and completely *mine*."

Ocean blue eyes and blue-black hair? Was he complimenting me again? Then the rest of what he'd said sunk in. I glared at him. "Yours?"

Alberic nodded smugly and released my chin. "As my personal body servant, it's your job to cater to my whims."

My mouth fell open. Okay, so he had a point. It *was* my job to cater to him, but *bed-warming* was taking things a bit too far, even for me. "Fine then, I quit! Get someone else to be your…body servant."

Alberic blinked and gave a small tight laugh. "You can quit if you like, Julian, but if you leave I'll only drag you back."

I scowled at him. "What the hell for?"

His lips curved into that gorgeously cruel smile. "Because what's mine *stays* mine."

A bell rang, and the elevator stopped.

Quick as an adder, Alberic grabbed hold of my neckcloth bow. "Time to become my love slave." He shoved open the gate and dragged me out into the mortared stone hallway of the castle's tallest tower. The alchemist hated the smell of the smoke from the gas lamps that lit the rest of the castle, so the windowless hallway was lit with small glowing baubles

57

connected by a cloth-covered wire. Theo called them electric lights. The shadows cast by the small yellow-white lights made my prince look positively demonic.

I grabbed onto his wrist with both hands again and dug my heels in once more. It still didn't do a damned bit of good. "But I don't want to be your love slave!"

Alberic chuckled while dragging me down the hall. "Well then, don't you think you should have escaped from my clutches long before now?"

"I didn't have a reason to escape your clutches!"

He stopped dead.

I froze in surprise. What the hell had I said this time?

Alberic turned slowly to look at me with narrowed green eyes and a puzzled frown. "You can't tell me that you honestly *like* being my personal punching bag?"

"Sparring partner." It was an old argument. "You may be better with a gun, but I'm your equal at sword and dagger, and better at hand-to-hand. I might have been your personal target, but I was never your punching bag."

It was true, actually. He'd never punched me. I can't say he never swatted me upside the head for no apparent reason whatsoever; he did all the time, although lately, he'd been smacking me with his gloves rather than his hand. I'd also worn the occasional bruise on my shins, and my butt from random kicks, but never a black eye. Not from him anyway, and he stopped kicking me when I finally got pissed off enough to kick him back.

My prince waved his hand. "Semantics." He leveled a hard glare at me. "And what about all the crazy games I made you play and the work I make you do, caring for my clothes, dressing me, picking up after me, caring for my horse, delivering dirty sonnets to my lovers, paying my informants?"

I rolled my eyes. "I'm your personal servant. I'm supposed

58

to play your games. As for the other stuff, all valets take care of their masters the same way."

His frown deepened. "They do not."

"They do so." I crossed my arms over my chest. "I asked."

His gaze narrowed. "Asked *who*.?"

I lifted a brow. "Considering the sheer number of nobles living in this castle, not including all the visiting outer kingdom dignitaries, do you have any idea just how many valets are running around in the castle?"

"Um..." His gaze slid off to the side. He looked at me and smiled. "I have no clue."

I sighed. "Why am I not surprised?" I waved a hand. "Never mind. Suffice it to say that when I first started acting as your valet, I asked several of the other valets exactly what I should be doing for you. What I didn't know I had someone teach me." Learning how to wash and iron silk had been a total pain in the ass.

His eyes widened and his jaw slackened. "Why would you do that?"

I glared at him, and the shout came leaping out of my mouth. "Because *somebody* had to care for you!" The stone hallway amplified my voice rather nicely.

He actually flinched.

It might have been from the sheer volume of my shout, but it also could have been because I hit a sore point. No one, and I mean absolutely no one, went anywhere near Prince Alberic if they could avoid it—except me. The servants were all scared to death of him. I brought him his meals, cared for his clothes, kept his chambers tidy, carried his bed linens and curtains down to the laundry, and collected them afterward. In short, if it had anything at all to do with the prince, I was the one who did it.

I sighed and dropped my voice to a softer decibel. "I owe you my life. Looking after you was the least I could do to return the favor."

His golden brows lifted. "In that case, you shouldn't mind looking after my physical needs, too." With that, he turned and started hauling me down the hallway again.

"What?" I continued with my struggles. "How the hell did you come to *that* conclusion? You have plenty of bedpartners!" He did. Dozens, in fact.

"None that I can trust." His voice was so soft that I almost didn't hear him. He raised his voice a little louder. "Sneaking all the way into town at night to get laid and then sneaking all the way back before dawn is tiresome. Why go through all that when I can just do you?"

It was such a typical answer from him that I merely rolled my eyes. "You have lovers in the castle too."

He sniffed. "I'm bored with them."

I groaned, still dragging my feet. "You'll get bored with me too!"

He glanced over his shoulder at me. "I doubt you'll ever be that lucky."

I frowned at him. That almost sounded like another back-handed compliment, except that I knew for a fact that it was a bald-faced lie. He never kept a paramour longer than a week.

We reached the end of the windowless hall, and Alberic kicked open the door to the alchemist's private lab. "Theo! It's time!" He dragged my struggling body through the doorway and slammed the door closed behind us.

THREE

Magister Alistair Theodoric, court alchemist, and royal physician sat up behind the broad oak desk where he'd apparently been perusing some monstrous book. He swept his elegant fingers through his long, sleek mane of silver hair, and his brows rose over his coin-gold eyes. He looked from the grinning Alberic to my heated and furious face and rose from his red leather chair. "Alberic, have Julian take off that coat and roll up a sleeve. I need to do a blood test to make sure I have the right one."

I frowned, suddenly confused. Had I missed something? "The right one...what?"

Theo smiled warmly and tugged on his lapels to straighten his black velvet robes. "The right contraceptive for you."

I stared at him slack-jawed. "You're in on this?"

Theo snorted and his smile tightened. "This is merely to keep you from getting pregnant, should an assault occur."

"Pregn...from *an assault*?" I was suddenly more confused than ever. I understood that there were those who'd attack me simply because they couldn't touch the prince without lethal repercussions, but *that* kind of an assault? "You're kidding, right? Who would want to...assault me?"

Alberic grabbed my arm, turning me to face him, then tugged my red sash from its bow at my hip. "You've been drawing entirely too much attention to yourself lately." He started unbuttoning my sable brown frock coat at an ungodly speed. "And everyone knows that you have no head for liquor whatsoever."

"Of course I draw attention. I'm *your* valet! And what does liquor have to do with anything?"

Theo chuckled. "When was the last time you looked in a mirror, Julian?"

I looked over at Theo, still thoroughly confused. "When I brushed my hair this morning?"

My prince groaned loudly and rolled his eyes. "Thick as a brick." He jerked off my coat, dropping it and my sash on the flagstone floor. He pulled on my neckcloth, jerking me against him, chest to chest. "I have no intention of losing you to some lowly peon who knocked you up simply because he got you drunk enough to find out what was really under your clothes."

I winced. Unfortunately, one of the laws of the kingdom stated that any unmarried man who impregnated an unmarried woman had to marry her and care for his offspring, whether he wanted to be married or not. Suddenly, contraception sounded like a really good idea.

His lips brushed against my ear. "If you get pregnant, it'll be because *I* want you pregnant. Understood?" He reached down with his free hand, cupped my ass cheek, and squeezed.

My temper exploded. *Son of a bitch!* Screw the penalties for hitting my prince! I slammed the heels of both hands against the center of his chest, hard.

Alberic tripped back, gasping for breath, the wind knocked from his lungs.

I curled my lip baring my teeth in anger, while rolling up my sleeve. "If I get pregnant, it'll be because *I* want to be pregnant. Not because someone wants to breed a half-royal bastard on me." I turned to stomp toward the archway leading into the far room.

62

Okay, so I could have just slapped him, but that was a female thing to do. I hadn't been female in any way other than anatomically since the day my mother started dressing me in my brother's clothes to help with the farm chores. Punching him was right out. It would have left a far too visible mark.

Standing by a small table that held a few oddly shaped bottles bubbling over small flames, the alchemist pulled on a pair of black stretchy gloves and presented me with a small silver lance. "Hold out your middle finger."

I did so, curious in spite of myself.

He stabbed my finger with the lance. A small bead of scarlet welled up. He collected the bead with a small eyedropper and released it into a flat-bottomed round beaker half-filled with a yellow solution. The solution turned pale green. He nodded. "It's a match." He set down the eyedropper. "Roll your sleeve up to the shoulder and follow me to the chair." He strode through the archway into the next room.

I followed him into a room that was brilliantly lit with large blue baubles suspended from the ceiling. Along the far-left wall was a large oblong metal counter and sink. In the very middle was a leather and steel contraption that only vaguely looked like a chair. It looked far more like what one would strap a criminal into for extremely painful interrogations. Leather straps hung from the chair's arms and legs.

Theo waved his hand toward the chair. "Sit here."

With extreme suspicion, I climbed up and sat in it.

Theo wheeled over a small decorative cart covered by a linen cloth that held a delicate scalpel, an ornate syringe filled with a clear liquid, and five tiny slivers of…something. With a cotton ball, he daubed rubbing alcohol all over the bend of my elbow.

My prince tromped over to my side while rubbing the center of his chest. "Hitting your prince is a crime in this kingdom."

Yes, it was, but I was too damned pissed to care. I shot a glare at him. "So is human slavery."

Theo took that moment to stab me in the arm with his syringe.

I winced.

Theo smiled. "This is to numb your arm."

I rolled my eyes. "Great, you cause me pain to remove my pain?"

Theo snorted. "Would you rather I cut you open without it?"

I stared at him. "Cut me open...?"

The alchemist lifted the scalpel and pointed at the five tiny slivers. "To prevent pregnancy for the next five years, these need to be inserted in your arm."

I frowned at the small slivers. "What are those?"

Theo shrugged. "It's from the *noir plant*. Something I collected from the neighboring world."

I looked up at him in awe. Our land of Nod was ruled by magic, but right next door was the extremely dangerous world ruled by science. It wasn't a place anyone wanted to live, but the clever alchemist had been known to pilfer a marvel or two, such as the bulbs in his quarters that lit up like candles without using live flame, the plans for the cable-lift elevator, and the indoor plumbing system. He also set up the huge ice box in the castle kitchens that didn't need ice blocks to keep the food cold, and in fact made small chunks of ice all year around. Theo was a very brave man. "How often do you cross over?"

Theo lifted one of the slivers, examining it closely. "I cross a few times a year. It's where I get my extremely rare pain-numbing anesthetics *novo-cane* and ether, as well as other rare medicines such as *perry-ox-hide* and *penny-sullen*, both of which prevent infections. The *noir plant* was a special request." He nodded toward Alberic.

My prince looked away. "I didn't want to use an enchantment on you. They work fine on men, but they tend to have nasty side effects when used on females."

My hands clenched on the padded arms of the chair. "Side effects?"

Theo shrugged and set the sliver back down. "Magic tends to take the shortest route to achieve its goal. When one uses magic for female contraception, there are far too many options a spell could take to ensure results."

Alberic curled his lip. "Such as extreme ugliness."

Theo smiled. "Or changing their gender."

I shrugged. "I wouldn't mind changing genders." I was already masquerading as a male, why not go all the way?

"Julian..." My prince lifted one brow, and a particularly cruel smile curved his lips. "Are you absolutely sure you wouldn't mind taking it up the ass?"

I flinched back from him. "What?! I thought you didn't like...doing men?"

Alberic leaned over me, his smile widening to include teeth. "For you, I would most definitely make an exception."

I stared at him in horror. I *so* did not need to know that, especially since my twin brother should have been his companion rather than I.

Theo poked at the inner side of my upper arm. "Is your arm getting numb yet?"

I stared down at my arm. I had only known that he poked me because I had seen him do it. I hadn't actually felt anything. "Wow... That's some potent stuff."

The alchemist nodded and raised his scalpel. "Hold your arm flat and do not move."

I held my arm as requested and watched in fascination.

Theo made a very tiny incision on the inside of my upper right arm. It bled only a small amount. He set down his knife and then pushed the slivers into the small cut, one by one until all five rested just under my skin in a fan pattern.

I didn't feel a thing.

Theo then held two fingers above the cut and chanted out a small line of words. The cut knitted closed. Magic was occasionally practical. Occasionally...

Alberic leaned over my chair to catch the alchemist's eye. "When will it take effect?"

Theo turned away to pull off his stretchy black gloves and wipe his hands with a cloth that stank of rubbing alcohol. "Two weeks."

Alberic nodded. "Excellent."

I jerked my sleeve back down and shoved my prince out of my way, practically flying from the chair. I left the inner lab and grabbed my coat and sash from the floor, heading for the door. I was in dire need of a nice quiet corner in one of the attics where I could tear apart a few old feather pillows and scream my head off in complete privacy.

Alberic was leaning against the door with his arms folded across his chest.

I jerked to a halt. *Crap...* I kept forgetting how fast he could be when he set his mind to it. Clearly, someone among his antecedents was a witch. There was no way in hell he could move that fast without magic.

My prince's smile radiated feline satisfaction, the kind where the cat had already digested the canary. "Going somewhere without me, Julian?"

I shrugged into my sable frock coat while dredging my brain for a good excuse to gain some privacy, then I remembered. "Breakfast!"

His golden brows lifted. "Hm?"

"I haven't brought up your breakfast. I need to go get it." I was so proud of myself that I even smiled. Unfortunately, my hand was too numb to work my coat buttons.

Alberic sighed and reached out to jerk me toward him by the lapels. His fingers practically flew up my buttons. "You realize I'm doing this for your own good?" His green gaze caught mine. "And I don't mean your coat buttons."

I knew damned good and well what he was referring to. "Oh, really?" I narrowed my eyes at him. "How is being *your* bed-warmer good for *me*?"

He blinked, and then the most god-awful smile graced my prince's lips. "Surely you know that denying yourself sexual release is unhealthy?"

I turned my gaze away. "I can take care of myself." As I said before, I had a hand, and I knew how to use it.

His voice dropped to a husky whisper. "Oh? Do you think of me when you touch yourself?"

I stared at him in shock. "What? No!" My face heated and I looked away. "I don't think of you in that way." I was lying of course. He was the only man I'd ever fantasized about. Seriously, there wasn't anyone as beautiful or as terrifying as my prince.

My prince wrapped my sash around my waist, leaning close to tie it in a simple bow at my hip. The heat from his body pressed against me, making my heart beat faster. His breath burned against my cheek. "Lying will get you punished, Julian, you know that."

I took a deep breath to steady my nerves and my voice. "Can we go now?"

Alberic chuckled and turned, waving a hand at the door. "By all means." That was my cue to open it for him.

I did so.

My prince swept past me and practically danced down the hallway toward the elevator, looking entirely too smug for anyone's comfort.

I followed him with my teeth clenched and my heels thumping hard on the carpets. I was furious, though not quite sure what to do about it. I had only two weeks to come to terms with being my prince's bed-warmer or find a way out of the kingdom. Maybe I could take a ship...?

At the elevator gate, he stopped and held up one hand. "Oh, wait!" He turned to face me with narrowed green eyes and smiled, sweeter than sugar. "I almost forgot."

A shiver ran up my spine. I knew that smile all too well. He was up to something. I narrowed my eyes at him in deep suspicion and took a half-step back. "Forgot...what?"

Alberic lunged at me lightning fast.

I threw up both arms to guard against a punch. Truthfully, I'd been expecting some sort of retaliation for hitting him earlier.

"Relax. I'm not going to hit you."

I lowered my hands a little and peeked past them. "You're not?"

He grabbed me by the upper arms and shoved me up against the wall. "No." His gaze focused below my nose and his voice rumbled low and deep like a purr. "I want a kiss." His head lowered, clearly aiming for my lips.

A...what? I turned my head sharply to avoid him. "What for?"

Alberic's lips brushed right under my ear. "Because I want one. Do I need any other reason than that?" His hot, wet, skin-tingling tongue swept under my jaw.

I'd never felt anything like it, so I was completely unprepared when the strength drained right out of my body and my neck arched back all by itself as though someone else inhabited my skin. "But I d-don't...k-kiss." I'm ashamed to say that my voice actually wavered with breathlessness.

"Hmm...?" He lifted his head from my neck and his brow lifted. "You *do* know how to kiss, don't you?"

I winced. "Uh..." Actually, no, I didn't. I'd never kissed anyone. I'd never *wanted* to kiss anyone. I looked away, avoiding his sharp green gaze. "I don't want to play this game."

Alberic's eyes widened. "You've never been kissed?"

I shot him a glare and curled my lip in a scowl. "Hello? Hiding my gender! Kissing would give it away, yes?"

He frowned. "You could have kissed a girl."

I rolled my eyes. "I'm not attracted to girls."

He lifted his brow and smiled. "Then why didn't you just kiss a guy?"

I shook my head. "I didn't want anyone to think I was interested in men!"

Alberic snorted and rolled his eyes. "Well, there's no avoiding that. The entire court thinks that I've been giving it to you up the ass since we were kids. Theo is the only one that knows that you're untouched."

The entire court thought...*what?* Ice filled the pit of my stomach, and the breath literally escaped my lungs. Suddenly the sly looks and comments I'd heard from certain visiting dignitaries began to make an awful kind of sense. Not to mention the pitying looks the chambermaids had been giving me all along. "Oh my God..."

Alberic rolled his eyes. "Julian, pay attention when your prince is speaking."

"What?" I stared up into his hooded cat-green eyes, suddenly reminded that I was trapped in my prince's embrace. My heart slammed up into my throat, almost choking me. I stiffened. "Eh..."

"Kiss me." His perfect lips curved into a smile that stole my breath. "Because I'm not letting you go until you do."

I hissed in an angry breath. "You're a complete bastard, you know that?"

His tongue darted out to flicker against my bottom lip. "So?" His lips captured my bottom lip, then his teeth. He tugged ever so gently.

Tingles of shock and feminine alarm raised the small hairs all over me, and I'm ashamed to say that a small whimper escaped. I would like to say that it was from fear, but I would have been lying. I had been longing for a kiss from his lips for almost as long as I'd known him. He was that damned beautiful. I licked my lower lip in reaction and brushed against his tongue.

He responded with a soft sound of pleasure then tilted his head to cover my mouth entirely with his lips, his chest pressing up against me.

Startled by the pressure of his body against mine, I gasped.

His tongue surged past my parted lips to engage my tongue with an aggressive sliding caress.

In pure self-defense, I parried his tongue with mine. I couldn't help but notice that he tasted of fresh clean water and something else, something musky and *interesting*.

His moan of pleasure was loud. His tongue redoubled its efforts while his hands slid up my arms and into my hair. Holding my head firmly in place, his lips captured my tongue and suckled on it.

Shivers erupted all over me and my thoughts began to shred. A warm melting sensation began to pool low in my belly and moisture dampened my drawers. My knees weakened. I grabbed onto his coat sleeves to keep from collapsing.

While his tongue worked to conquer mine, his knee slid between my legs, his thigh pressing up against my crotch. He rubbed intimately against me.

Something deep in my belly tightened deliciously, triggering a strange, powerful urgency that pulsed deep inside me. A moan erupted from my throat.

Abruptly, Alberic pulled back, releasing me.

I slid down the wall to sit on the floor utterly dazed, yet at the same time wound tight as a spring. An urgent ache throbbed in my core. I'd gotten mildly excited in my prince's presence before when I'd dressed him, or bathed him, but nothing like *this*. I had to clench my hands at my sides to keep from diving into my own pants to find relief.

He leaned down and smirked directly in my face. "I think you rather enjoyed that."

My temper flared enough to glare at him, but it didn't help the frustrated hunger boiling in me. In fact, it actually aggravated it. I pushed against the wall and rose to my feet with as much dignity as my wobbly knees would allow. I couldn't think of a single thing to say to him. He was right. I *had* enjoyed it, but I had no intention of admitting it.

Alberic snorted, then turned away to open the elevator gate.

I followed him into the elevator and rode it to our floor without looking at him. I didn't need to look at him to know that he was more than pleased with himself. By the time we arrived on our floor and headed up the hallway toward my prince's suite, I had my…problem under control, more or less.

Just in time for yet another complication to appear. At the door of my prince's chamber door was a young page dressed in a bright yellow overtunic sporting a white crown.

Both of us stopped dead staring at the small boy in the oversized tunic. We traded fleeting glances. Apparently, the king wanted to see Alberic.

That was never good news, for either of us.

I dashed into my prince's rooms to collect his formal coat from his wardrobe and dashed back out just in time to see my prince whispering to the nodding page.

I frowned at them.

My prince straightened and held out his arm, waiting for me to help him into his coat.

I did my best, but unfortunately, my hand was still too numb to button it or tie the burgundy sash. "I'm completely useless, you should leave me here."

Alberic turned to glare down at me.

I cringed back and swallowed hard. "Or not."

Alberic snorted and tied the bow on his sash. "This summons concerns you, too." He turned on his heel and led the way to the elevator.

I followed after him and the little page. "Me? How does this concern *me*? *You're* the heir to the kingdom, not me!"

My prince opened the gate to the elevator and turned to smile sweetly. "Anything that concerns me, concerns my minions by default."

Clearly, that was just an excuse to keep me at his side. I stepped into the elevator car and fisted my hands at my sides.

My prince closed the door to the elevator with a loud clang. "My guess is that he's found another kingdom he wants to add to his, by way of marrying me to their princess."

I rolled my eyes. "In the hopes that you'll bump off the legitimate male heir and inherit through marriage?"

He smiled and grabbed the brass lever to pull it down. "I see you know the king well." The elevator car began to lower.

I should, I'd sat through more than my share of the man's lectures to his son on politics.

"There is absolutely no need for concern that he'll succeed in finding me a proper bride." My prince scowled. "The king has abysmal taste in women."

I looked away and snorted. "Rather like your own?"

My prince turned sharply, his brows lowered in definite suspicion. "What was that?"

I opened my eyes wide and gave him my most innocent smile. "He should leave you to find your own."

Alberic rolled his eyes and sighed. "I'd have to wait until his death for that." He blew out a sigh. "Pity he's even more resistant to poisons than I am."

It *was* a pity. Seriously. The man was practically insane,

though he *was* smart enough to leave law-making and actual governing to his council.

On the other hand, if I wanted to save myself, finding a suitable bride for my prince might be my only hope. It wasn't that my virginity meant so much to me; it was more that his kiss had shown me, in no uncertain terms, that once he'd taken me to his bed, I might not ever want to leave it.

I needed to get him a bride, and I needed to get him one fast.

Four

One would think the king's private chambers would be quiet, subdued, and genteel. Nope. It was a madhouse of over-dressed lords and ladies with servants rushing back and forth carrying drinks, snacks, documents, and the occasional small pet.

Resplendent in his gold silk frock coat embroidered with cream roses, my prince followed the young page beyond the wide-flung doors.

I stepped to the side, perfectly content to wait out in the hall, or rather, perfectly content to be left out in the hall long enough to make an escape.

My prince promptly ducked back out and snagged me by the lapel. "Oh, no, you don't! If I have to go in there, you're coming too." He hauled me in behind him, diving straight into the crush.

The crowd parted around him with wide eyes, choked off whispers, and almost unseemly hastened. Clearly, no one wanted to bump into him.

I sighed heavily. I couldn't say that my prince was misunderstood; he *was* rather temperamental. However, while my prince very much enjoyed scaring the living daylights out of people with his pranks, he didn't believe in killing anyone who wasn't actively trying to kill him first. Though he had absolutely no compunction about sending them to the palace dungeons to be *entertained* by the royal guards for a few weeks or months.

Eventually, he released me, but by then, I had no choice but to follow at his heels. Unfortunately, kicking and screaming in protest in front of the nobility was out of the question. Anything I did would reflect badly on my prince. Not that my prince wasn't perfectly capable of making his own bad impressions.

I followed Alberic to the far wall, with its monstrous balconies and glass doors that shed light on the tall throne draped in red velvet and trimmed in white ermine atop a six-step dais. It was the only chair in the room, and upon it sat the king.

His royal highness was a flushed and corpulent man who had taken to wearing floor-length robes to hide his steadily increasing waistline. Extravagant curling white horsehair wigs hid his utterly bald pate. His jawline, almost completely encased in rolls of moist flesh, was brutally square, whereas my prince's was gracefully rounded, almost pointed. His nose was squashed and a bit crooked, whereas my prince's was delicate and defined. Thick black brows rose and met in the middle over bulbous black eyes. My prince's eyes, however, were almond-shaped and tilted slightly upward, the green of cut emeralds.

There was absolutely no trace of bloodline similarity between my golden prince and the king. I often wondered how such a beautiful prince could possibly have come from that man's seed.

The king's fevered and bloodshot black gaze locked onto my prince, and his smile twisted into an open leer dripping with absolute malice. "I found you a bride, my son."

Alberic's lips twisted into a smile that was equally malicious. "You do remember what happened to the last one you found me, yes?"

75

That would be Princess Isolde, also known as Princess Snow. She died from eating her own poisoned apple. It hadn't exactly been her idea to eat it; she'd intended it for my prince. However, my prince was a little too familiar with poisons not to recognize it on the first taste, if not by scent alone. From that moment, her fate was sealed.

My prince can be very...*persuasive*, especially when wielding the cold, hard evidence of an attempted murder. However, the cold, hard evidence of a previously successful murder didn't help her case one bit. According to my prince's spies...err, *sources*, no one knew what had become of her royal father, but Isolde had put her royal mother to death in front of a few too many witnesses by having her dance her life away in red hot iron shoes, which was of course how she'd gained a kingdom.

A murderess was never a good choice for a queen.

The king waved his hand in dismissal. "That was then, this is now. The kingdom of Swanstone is hosting a unicorn hunt. The one who succeeds in capturing a unicorn will be awarded the hand of the princess Rosette and become heir to the kingdom." The king leaned close to the prince. "Bring me that kingdom."

Alberic's smile widened. "Do you happen to have the princess's measurements?"

The king blinked. "What?"

"Hips, waist, bust line?"

The king scowled. "Hell no, I don't have that!"

Alberic rolled his eyes. "What's the point of winning a less-than-satisfactory princess?"

The king swatted at his only legitimate heir with his long and pointy scepter. He missed, of course. "I could care less what you do with the princess, I just want that kingdom! So, go and get it!"

My prince promptly launched into a lecture on the

importance of princesses being *physically* worth marrying.

The king naturally, had to launch into a counter-lecture on the greater importance of expanding the kingdom.

Meanwhile, I ducked back into the crowd and made my escape. Weaving and dodging lords, ladies, and servants, I hauled ass as fast as politeness would allow. If I could get to the attics and hide myself long enough, my prince would be forced to leave without me. This would allow me to make a nice clean escape to the nearest faraway place with my virginity — and my sanity — intact.

I made it out the double doors and into the hallway, only to be brought up short by a hard, choking jerk on my coat collar.

A very amused yet deeply malicious voice whispered in my ear. "You wouldn't be thinking of hiding until I was gone and then escaping, would you?"

I swallowed hard. "Not at all, my prince. I was rushing off to pack our things for the journey."

I was patted on the head rather heavily. "Good peon. Let's get to it."

It was then that I realized that the Fates truly had it in for me.

Back in his suite, I packed my prince's saddlebags with spare traveling clothes and weapons, making sure that his black-powder horn was full and fresh and the bag holding the lead balls for his pistol was full. I also ordered traveling provisions from the kitchens, arranged for maps to the kingdom of Lyoness, and notified the grooms that our horses needed to be saddled.

All with Alberic practically hanging over my shoulder.

My only chance for privacy came when he started stripping down to change into his riding attire. As soon as his back was turned, I slipped through the small door from the prince's room into my room to change my clothes and pack for traveling.

I hung my sable velvet waistcoat and frock coat neatly on the wall pegs and grabbed my saddlebags. With extreme haste, I changed out of my silk shirt and neckcloth to don sturdy cream muslin. My velvet breeches were swapped for a pair of deep brown deerskin. Luckily, my hand had finally recovered, so I was able to button them, as well as my matching deerskin waistcoat. I stomped into my thigh-high riding boots and then set to packing my saddlebags. I tossed in clothes, weapons, powder, ammunition, my compass, and the small journal I kept during my travels, which included an annotated list of inns I'd visited.

After handling the necessities, I slid into the shoulder harness for my throwing knives and strapped my gun belt around my hips. I took a moment to check my pistol to be sure that it was in working order. It was. I cleaned it regularly. Then I shrugged into my dark brown deerskin riding coat with the plain horn buttons. I grabbed my bedroll, which also held my rolled-up foul-weather coat, and collected my broad-brimmed hat.

Time to go.

Knowing that Alberic was bound to come through the door to check on me at any moment, I grabbed the handle to the outer door to make my escape into the hall.

The handle moved, but the door didn't budge.

I pushed.

Nothing.

I shoved.

Still nothing.

I tried everything short of slamming my foot into the door,

which would have made a horrendous amount of noise and given me away.

Big fat nothing.

I couldn't open my door. "Shit!"

"Something wrong, Julian?"

I whirled around.

My prince was leaning against the rounded doorframe of the small door that led into his suite. He was already dressed for traveling, his white cotton neck cloth neatly tied around the collar of his white cotton shirt and his sleek black leather frock coat buttoned over his red leather waistcoat. His sword belt and gun belt were buckled over his knotted red sash, and his black breeches were tucked neatly into his gleaming thigh-high riding boots with their wickedly sharp silver spurs. His smile radiated as much amusement as it did annoyance. Not a healthy combination.

I glared at him. "I can't open my door." There was no question in my mind that he was behind it.

Alberic waved toward the door leading into his chambers. "This one works just fine." He smiled with all his teeth. "Why don't you try it?"

I shouldered my saddlebags and tromped toward my prince and out the small door. What other choice did I have?

While musing aloud about the Princess Rosette, or rather about the size of her bustline, and whether or not she was still virginal, my prince gleefully proceeded to toss his saddlebags on my other shoulder. He then shoved a valise into each of my hands and tucked his bedroll around my neck. Lifting a third valise, he led the way out his perfectly functional chamber door.

Bowed under the weight of his possessions and mine, and feeling distinctly like a pack horse, I followed him. When we passed my chamber door, I suddenly noticed the half a dozen boards that had been nailed across my door frame. Kicking my door would not have opened it.

Feeling more than a little put out, I scowled at my prince. "When did you nail my door shut?"

Alberic waved his hand negligently. "I arranged to have that done while we were visiting the king." He turned to smile at me. "That little page was very helpful in fetching a workman on such short notice."

I stared at him in open-mouthed shock. "What? Why?"

My prince opened the elevator gate and turned with a pleased smirk. "Don't worry. I'll have the boards removed."

"Is that so?" I stomped into the elevator behind him. "When, exactly?"

Alberic slammed the gate closed. "As soon as I have you thoroughly addicted to my body." He pulled the brass lever down.

The elevator descended, and I had the distinct impression that I was falling headlong into hell. I couldn't help but feel that all of the trials I'd gone through and the terrors I'd survived were nothing compared to what awaited me in two weeks' time.

And so, with my prince mounted on his dapple-gray gelding and me on my chocolate brown mare leading the equally chocolate brown gelding pack horse, we rode out of the castle bailey, across the drawbridge, and onto the forest road heading for the kingdom of Lyoness.

One would think that a prince of such a powerful kingdom would ride to his bride in a coach pulled by six white steeds accompanied by a troop of soldiers. Nope, not *my* prince, though I did suggest it when we originally went to visit Princess Isolde.

He'd turned to me with a sneer. "What? Are you stupid? We might as well wear a sign alerting every brigand from here to there that says, "I'm rich! Come rob me!'"

Anyway...

Keeping to a slow but comfortable trot, we made good time through the forest and into the farmlands beyond. A lunch of meat and bread with a bottle of cooled tea was partaken of while in the saddle.

When early afternoon finally melted into evening, we came to an inn we'd visited fairly frequently over the past few years.

The main tavern room was, of course, filled to the brim with locals having dinner and a few pints of the local ale. However, it appeared that Alberic and I were the inn's only overnight occupants.

While I made arrangements for our rooms, my prince grabbed a literal double armful of giggling barmaids and hauled them into a private dining room, slamming the door closed behind him.

I did not want to know what he was doing in there. I could pretty much guess, anyway. Sighing, I went back out to the stables to unsaddle and feed our horses and collected our belongings.

I hauled all three of my prince's valises plus his saddlebags up to his room, lit his fire in the small fireplace, turned his feather mattress over, and then made his bed with the sheets and blankets he'd brought. In case you haven't guessed, my prince did not believe in 'roughing' it.

Finally finished, I dropped my saddle bags in my tiny cubby hole of a room next door, turned my straw mattress over, and spread out my saddle blankets. My room didn't come with a fireplace. Prepared for the night, I pulled off my deerskin frock coat and gun belt, leaving them on the hanging pegs by the door. Armed with only my knives, my heaviest towel, and a thick bar of milled soap wrapped in wax paper, I went back downstairs to inquire about their bath.

This was one of my favorite inns, as it had a luxury few had. A monstrous fire-stoked hot bath that was large enough for six people to soak in. It cost a few extra coins to ensure that I was the only occupant in the outdoor bathhouse, but I was perfectly happy to spend my prince's silver for that pleasure.

The bathhouse was not much more than a circular hut of cut spruce logs with a thatched roof over a deep sunken stone-lined pool fed from a hot spring. But to me, it was the height of luxury indeed.

My prince had a private bathing chamber all to himself with piped-in hot water. I had a copper tub set before the fire in my bedroom, filled by way of half a dozen tin buckets of water heated in my fireplace. My prince *had* offered his chamber for my use...as long as he got to watch while I bathed. An offer I refused. Often.

After stripping down, I scooped out a bucket of water and scrubbed myself down with the soap I had brought. One did not wash in a hot bath. That would make the water dirty. One also did not use the soap provided by the inn, if one was intelligent. Coarse lye soap was fine for thick-skinned farmers, but it had a nasty habit of scouring my skin right off.

With my towel and throwing knives well within hand's reach, I slipped into the steaming water and sat down on the stones, sinking to the neck. Comfortably seated, I proceeded to let the exquisite heat force all the road kinks and the day's stress from my muscles, leaving me in a blissful state of complete relaxation.

A wooden thunk announced that someone had lifted the latch to the bath's door.

I grabbed a knife and positioned it for throwing. "Open that door, and you'll get a knife in your gut!"

From the other side of the closed door came a frighteningly

familiar voice. "Julian, you will allow your prince to enter, or you will suffer very dire consequences when you get out of there."

My heart stopped in shock, then redoubled in speed from sheer terror. Unlike your average person, my prince *never* made a threat he wouldn't carry out. "I'm bathing!"

There was a low chuckle. "Well, obviously, as this is a *bath* house."

I scrambled up from my seat and grabbed for my towel. "Gimme a minute to get dressed!"

"Don't you dare!"

Five

I froze halfway out of the water. Behind me, the door opened and slammed closed. The latch dropped into place. I dropped back into the water, neck-deep, and turned to face my prince.

He was already stripping out of his waistcoat and shirt. "Julian, I've seen you naked before, so there's no need to act so…virginal." He shot me a narrow-eyed smile and proceeded to pull off his boots and breeches.

I didn't bother averting my eyes. After all, I had been bathing and dressing him for years, so I was quite familiar with nearly every inch of his lean, muscular form. I was far more perturbed by what he'd just said. "You've *seen* me?"

He set his clothes on a nearby bench and snorted. "I've been peeking on you when you bathe for years now."

My eyes went very wide and my mouth fell open. "What?"

My prince scooped a bucket of water from the monstrous tub. "There's a peephole from my room to yours that overlooks your fireplace, where you always put your hip bath." He dumped the water over his head, letting it sluice down his long body. He shook his head to clear his eyes and grinned. "I had it made when I was sixteen." He picked up my soap, lathered up the nubby cloth provided by the inn, and began scrubbing down. "I was very interested in how you were…developing."

I ground my teeth. "You wanted to see my breasts."

Alberic nodded, completely unashamed. "Among other

feminine parts."

Under the water, I fisted my hands at my sides. "You perverted bastard…"

My prince set down the soap and waggled a finger at me. "I am not a bastard. My parents were dutifully married to each other when I was born."

I curled my lip. "I noticed you didn't argue the perverted part."

Alberic dumped another bucket of water over himself to rinse off the soap, then wiped at his eyes. "Of course not." He set the bucket down and climbed up the short stair to the rim of the tub. "I don't believe in denial."

I held out my hand. "Don't come near me!"

Alberic snorted and stepped into the water. "You're going to have to get used to me being near you." He leaned back against the far side of the tub, spreading his arms wide across the rim. "How else will we fuck?"

I hunched my shoulders. "But I don't want to f-fuck!"

Alberic chuckled merrily; it was almost a giggle. "I am definitely going to have to punish you for lying!" He narrowed his eyes and smirked. "I've heard you moaning my name at night."

If one could have died from mortification, I would have dropped dead on the spot. Alas, I was perfectly alive, painfully aware, and thoroughly annoyed. Long experience had taught me that defending myself would only dig my grave deeper, so I went on the attack. "Of course I moan your name." My lips curled into a sneer. "You're in most of my nightmares."

Alberic's smile sharpened. "That was cruel, Julian."

I lifted my chin and sniffed. "I learned from the best."

My prince waved his hand. "Anyway, I came in here because I have a plan."

I narrowed my gaze. "A plan?" Oh Gods, what was he up

to now?

"For catching a unicorn so I can win the princess." He curled his lip. "That is *if* the princess is worth winning."

I rolled my eyes and spoke very dryly. "Translation: If she's absolutely gorgeous with big breasts."

Alberic nodded. "Exactly." His brows lifted. "You know, Julian, I was wrong about you."

I looked at him, eyes wide. "What?"

Alberic's lips curled into a lascivious smile, and he stared pointedly below the level of my chin. "Your breasts are actually fairly sizable. How do you squish them down so flat?"

I looked down. Without realizing it, I had risen in the water until the tops of my breasts had emerged, practically to the nipples. I yelped in surprise, crossed my arms over my chest, and dunked lower into the water, submerging to my chin. I scowled up at him. "I thought you saw them already!"

Alberic shrugged. "I peeked, yes, but you always take your baths facing the other way." His brows lowered, but his bottom lip protruded. "So, all I've ever really seen is your ass."

I blinked. Was he pouting?

"Anyway, as I was saying before, I have a plan." He swept his hands through his long, wet hair. The water drops gleamed in the lamplight. "Everyone knows that to catch a unicorn, you need a virgin." He smiled at me with all of his teeth. It wasn't pretty. "And that's where you come in."

I curled my lip. "I am *not* wearing a dress."

Alberic rolled his eyes. "Unicorns rely on scent, not sight, idiot."

I frowned. "Okay…"

He leaned toward me and dropped his voice to a whisper. "So all I need you to do…"

I leaned closer to hear what he was saying.

86

Alberic lifted one elegant finger. "...Is camp out in the woods just out of sight and catch it as soon as it shows up. Once you have it, hand it over to me, and I'll do the rest." He smiled smugly. "Simple, no?"

The plan did sound simple, but... I frowned up at him. "Okay, so I get that I'm the bait, but how do I catch it once it shows up?"

My prince leaned closer. "Well, it's basically a horse, so one would think a rope would work and just tie it to a tree."

I scowled up at him. "I think you're forgetting one extremely important point here."

His brows lifted. "What's that?"

I curled my lip, baring my teeth. "The one on its head! Those things are not only armed with long pointy horns and pointy hooves, they're known to be very smart, and very temperamental!"

Alberic tilted his head and smiled brightly. "Then you'll just have to be careful, Julian."

Groaning, I lifted my hands and swept my long black hair back from my sweaty face. "And you wonder why you're in all my nightmares."

Alberic's gaze narrowed to hard green slits. "Only your nightmares?" Quick as an adder, he lunged, closing the distance between us. His hands slammed against the wall of the tub to either side of me, trapping me against the wall of the tub. "None of your dreams?"

I was naked, he was naked, *we* were naked...and he was much, much, *much* too close. Naturally, I panicked. I twisted hard to the side and scrabbled for the edge of the tub to get the hell out.

"Oh no, you don't!" He grabbed my shoulder, pulling me back down into the water, then shoved me back against the side of the tub none too gently.

The air whooshed out of my lungs, stunning me briefly.

This gave him enough time to grab my wrists and pin them both behind my back. With a twist of his hips, he jammed his leg between my thighs in a frighteningly intimate position. A profoundly hard, hot ridge pressed against my belly.

I guess I should have felt a small amount of feminine pride in the fact that he was clearly...*pleased* to be in my company, but at that moment, all I felt was absolute terror. I opened my mouth to shout.

He clapped his free hand over my mouth, stifling me. His lips brushed my ear. "If you scream like a little girl, someone will barge in to investigate. Do you really want to expose your gender to the entire inn?"

Scream like a little girl? My fear was abruptly scorched away by my temper. I jerked my face from his palm, tilted my head back to glare in his eyes, and spoke through my clenched teeth in a low growl. "I *don't* scream." It was the truth, actually. Despite my true gender, my voice was oddly incapable of producing a scream. I had no idea why not. It was just another one of life's little mysteries. Rather like the mystery of why I simply didn't clock my prince in the head for his perverted behavior. "Didn't you just have a double-armful of barmaids only a few minutes ago?"

Alberic rolled his eyes. "Yes, and they were extremely pleased to serve me dinner." He blinked, then leaned close and smiled. "Goodness, are you jealous?"

"What? No!" I looked away and twisted my hands in his grasp, not that it did a damned bit of good. "It's just... Why bother with me when you could have them?"

Alberic's hand tightened around my wrists, and he leaned in closer. His head tilted slightly to the side, his damp hair sweeping against my cheek. His breath brushed against my ear. "Why would I bother with them when I already have you?"

I turned to glare at him, eye to eye. "You don't have me

yet!"

"I don't?" Alberic smiled and leaned close until his lips were only a breath from mine. "Are you quite sure about that?"

"Eh..." Well, he did have me trapped against the side of the tub, so he sort of...*did* have me. I leaned away as far as I was able, which wasn't saying much. "B-but you can't do...*that* with me!"

Alberic's brows lifted. "That?" He rolled his eyes. "Oh, you mean fucking." He shook his head and chuckled. "So naïve." His brow lifted, and his narrowed eyes gleamed like sharp-edged emeralds. "Julian, my tender little virgin, I almost hate to break this to you, but there are *plenty* of other things that I can do to you."

I went rigid, every hair on my body rising to attention. I knew a threat when I heard one.

His smile widened. "Shall we begin?"

I flinched away and shook my head. "No! Let's *not* begin!"

Alberic leaned in and his lips brushed my cheek. "Too late." His scorching, wet tongue trailed down my throat, his warm breath bringing shivers.

I writhed away, only to feel the presence of his lightly furred bare leg intimately pressed between mine, reminding me how thoroughly I was trapped. A melting warmth bloomed within my belly, waking something hot and hungry. I gasped in a deep breath.

His deep velvety whisper caressed my ear. "Julian..."

I turned to look at him.

His gaze locked on my lips. He lowered his head.

He was about to kiss me, and I freely admit that I probably should have turned my head, but I just couldn't make myself do it.

His lips brushed mine in the lightest of caresses, then his tongue swept across my bottom lip.

89

My lips parted all by themselves.

He took the invitation and pressed his mouth fully onto mine, his tongue swooping in to engage mine in an exchange of caresses. His lips captured my tongue and suckled on it.

I shivered, the hunger deep in my core tightening further.

His free hand slid down my shoulder to cup my breast, his thumb brushing my nipple.

Shocked aware, I twisted in an attempt to move away from his hand. A kiss was one thing, but *that* was something else!

His fingers tightened to capture my nipple, pinching with punishing force.

A bolt of erotic fire in my nipple streaked straight down to pulse in my core. The smallest of whimpers escaped me.

My prince sighed, clearly pleased. He released his pinch, only to roll my nipple between his finger and thumb. At the same time, he slid his other leg between mine, spreading me open. The hard length of his cock centered on me and slid upward along my feminine core to rub directly against the tiny point that nestled above it.

The erotic jolts in my nipple streaked downward and combined with the delicious slide against my feminine point. Raw lust clenched hard in my belly. I moaned into his mouth, my hips bucking upward, instinctively chasing after more of that brutally pleasurable sensation.

He obligingly rocked his hips in reply, his cock sliding up and down against that tiny point. At the same time, his hand opened to cup my breast and squeezed.

The sensation was almost electric in intensity. Carnal urgency coiled deliciously in my belly. I lifted one knee to angle my hips better, and rocked against him, deliberately seeking more.

Grinding up against me, he pulled back, breaking the kiss with a wicked smile. "I knew you couldn't resist me." Before I could even think of a reply, he released my wrists and reached down with both hands, cupped my ass, and lifted me just enough to raise my breasts from under the water.

Off balance, I grabbed for his broad, wet shoulders.

He ducked his head to capture my nipple with his lips and sucked, hard. Then he proceeded to continue rubbing and grinding his cock up against my most intimate flesh.

A pulsing wave of carnal delight exploded in my belly, forcing loud choking gasps from my throat. I shuddered and arched under the onslaught, writhing to prolong the glorious sensations. The last vestiges of pleasure passed, and I was left decidedly limp and panting.

Alberic stared at me, his brows up, then chuckled. "That was quick."

Still trembling with minor aftershocks, I looked away, my face hot. Nothing I'd ever done in the depths of the night, hidden under the covers of my small bed had ever felt that intense, that overwhelming, or that addictive. My body was already hungry for more.

And he hadn't even fucked me.

I was so doomed.

Six

Alberic set me back down, caught my wrists, and tugged them from his shoulders. His voice whispered against my ear. "My turn."

I blinked at him, rather stupidly, I'll admit. "Huh?"

Staring straight into my eyes, he smiled and shoved both my hands under the water. "You got yours. Now, I want mine." His thumbs pried my hands open, only to close both of them around something long, round, and firm, yet silky smooth and hot.

He did not just...? I stared at him in utter disbelief. Unfortunately, my disbelief was short-lived. Though I couldn't see below the steaming water's surface, there was no mistaking what I held in my hands. I unconsciously tightened my fingers.

Alberic's green gaze was hooded, and a sigh passed his lips. "Oh yes..." He set one hand on my shoulder, the other firmly trapping my fingers around him and licked his lips. "Just like that."

I tried to swallow the lump in my throat. I wanted to let go, I needed to let go, but my fingers apparently had a mind of their own, because they *wouldn't* let go. I wasn't a complete stranger to his...lower anatomy. I bathed and dressed my prince almost daily, but I'd never actually *held* it before.

He leaned into me and his hips tilted back, drawing his

length through my fingers under the water until the edge of the hood caught against my curled fingers. Then the cap of his cock was in my palm. He pumped forward, sliding into my grip until the short curling hairs at his root pressed against the edge of my hand. A groan rolled from his throat. He pulled back and pressed forward a little quicker and harder, his breath expelling in a huff. "Nice... Very nice." His fingers tightened on my shoulder, and he began thrusting into my hands in earnest. The subtle scent of masculine musk, of arousal drifted from his skin. His jaw tightened and his brows drew together. His muscles tensed and flexed in stark relief. It almost looked as though he was in pain.

It was frightening and fascinating.

Alberic leaned in and covered my mouth with his. His tongue delved in to sweep along mine. His chest pressed against my breasts, forcing me back against the wall of the tub. Up against my belly, his fingers tightened around mine and he started drawing my hand along his length, back and forth in swift strokes.

My thoughts scattered and my fingers tightened, unable to think beyond the hungry kiss devouring my mouth, the needy groans in my ears, and the hot, hard, slippery length sliding along my fingers between us.

Alberic abruptly pulled his mouth from mine and pressed hard up against me. He stiffened, his muscles going taut. His lips parted on small choking gasps. His cock pulsed in my hand, and something hot spurted against my belly, only to fade in the water. He sighed and went limp against me.

I blinked, not quite sure what to make of what had just happened. I should have been disgusted, or at least annoyed, but oddly, all I felt was a spark of feminine pride. My prince had found me exciting enough that he'd actually climaxed in my hand — *my* hand.

Would being his bed-warmer be such a bad thing?

I slapped the thought down with all the force I could muster. Being his bed-warmer would be a *very* bad thing, especially once he'd found his princess and married her. Wives were notoriously nasty toward mistresses, and princesses married to heirs of kingdoms were particularly so. Being the prince's bed-warmer would mean a death sentence if…no, *when* she found out.

That didn't stop the cravings already coiling within me. *Crap…*

The thought crossed my mind that the prince might find a princess that didn't want sex? I eyed my gloriously handsome prince. *Nope, not in a million years.* Anyone who saw him would most definitely want to sleep with him. Repeatedly.

I was so very doomed.

Loud banging came from the bathhouse door.

I stiffened in shock.

Alberic turned toward the door, scowling. "Damned nosy innkeeper."

From the other side of the bathhouse door, a syrupy feminine voice called out, "Prince Alberic, are you still in there?" A high-pitched giggle followed. "Shall I wash your back for you?"

Alberic cringed against me. "Shit."

I frowned. I knew that voice. "Gabriella?" The busty redhead was a minor sorceress and one of the prince's most reliable informants. However, her most notable characteristic, beyond her immense bust-line and taste for sexual deviancy, was her obsession for the prince, an obsession that involved outright stalking. Any time we left the castle environs for whatever reason, sooner or later, she'd show up.

The door handle rattled. "Let me in, my sweet prince!"

Alberic turned toward the door with a scowl. "I'm busy!"

A smile crept onto my face. Normally, Gabriella was something of an annoyance, as she spent every waking

94

moment sidling up to my prince begging to be his full-time mistress instead of just his part-time spy. On top of that, her magic didn't always work quite the way she intended. However, at that moment, I could have kissed her. With Gabriella hanging around, Alberic would have far fewer chances of cornering me, because he'd be too busy avoiding her.

"We'll be out in a minute!" I twisted free of Alberic's hands and lunged for the ladder.

Alberic grabbed for me. "Julian!"

"Oh, is that you, Julian?"

I dodged my prince's hands and climbed out of the tub with all the speed I could muster, spilling water all over the raised wooden floor. "Yeah, it's me!" I grabbed for my towel. "We'll meet you in the taproom, Gabriella. Okay?"

"Okay, Julian! See you there!"

Alberic climbed out of the tub after me and whispered fiercely. "What are you doing?"

"I'm getting dressed." I tossed my prince's monogrammed towel at him. "And so should you."

Alberic caught the towel. His eyes narrowed and his lip curled into a scowl. "Julian, I wasn't done…"

I wiped down and smiled sweetly at my prince. "Your hands are starting to prune. Are you sure you want to stay in the bath?"

Alberic's eyes widened, and he looked at his hands. "Crap." He started scrubbing the water from his skin with his towel.

I turned away from him to hide my smile and started dressing. One thing I could *always* count on was my prince's vanity. He hated to look anything less than perfect.

In a matter of minutes, I had my breasts wrapped in their customary cotton strips to keep them unobtrusive and my shirt tucked into my breeches. I looped my neckcloth around my collar, tied it into a loose bow, and dragged on my knee-length waistcoat. I started buttoning and turned to see how my prince was doing.

Alberic sat on the wooden bench by the tub with one knee crossed over the other, his elbow propped on his knee and his chin resting on his upraised fist. He had his ruffled shirt tucked into his black leather breeches but hadn't bothered to tie his neckcloth or his necklaces. The ruffles on his shirt framed his smooth, muscular chest in a far too fascinating fashion. He frowned. "So, that's how you hid your breasts."

I scowled at him and stomped into my riding boots. "It's not like I had an option."

Alberic stood up, and his lips twisted upward in a breathtakingly cruel smile. "Of course not. You are, after all, *my* little secret."

Every hair on my body stood at attention. Even worse, something deep in my belly quivered and dampness slid from my core. I turned and bolted for the door.

Behind me, Alberic chuckled. "Are you running away?"

My fingers scrabbled with the lock. Yes, I was running away, and I didn't give a damn how much of a coward that made me. I got the lock unfastened, threw open the door, and tore down the gravel path as though pursued by the hounds of hell.

Alberic's laughter followed me all the way to the inn's back door.

I slammed the door closed behind me and strode up the narrow hallway and into the main taproom on shaky legs. I was determined to go straight to my tiny room under the attic eaves and lock the door behind me.

Halfway to the stairs on the far side of the taproom, my upper arm was grabbed with bruising force. I slipped a knife into my hand and turned.

A half-plastered Gabriella grinned slyly with plump,

bright scarlet lips. She wore a black satin gown that was corseted within an inch of her life. Her breasts spilled almost completely out of the low, ruffled neckline. The busty, blue-eyed sorceress tossed her blood-red curls and pressed her exceedingly full bosom against my arm. The multiple ruffled crinolines under the skirt that barely came to her knees were so stiff that they forced her to lean almost halfway over just to reach me. "Julian, where's his tall, blond, and vicious highness?" The half-empty tankard in her other hand tipped toward me dangerously.

While surreptitiously sliding the knife back into its sheath, I used the index finger of my other hand to tip the tankard more toward her. "He'll be in any moment now." I took a quick look over my shoulder at the hallway I'd just left.

Lamplight glinted on long gold hair falling over broad shoulders, and my tall, handsome, and frowning prince, sauntered into the taproom.

I blinked. His hair was perfectly dry, and my black mane was still dripping. I rolled my eyes. The man definitely had a witch or two among his antecedents.

"There you are!" Gabriella shoved me away from her hard enough to very nearly throw me to the floor. She threw out her arms, tossing her tankard across the room in the process. "I've missed you, darling. Did you miss me?"

Alberic rolled his eyes and set his hands on his hips. "I keep trying to, but you never let me."

I ducked my head and headed for the stairs.

Alberic's voice lashed out. "Julian!"

I froze in my tracks and then turned slowly to face him.

Alberic smiled, his eyes narrowed to green slits. "Fetch me a bottle of wine." He sauntered into one of the private rooms with Gabriella cooing at his heels.

I sighed in defeat and turned back toward the bar.

The next hour was spent in a small wood-walled room,

97

standing by a battered table, keeping my seated prince's wineglass full while trying to eat a bowl of stew I'd managed to grab.

Gabriella pouted while straddling a chair at his side. "So you're finally getting married?"

Alberic spat a mouthful of wine and scowled at the sorceress. "What makes you think that?"

Gabriella snorted. "Oh, come on! Like what goes on in the throne room can be hidden from me?" She shrugged. "I just didn't hear *where* you were going to get married."

I yanked the bar towel off my arm and wiped at the wine my prince had spat all over the table. "We're going to the kingdom of Swanstone in Lyoness."

"Oh!" Gabriella clapped her hands to her cheeks rather dramatically. "You're going to the unicorn hunt?"

Alberic frowned at Gabriella. "You know about that?"

Gabriella stepped away from the table, threw out her arms, and twirled. "Everybody knows about the unicorn hunt!" She set her elbow on the table and smiled at Alberic. "The Princess Rosette has been refusing suitors since she came of marriageable age because of her twin sister, Princess Blanchette."

"Oh?" Alberic tilted his head in a bored manner, but his gaze slid to Gabriella.

Gabriella nodded. "It seems that Princess Rosette refused to be parted from her sister. However..." She set one finger beside her nose. "The king declared that if Rosette didn't choose a suitor by her eighteenth birthday, he would marry off Blanchette to the first man that offered." She grinned. "So, Rosette declared that she would marry the first man to bring her a unicorn." She leaned closer to the prince. "Rumor has it that the lucky man who brings in this unicorn will not only get half the kingdom but two princesses for the price of one! Snow White and Rose Red, isn't it cute?"

Alberic leaned back in his chair, his lips curling into a sour smile. "This Snow White, she doesn't have black hair, does she?"

I winced. The prince's original fiancé, the one who had tried to poison him with an apple, had also been known as Snow White. She'd had hair like night, lips as red as blood, and skin as white as snow, but a heart as cold as ice.

Gabriella shook her head, sending her blood-red curls bouncing. "Blanchette is said to be a willowy platinum blonde, and Rosette a buxom and full-bodied redhead."

Alberic blinked. "Well now, that *is* interesting."

Gabriella grinned. "Pity you'll miss it!"

I stiffened in shock. "What?"

Gabriella plopped down on the bench and grinned at me. "Lyoness is on the other side of the northern ocean. Princess Rosette's birthday is in two weeks. Even the fastest ship leaving today will never make it to Lyoness in time for the hunt."

Alberic's eyes narrowed, and his lips curled into a smile that practically dripped with malicious intent. "Two weeks is plenty of time."

I cringed. Oh gods, he was up to something.

The sorceress leaned back, setting her elbows up on the table. "You could just marry me." She fluffed her blood-red curls.

Alberic snorted and rose from his chair. "You're not a princess."

Gabriella set her hands on her ample hips and stuck out her bottom lip. "So?"

Alberic strode for the door, waving his hand negligently. "The king wants a pedigreed princess for a daughter-in-law." He turned to me. "Julian, I'm going to bed. Make sure to wake me at noon."

I nodded. "Good night, my prince."

Alberic strode out.

Gabriella chased after him. "If not your wife, then how about making me your mistress?"

I rolled my eyes. Did she have to ask that *every* time she saw him?

"I have too many already."

I sighed. That was true enough.

Gabriella's voice carried very clearly from the tap room. "Then how about your love slave?"

"Have one of those too."

I didn't quite flinch.

With a sinking heart, I gathered the three empty wine bottles, my stew bowl, and Gabriella's tankard to deliver them to the innkeeper. My feet dragged up the stairs to my attic room. How the hell was I supposed to get my prince to Swanstone and married off in time to save my virginity? It was seriously beginning to look hopeless for me.

Gabriella knelt in the hallway before Alberic's door in a black lace *peignoir* that didn't leave anything to the imagination at all. She was fiddling with the lock.

Ignoring the lock picks in her hands, I nodded at her. "Good night, Gabriella."

She jerked both hands behind her and smiled. "Good night, Julian!"

I passed her by, biting back a smile. Gabriella would be a more than adequate distraction for my perverted prince. I unlocked and opened the door to my attic room anticipating an undisturbed night's sleep.

Long fingers burrowed into the back of my collar, jerking me to a choking halt. Behind me, the door slammed shut and I was slammed back into the wall. A tall heavy weight pressed bodily against me, knocking the air from my lungs.

I gasped for breath, more than a bit stunned and partially blinded by both the dark and my assailant's long hair. Even so, I managed to pull a knife from my shoulder harness.

A soft masculine voice whispered against my ear. "Julian…"

I knew that voice. Hell, I knew the scent of the soap perfuming my assailant's hair. I stiffened, even more alarmed than I was before. "Prince…?"

Alberic leaned back so that I could see his face. "Pack everything. We leave for Swanstone within the hour."

I blinked. "What about your belongings?"

He turned to the side, revealing that he was dressed in his long black leather traveling coat, and his valises were already packed and piled on my bed.

I slumped against the wall. "Oh." So much for an undisturbed night's sleep. I lifted my brow at my prince. "Gabriella is camped in the hallway. How do you plan to get past her?"

Alberic smiled, and it wasn't pretty. "We won't need to. We're leaving from the roof."

My jaw slackened. "The roof?"

Seven

My golden-haired prince strode for the attic room's only window and threw open the shutters. He leaned out, reached up, stepped onto the windowsill, and climbed upward, disappearing from my view.

Terrified that my prince was about to fall to his death, I chased after him. "Prince, what are you doing? We are on the third floor!" I shoved my head out the window just in time to get a face full of rope ladder. "Oof!" I had no idea where he'd found it, and at that moment, I didn't particularly care. I turned to look up at the top of the inn's thatched roof.

Alberic stood on a broad section of roof that was relatively flat in the shadow of the main peak. Beyond the roof, the moon glowed, three-quarters full. "Tie the bags together and rope them around your waist, then climb up."

I winced. I'd done just that a few times before for random cliff climbs, and I had not once enjoyed the experience. Unfortunately, I didn't have a choice. My prince had given me a direct order.

I did as ordered and tied the bags together, looping the rope's end around my hips, then lowered them out the window. Grabbing a good hold of the rope ladder, I stepped out of the window and climbed up to the roof with the heavy baggage swinging at the far end of the rope. Once I reached the rooftop, I pulled the bags up, hand over hand, and set them beside me on the thatch. I then collapsed beside them, gasping for breath.

Alberic's brows rose. "Your strength has improved."

I eyed my prince with a scowl. "Gee, I wonder how *that* happened?"

Alberic snorted. "However, your stamina needs work."

I flopped onto my back. "Great." I looked up at my prince. "So, what exactly are we doing on the roof?"

Alberic looked up and pointed beyond the edge of the roof. "See that shooting star?"

I sat up to look where he pointed. A blue-white shooting star was indeed racing across the night sky. I then noted that it was heading straight for us.

"Oh shit!" I scrambled to get myself and our belongings, which were still tied to me, to the far side where the roof rose to its peak and crouched unashamedly by my prince's boot. "What the hell is *that*?"

Alberic smiled and reached down to pat my head by his knee. "Our transportation to the kingdom of Swanstone."

The shooting star coalesced into a black carriage outlined in blue-white spectral flames, drawn by four sooty horses with blue flaming manes and tails. The driver of the carriage wore a broad-brimmed tricorn hat and a long coat. His dark cape flared out to either side. A long whip flicked out, and lightning lashed out from the very end.

I swallowed hard. "Please tell me that's not Death's coach?"

Alberic snorted. "Julian, you know I don't believe in lying."

I looked up at my prince. "How the hell did you arrange for this?"

Alberic shrugged. "He owes me a favor."

Death owed him a favor?

The four incandescent black horses, snorting blue flames

and tossing sparks from their flaming heels, drew the coach in an arc and slowed to a long-legged trot that brought them and the coach they drew to land on the rooftop with feather lightness alongside us. Strangely, neither the coach nor the horses gave off any heat.

I noted that the coachman had the beaked face of a raven, though long black hair spilled from under his tricorn hat in waves to his waist. His cape shifted against his back, revealing that it wasn't a cape at all, but a pair of enormous raven's wings.

The coachman gathered the reins into his whip hand, then lifted his free hand to his face. He pushed up on the beak, raising a mask from his face. He turned to face us. His eyes were the color of gold coins in a hawkish, yet quite handsome face. His golden gaze focused on me. "Have you brought me my bride, Prince Alberic?"

I stiffened. *Bride?*

"Who? This?" Alberic knocked on my head with his knuckles.

I flinched. "Ow!" His knuckles hurt, damn it.

Alberic snorted. "This is merely my minion." He looked down at me. "Right, minion?"

I rubbed my head and spoke through my clenched teeth. "Yes, my prince."

The coachman's brows lifted, then fell, and he sighed. "Pity." He smiled directly at me. "This one would be a most acceptable bride."

I did not like the smile he was giving me *at all*.

"Minion." Alberic grabbed me by the coat collar and dragged me upright. "Stow the bags in the boot." He strode for the coach door. "And make it quick. Master Corwin is a very busy man." The coach door swung open for him, and steps dropped down.

Under the coachman's watchful gaze, I untied the bags and

104

myself and dragged them over to the covered boot at the back of the coach. I unlatched the leather covering and stowed each bag neatly, then coiled up the rope and stowed that, too.

Alberic stuck his head out of the window and looked back at me. "Are you done yet?"

"Yes!" I buckled the boot's covering and strode for the coach's open door. The door slammed closed on me. I recoiled in surprise. "What?"

The coachman leaped from his seat, his wings flaring wide. Before I could take a single breath, Master Corwin held out a massive arm, blocking me from the door. "You cannot sit within the coach."

"What?" I blinked up at him. He was ungodly tall and very broad in the shoulders. "Why not?"

"Prince Alberic paid the price to travel among the dead. You have not." Between one breath and the next, he looped an arm around my waist and jumped with me in his arms. His wings flared out, and we twisted in midair. I was forced to grab onto his shoulders for balance.

He landed in his coachbox, facing the bench. "So, you will ride with me." He set me on the bench seat, then turned and sat down on my left.

Alberic craned his neck, staring out the window. "Julian!"

I turned to look down at him. "Prince?"

Corwin grabbed me by the lapel, forcing me to sit upright. "Your servant is safe, Prince Alberic." He gathered up the reins and smiled at me. "She rides with me."

She? I stiffened and stared at Corwin. "How did you know?"

Corwin snorted and lowered his raven mask over his face. "It's obvious." He raised his whip, and his wings flared out, one sliding right behind me. He cracked the whip.

The horses snorted blue-white flames and lunged forward in the traces, drawing the coach after them. They dove from the rooftop to skim the tops of the trees.

I was thrown back against the black wing behind me. Gasping in fright, I gripped the low armrest as though my life depended on it, but I am proud to say I didn't yell.

Corwin freed a hand from the reins to grab my arm and pull me up against his side. "Hold onto my belt."

More frightened than I'd ever been in my entire life, and that's saying something, I grabbed onto his wide leather belt with both hands, my knuckles going white.

He pulled on the reins, and the horses lunged upward, pulling the coach high into the sky. The trees below us looked like mere blades of bushy grass, and the towns not much more than tiny candle flames amongst the greater forest. The coach leveled out and soared onward across the sky.

Despite the fact that the breeze was rather chilly, it was the most comfortably smooth coach ride I'd ever had. I watched the land under us pass with incredible swiftness and frowned. "Um, considering our speed, shouldn't the wind be a lot stronger than this?"

Corwin gathered the reins and the whip into his far hand and slouched back into the seat. "A barrier has been cast around the coach and team. It keeps the rain off, too." He lifted his free arm and set it around my shoulders.

"Oh." I looked up at my unusual host. I didn't have the guts to tell him to remove his arm. He *was* Death, so to speak, or at least worked for Death. Also, I couldn't help but feel a bit safer, considering that there wasn't much holding me to the airborne vehicle beyond my hands on his belt. "So, um… How did you end up driving…this?"

Corwin looked over at me, his eyes glowing bright gold behind his mask. "Death's coach?" He shrugged and looked toward his horses. "I inherited the position from my father, as someday my child will inherit the position from me."

I blinked. "You have a child?"

"Not yet." He turned toward me and chuckled. "I need a bride first." His arm tightened around my shoulders. "Would you consider being my bride?"

I thought about it. He was handsome and showed no sign of Alberic's level of sadistic cruelty, and he did have a steady job, even if it was a bit unusual. On top of that, being his bride would be one way to escape Prince Alberic. However, one thing bothered me. "What makes you think I'd make a good bride?"

Corwin turned to face the sky ahead. "You are lovely and unafraid."

I stared at him. *Lovely?* He thought I was lovely? I shook my head to get myself off that thought. "What do you mean by unafraid? I'm scared to death of falling off this thing!"

He snorted. "But you do not fear *me*."

I frowned. "You seem nice enough. Why would I be afraid of you?"

He lifted his chin and looked away with a groan. He looked back at me. "Perhaps because I drive Death's coach and I'm not quite human?"

I snorted. "You're not the only not-quite-human I've met." That was an understatement. To begin with, I'd always suspected that my prince wasn't quite human. His sadistic streak was downright demonic. Then there were the phantoms, witches, sorcerers, evil princesses, psychotic princes, lake nixies, pond naiads, garden fairies, and forest fey that had a tendency to harass us whenever the prince decided to leave the castle. I shrugged. "One gets used to such things."

"Is that so?" His voice was soft. "Do ghosts bother you?"

I rolled my eyes. "Only the ones that try to kill me." I gave him a half-shrug. "Though the ones that look half-rotted do give me the creeps."

Corwin chuckled and shook his head. "I'm not particularly fond of those either."

The coach dove into a cloud, and the wind became decidedly icy. It cut right through my coat and clothes. I shivered hard.

Corwin's wing closed around my right side all the way down to my ankles, practically tucking me against him. It might have been a bit too cozy for propriety, but it was definitely warmer. He glanced down at me. "You are welcome to put your feet up and lean against me. We will be traveling over the sea soon, and the air can be quite cold."

I took him up on the invitation to lean against him. The air was beginning to be bitingly cold, and it was very warm under his wing. My eyelids drifted closed. I was dead tired. It had been one hell of an exhausting day. A yawn escaped me. I clapped a hand over my mouth and glanced up at him. "Oh, sorry."

He chuckled. "Feel free to sleep if you like. We won't arrive until sometime after dawn."

"Oh, okay." Without further ado, I tucked my feet up on the seat and snuggled against him.

Corwin's arm slid down around me, his hand cupping my hip.

I freely admit to falling fast asleep. I also freely admit to seriously wondering what Corwin's kiss would be like before I did so. Would it be anything like my prince's?

I awoke with my cheek resting on a rather hard, if warm pillow that smelled strongly of leather and pleasantly of something else, something masculine. I turned over and opened my eyes to the most incredible sunrise I'd ever seen. Delicate pinks, violets, and soft butter yellows spilled across the tops of the clouds under a sky of china blue. "Wow!" I sat up to get a better look and suddenly realized that not only was I looking down on the sunrise from the driver's box of a flying carriage, my pillow had been the coachman's leather-clad thigh. I looked back at Corwin, and my face heated despite the chilly breeze against my cheeks. "Eh... Sorry."

Corwin merely snorted. "I didn't mind." He turned toward me and nodded, the yellow beak of his raven mask dipping. "I never tire of seeing the sun rise from above the clouds."

I rubbed the sleep from my eyes. The clouds warmed to pale orange with hints of violet. Below us lay a wrinkled sheet of deep blue--the ocean. "It really is gorgeous."

Corwin pointed dead ahead, toward the North. "Do you see that line of green?"

I narrowed my eyes. There was indeed a smudge of green on the edge of the wide blue expanse. "Yeah."

He nodded. "That is the country of Lyoness."

"Oh." The ride was nearly over. Oddly, I felt somewhat disappointed.

He pointed to his left. "My home is on an island in the far west."

I dutifully looked past him. "Oh?"

Corwin shrugged. "It's not a particularly large island, but the view of the sea from the manor overlooking the cliffs is nice."

I looked up at him in some surprise. "You have a manor?"

He chuckled. "I have to live somewhere."

I ducked my head to hide the heat filling my cheeks. "Well, yeah, I guess you do."

A shout came from within the carriage. "Are we there yet?"

I flinched and felt a small stab of guilt. I hadn't even considered how Prince Alberic was doing back there.

Corwin turned to shout back. "Twenty more minutes."

Alberic stuck his head out of the window. "Good! Make sure you drop us off near civilization. I'm starving!"

Corwin raised his whip. "As you wish, Your Highness."

EIGHT

The flying coach eased down amidst a forest and settled surprisingly gently on a deserted road. The blue-white flames on the horses winked out as though they had never been, and the carriage rattled and swayed down the rutted dirt road like any other conveyance. Corwin removed his mask, and his wings faded into a tattered leather cape. Only minutes later, the forest became farmland on the edge of a huge walled town surrounding a magnificent white stone castle.

All too quickly, the coach clattered across the wide stone bridge and through the town's arching portcullis. According to the name carved into the arch, we had arrived in Kingston, the capital city of Swanstone, with nearly two whole weeks to spare.

Corwin pulled his team to a halt before a rather imposing marble and gilt hotel. He turned to me with a warm smile and a touch to his tri-corn hat. "I enjoyed having your company, Julianna."

I nodded and smiled. "Thank you, Corwin. I enjoyed the ride." It didn't even occur to me to ask how he knew my name — my *feminine* name.

"Julian! Get your scrawny ass down here and make like a baggage mule!"

I turned to see my prince scowling up at me. I turned back to Corwin and rolled my eyes. "Duty calls."

Corwin's brow lifted and his gaze narrowed above his smile. "So I see." He offered me his hand to help me down from the driver's box. Before I took that last step down, his fingers tightened around my wrist, stopping me. His voice dropped to a whisper. "If you should wish to see me, whisper my name to any crow or raven, and I will come."

I nodded. "I'll remember that."

"Peon! Quit flirting with Death and get your ass moving!"

I dropped to the ground and turned to face my prince. "Proceeding!" From the corner of my eye, I caught the sight of his boot swinging for my butt. I lunged forward and dodged it—barely, then hurried off to retrieve our bags from the coach's boot.

I pulled our bags from the carriage with all due haste, waved goodbye to Corwin, and turned around to face my prince. He was nowhere to be seen on the sidewalk or the road. We hadn't brought our horses, so he couldn't have gone far. On a whim, I looked through the hotel's glass doors and discovered him on the far side of the lobby.

Not quite sure what was going on, I hauled all our bags into the hotel's marble-floored lobby.

My prince took a heavy brass key from the girl at the carved oak counter. With a pointed glare aimed at me and a lift of his chin, he headed farther into the hotel.

I hefted the bags to my shoulders and followed him, frowning. "We're not staying at the castle?"

Alberic spoke without looking at me. "No."

No? But that was where the unicorn hunt was supposed to be, wasn't it? Bowed under the weight of the bags, I lurched after him all the way to the cast-iron gated lift. "You know, we could have used a porter to carry the bags."

Alberic shot a quick, narrow-eyed look at me. "No." By the chill in his narrowed gaze, the lift of his chin, the slight tightness in his jaw, and the stiff way he held his shoulders, I could tell that my prince was on the edge of a temperamental explosion.

I cringed. *Oh shit…*

The bellman in the lift closed the gate behind us. "Floor, please?"

My prince crossed his arms and lifted his chin. "Penthouse."

"Yes, sir." The bellman moved the lever on the right-hand wall into the upward position. The lift rose under us.

The higher we rose, the tighter dread coiled in my belly. I had no idea what had upset my prince, so I had no idea how to diffuse the situation. My only hope was that someone supremely stupid would cross his path, allowing him to vent whatever frustration was seething within him.

The lift opened onto a short hallway with only one carved white door at the end. The door opened onto an opulent suite of rooms that rivaled the Prince's own bedchambers for elegance.

I blinked in open-mouthed surprise. "Wow… Posh."

The main receiving room was painted sky blue with white molding, and the ceiling was domed with a huge floral motif in white. A white marble fireplace commanded the back wall flanked by tall windows. In the center of the room, on a huge circular Arabian carpet, was a low oval table of white oak surrounded by loungers upholstered in midnight blue velvet and silver braiding. An ornate door opened into bedrooms with magnificent canopied beds on either side of the main room.

The far door on the right, closest to the fireplace, held a private bathing room with a pull-chain flush toilet. I dropped the bags on the carpet and rushed in to take advantage of that particular amenity. It had been a *very* long carriage ride.

I walked back out of the bathing room feeling quite…relieved. "Now, *this* is a hotel!"

Alberic shrugged out of his black leather traveling coat, tossed it over the back of one of the lounges, then flopped down on the lounge and threw out his arms across the back. "It *is* nice." His eyes narrowed to green slits and his lips curled up in a chilly smile. "Too bad you won't be staying here."

I turned to stare at him. "I won't?"

His smile broadened, and I swear the temperature in the room dropped about ten degrees. "You'll be camping out in the woods."

My jaw slackened. "I will?"

Alberic folded his arms across his chest and one golden brow lifted. "You have a unicorn to catch, remember?"

My shoulders slumped. "Crap." Resigned to my fate, I crouched over the bags and started unpacking my prince's things.

My prince's chilly gaze followed me. "No argument?"

I scowled in his general direction. "Since when has arguing ever gotten me anywhere?"

He shrugged. "Good point."

I hung his coats on the pegs in the closet and set his shirts and sundries in the dresser drawers, basically arranging for his stay. If left to his own devices, he'd just pull what he needed from his valises, then just drop it on the floor until everything was scattered around the room. However, if it was hung up to begin with, he'd hang it back where he'd found it. I couldn't even begin to understand why that was.

Once my prince's belongings were in their proper places, it was time to take care of mine. I pulled the bell cord to call the bellhop.

The man arrived in seconds. Apparently, he'd been warned about my impatient prince. According to him, there was a good livery stable nearby where I could rent a horse. I was *not* walking all the way out to the outskirts of the city with all that camping gear. He then took the order for my prince's dinner and left.

"I suppose I better get started." I hefted my saddlebags to my shoulder, grabbed my valise, and lifted the heavy canvas tent bag to my other shoulder.

My prince rose from his lounge. "Meet me at the castle gate tomorrow at noon."

"Yes, my prince." I smiled at him. "Sleep well." I turned and headed for the door.

Lightning fast, Alberic passed me and slammed his hand against the door, preventing me from opening it. "Before you go..." His green gaze narrowed. "Did he kiss you?"

The warmth from his body washed across my back, carrying the intriguing scent of clean sweat with a trace of expensive soap and leather. It was so distracting; it actually took me a bit to realize that my prince had asked me a question and another to recall what the question had been. I looked over my shoulder at him, blinking in confusion. "Did who kiss me?"

Behind me, Alberic spoke through clenched teeth, his gaze narrowed. "The coachman, Master Corwin. Did he kiss you?"

My mouth fell open. "What?" I whirled all the way around to face him and glared in indignation. "No! He was a perfect gentleman in every way."

Alberic blew out a breath. "Good." Abruptly, he shook his head, then frowned. "Wait a minute, what are you trying to imply?"

Oh crap... I'd just implied by comparison that a commoner was more of a gentleman than my prince was. *Time for some damage control...* I rolled my eyes, contriving to look as bored as I possibly could. "About what?"

He frowned, clearly confused.

God bless my prince's short attention span. I lifted my brow. "Can I go now? I'd rather not set my tent up in the dark."

Alberic curled his lip. "You've done it before."

"Yes, I have." I lifted my chin. "But I never *liked* doing it."

"Julian..." Alberic leaned closer, framing me with both hands against the door. "Aren't you forgetting something?"

Forgetting something? I cringed back against the door and did a fast survey of all my belongings and camping equipment. "I don't think so."

Alberic pressed up against me, his ridiculously muscular chest pushing me flat against the door. His voice dropped to a whisper. "My goodnight kiss?"

I stared at him wide-eyed. "Your...*what?*" I'd never kissed him goodnight in my life! The memory of our kiss in the castle hallway burned across my mind. My gaze fell to his lips and focused. Suddenly, memories from the bathhouse flashed across my inner eye. His damp, half-lidded gaze filled with heat, his wet hair falling across his bare, wet shoulders, his hot lips on my throat, his warm hands...

Despite the binding that flattened my breasts, my nipples tingled into hardness. I swallowed hard and turned away, tearing my gaze from his mouth. "That's all you want, just a kiss?"

Alberic smiled. "Would you prefer something more...?" His knee slid between my legs and rubbed upwards. "...Substantial?"

The pressure and friction right up against my crotch triggered a hungry clench deep in my belly. Melting warmth spread through me so fast that it made my knees weaken and very nearly forced a moan from my throat.

Alberic's knee ceased rubbing against me, but he didn't withdraw it. "Well, which is it?" His smile was entirely too smug.

I couldn't believe how easily my body gave in to him. My face filled with heat. *Damn it!* I sucked in a breath in an attempt to gather my scattered wits. "You can have a

116

goodnight kiss, but that's all!"

Alberic grinned. "Done."

My gaze dropped to his mouth, and I licked my lips. A chill ran through me. I suddenly got the distinct impression that I had done something monumentally stupid, but... *It's only a kiss, right?*

His brow lifted, and his smile curled a bit at the corners. "I'm waiting."

I glared up at him. "Don't rush me!" I took a deep breath to brace myself and lunged upward to close the distance between us.

Alberic's upraised finger intercepted my lips. His gaze narrowed. "A proper kiss. No quick pecks."

I jerked back from his finger and ground my teeth in annoyance. "Fine." *Bastard...*

Alberic nodded and set his hand back on the door to lean over me, his breath whispering against my lips. "Go on."

I licked my lips again while my heart tried to pound its way out of my chest. I leaned close and pressed my lips against his, not hard, but not so soft that he'd think I was frightened of him either. Not that my trembling didn't give that away.

His lips parted under mine, and his tongue flicked out to brush fleetingly against my bottom lip in a clear invitation.

Determined to see this through, I replied by parting my lips and stroking his bottom lip with my tongue. I encountered his tongue in passing.

He turned his head and pressed in, not voraciously, merely sealing our lips together. He reached in and stroked against my tongue as though it was a delicacy, gentle, slow, and almost...tender. It was completely unlike the other kiss he'd given me.

I stilled for half a heartbeat, a little puzzled that he hadn't tried to take over completely, then tentatively slid my tongue along his, returning the gentle caress.

He sighed directly into my mouth, and his eyes closed. He coaxed my tongue into his mouth and then ever so gently suckled on it.

The tingles that erupted from my mouth up into the back of my skull, then down my spine, emptied my head of every thought I had. I let go of everything I held, letting it drop to the floor with a thump so I could grab onto his shoulders to keep myself from sliding to the floor. The tiny point at the apex of my crotch throbbed. I barely restrained myself from sitting down on his thigh and rubbing to get some form of relief.

Alberic abruptly released me and stepped back, licking his lips in obvious relish. "That mouth belongs to me. Remember that."

I only managed to stay on my feet by leaning back against the door, but there was no help for the heat burning in my face. Barely able to string two thoughts together, I quickly gathered my fallen equipment, reached behind me, and grabbed onto the door handle. A quick twist opened the door. I practically fell out into the carpeted hall.

My prince followed me.

I looked back at him, not quite sure what I would see.

Alberic frowned with his arms crossed over his chest, but his head was tilted, as though trying to work out a puzzle.

"Good night." I sketched a short bow and turned on my heels to leave.

A whisper came from behind me. "You, too."

I hurried down the hall, not quite able to pinpoint where the sudden ache in my chest was coming from.

The livery stable across the street from the hotel was neat,

118

clean, and not all that expensive. They provided me with a placid, dark chestnut gelding with a smooth but ground-eating gait. About two hours later, just outside the king's forest, I made it to a nice little clearing under tall oaks with the occasional flowering dogwood. A freshwater brook meandered along the very edge.

I unsaddled the gelding and tied his halter to a line strung between two oaks, then got to work. The nine-foot by twelve-foot square tent went up smoothly, for once. After unrolling the tent carpet and stuffing my mattress with meadow grass, I made the bed with my cotton sheets and saddle blankets. I then unpacked my peg-joined clothes rack and hung my things on the hooks. Living quarters all set up, I dug a nice little fire pit and set a pot of water to hang from the tripod for a stew from the smoked and dried provisions I carried.

With my dinner bubbling and at least an hour from ready, I relaxed on a convenient log and looked around at the forest. The trees were all new with leaves, and the undergrowth was still short. Despite the fact that the late afternoon sun was warm, it was pretty much a guarantee that the night would be cold.

I eyed the creek at the edge of my campsite. Bathing would definitely have to be done during midday, as with my luck, there'd be frost on the ground around dawn. That was *if* I could escape my prince long enough to *have* a private bath.

Better to be safe and bathe immediately, than sorry later. I put another larger pot of water on the fire to heat. I didn't want a repeat of the 'bathhouse incident.'

Though parts of it had been rather nice.

I slammed a lid down on those thoughts and went to get my soap and towel.

An hour later, I was squeaky clean and wearing fresh doe skin pants, clean breast bindings, and a warm flannel shirt I planned to sleep in. I didn't bother with my waistcoat, but I put on my shoulder harness for my knives. By then, the stew was ready to eat. I ladled a healthy amount into one of my wooden camp bowls with relish.

A small but noisy flock of crows landed in the tree right by the fire.

"Might I impose upon you for a bite of that?" The voice was deep, masculine, and right behind me.

Alarmed, I whirled into a crouch, bowl in one hand and throwing knife raised in the other.

A tall, dark-haired man stood in the shadows of the trees. I couldn't make out his face, but I could see that he wore a black leather waistcoat over a gray full-sleeved shirt negligently tied at the throat with a black neckcloth, dark gray buckskin breeches, and tall black knee boots. He stepped from the shadows, and sunlight caressed the strong planes of a very familiar smiling face with coin-gold eyes.

My mouth fell open. "Master Corwin?" I lowered my knife and frowned. "What are you doing here?" I glanced around but saw no sign of his coach or his flame-breathing horses. "Don't you have to, um…" *Collect the dead?* I didn't want to say that. It sounded rude. "A job to do?" I shoved my knife back into its sheath.

Corwin shrugged and stepped closer. "I…took a few days off." He smiled. "My brother is covering for me."

I tilted my head to the side. "Your brother…" I let out a sigh, then smiled in pure envy. "Must be nice to have someone that can take over your duties for a few days." I turned back to my pot of stew. "I haven't had a day off in…" I pondered for a bit, then snorted. "…Ever." My prince did not believe in 'days off.'

120

Corwin approached the fire and eased onto the log where I sat. "No days off?"

I shrugged and smiled sourly while reaching for the other camp bowl in my pack. "I don't mind." I didn't...really. The prince kept me very busy, and every day always held something new and exciting, though occasionally traumatic. I scooped some stew into the other bowl and passed it to Corwin. "Here."

He took the bowl and reached into his belt pouch to pull out a tin spoon. "Thanks."

I sat down on the ground on the opposite side of the fire with my bowl, and something occurred to me. "So, what did you do with your coach and team?" I couldn't see him leaving it or those six spectral horses in an ordinary inn stable.

"The horses are there." He pointed his spoon toward the tree over my head.

I turned around and looked up at the crows cawing and fluttering among the tree's branches. "The crows...? Seriously?"

Corwin nodded and reached under his long coat and tugged at something connected to his belt. "This conjures the coach and the crows become the team." He pulled out his raven's mask.

I stared at his wood and feather mask. "I'd heard rumors of a half-fae that turned a pumpkin and some mice into a coach and six to catch the interest of a prince, but it only lasted a few hours." I waved my spoon toward his mask. "*That* is an impressive piece of enchantment."

Corwin tucked the mask back under his coat and smiled a little sourly. "Technically, it's a curse, one that's passed down through the generations."

I nodded, chewing. "How old is it?"

Corwin shrugged. "Great Grandfather said that the first reaper didn't even have a coach, just a huge flock of ravens.

121

He simply swooped down with the ravens as horses and the restless spirits rode into the sky after him."

I chewed thoughtfully. "That must have been a sight to see."

Corwin smiled. "Only you…"

I blinked at him. "Hm…?"

He shook his head. "It's nothing." He lifted his spoon. "You're a good cook."

Heat filled my cheeks. "It's nothing special, just stew." I shoveled more food into my mouth.

He smiled and chuckled. "I've had worse, much worse."

I looked over at him with one raised brow, unsure if I should be flattered or not.

His smile broadened. "My own cooking, for example."

I snorted and rolled my eyes. "Oh, I feel so much better now."

He chuckled and kept eating.

It didn't take long for the two of us to finish off the entire pot. Afterward, I collected the bowls and pot, then took them to the brook, washed them, and came back with the wet bowls.

Corwin lit a long-stemmed clay pipe and stretched out his long legs. "Thank you for dinner."

I crouched to tuck the bowls back into my pack. "You're welcome." I rose and carried my bag into my tent. I came back out and settled back on the log only a foot or so away from Corwin to sharpen my knives.

Corwin took a deep draught from his pipe and blew out a stream of smoke. "Is he your lover?"

I froze. Heat filled my face so fast that I thought my cheeks were about to go up in flames. Then my temper flared. I ground my teeth. "No, he is *not*." Though not from lack of effort on *his* part.

Corwin turned toward me, with half-lidded eyes and a

satisfied smile. "Good."

I frowned at him.

Corwin leaned toward me. "Because I intend to woo you away from him."

My brows lifted and my eyes opened wide. *Woo me away?*

He closed the distance between us with the clear and obvious intent to kiss me.

Suddenly, my prince's words echoed in my head. *"That mouth belongs to me. Remember that."*

I turned away.

Corwin's lips pressed against my cheek in a butterfly light and fleeting kiss, and then he whispered against my ear, "Good night, Julianna." He rose from the log and walked into the trees.

I stared at the darkening shadows between the trees, wondering why I hadn't let Master Corwin kiss me. He was an obvious escape from my fate at the prince's hands.

I buried my face in my hands. "I'm an idiot."

Nine

The morning sun brightened the white canvas of my tent to almost painful intensity. I had slept like crap. My dreams had been filled with disjointed scenes of the prince, mainly from our rather insane childhood. One dream in particular was very vivid. It was during the Winter Festival, and I was following him around carrying an ungodly amount of packages with a pony bit in my teeth.

I wasn't kidding about him being in most of my nightmares.

I rolled out of my straw-filled bed and shivered. The air was frosty enough to see my breath. I hurriedly pulled on my stockings and boots, then tugged on my camp robe made from an old saddle blanket. Yawning, I added a few branches to the embers of the fire to bring it back to life, then set a small pot of oatmeal to cook along the edge and propped the small cast-iron teapot on the tripod.

It was amazingly peaceful. The sky was blue, the birds were chirping. Over on his picket line, the gelding munched his oats contentedly. Best of all, no crazy princes were there to ask for impossible things, like poached eggs and toast for breakfast, with chocolate. It *could* be done over a campfire, but not without an ungodly early trip to a local farm. One didn't carry fresh eggs or bread in a saddlebag.

I was not lonely at all, not one tiny bit. I wasn't worried

about my prince either. He was an adult, so to speak. He could handle himself. He could even be polite, on occasion.

Even so, he simply refused to leave my thoughts.

No matter how hard I tried to keep busy and think of other things, that last kiss my prince and I had shared kept sneaking into my thoughts, along with that last whisper in the hall. It had almost sounded like…regret. Like I would be missed?

I shook my head to clear my thoughts and grabbed my hand-axe to chop deadwood for the evening fire.

The memory continued to haunt me.

The hour before noon came far more swiftly than I expected. Considerably warmer than it had been at dawn, I washed off with a rag, then exchanged my flannel shirt for one of creamy unbleached cotton and tied a dark blue neckcloth around the collar. After a quick straightening of the campsite, including dumping a bucket of water on my dying fire, I donned my gray leather waistcoat and went to saddle the dark chestnut gelding.

The gelding had apparently appreciated his breakfast of oats and fresh grass. He gave me no trouble taking the bit or the saddle's cinch.

I pulled on my gray buckskin frock coat, double-checked the set of my throwing knives and pistol butt for quick access, then stepped up into the saddle. At a light canter, I went to meet my prince at the castle gate.

It didn't even occur to me that I hadn't thought about Corwin's surprise visit and almost-kiss the night before even once.

Ten

Alberic hustled Gabriella and me down a small side corridor and into an intimate sitting room with potted palms framing the windows on the far wall. A white marble fireplace was centered on a pale green wall on the left, and bookshelves took up the right. In the very center of the room, on a very expensive Arabian carpet in gold and green, was a small golden oak oval table beyond which was a green velvet loveseat flanked by a pair of matching wing-back chairs. The floor-to-ceiling paned windows along the back wall opened to an exquisite view of the palace gardens.

Alberic closed the door behind him quietly. There was a click.

My brows rose. *He locked the door?*

Alberic turned to face us, rubbing his palms together. "I have it on excellent authority that there is indeed a unicorn in these woods."

I grinned. "Great!"

"However…" Alberic lifted a finger. "It only appears after the first snowfall in winter."

It was early spring.

"Crap." I slumped into the left-hand wing chair. "Now what do we do?"

Alberic dropped into the right wing chair and folded one knee over the other. "Supposedly, this beast is not only highly

126

intelligent and capable of speech but also a personal friend of the princesses."

I leaned forward in my chair. "Oh! Then, we might be able to talk the creature into allowing us to take him to them?"

Alberic's brow lifted. "*If* we can find it."

"Wait..." Gabriella folded her arms below her more than ample chest. "Does it have to be this unicorn in particular, or can it be any unicorn?"

Alberic shrugged. "I doubt anyone knows about this particular beast but the princesses."

I shook my head. "But the princesses' unicorn is the *only* unicorn in these woods, isn't it?"

Gabriella looked at me with narrowed eyes and smiled. It wasn't pretty. "Not necessarily."

Alberic looked over at Gabriella and lifted his brow. "What did you have in mind?"

Gabriella smiled ever so sweetly at Alberic. "I'll make one!"

Make? I frowned. "You mean, like you made your broom into a horse?"

She glanced at me from the corner of her eye and her smile widened. "Something like that, yes."

My frown deepened. Gabriella was definitely up to something, and I had a bad feeling that I wasn't going to like it one bit.

Alberic nodded at Gabriella. "How soon can you have the spell ready?"

"Yes!" Gabriella bounced on the loveseat cushions. "Tomorrow by dawn."

"Good." Alberic rose from his seat. "We'll meet on the far edge of that garden." He pointed across the room and out the window. "Tomorrow, one hour before noon."

Gabriella's brows rose. "But it'll be ready at *dawn*."

My prince curled his lip. "I do *not* get up at dawn."

"Pfft!" I covered my mouth and hunched my shoulders to hide the snickers trying to escape. No, my prince did not get up at dawn, ever. Not even to kick a lover out of his bed. That was my job.

Alberic lifted his hand. "And you!" He pointed straight at me. "Make preparations for my appearance at tonight's ball."

I leaped from my chair in utter shock. "A ball, *tonight*?" Did he even have something fancy enough to wear to one? I quickly ran through my memory of what my prince had brought with him. Yes, he had one whole outfit in forest green and gold that might work... "I'll have to brush out the velvet, iron the silks, and starch all the lace..." I think I actually had some starch in my bags. I looked at my prince in a panic. "Did you remember your curling irons and the good razor?"

Alberic headed for the door. "I never leave home without them." He turned back and smiled. "You know that." He stepped out into the hall.

Gabriella's eyes widened. "He uses curling irons?"

I snorted and headed for the door after my prince. "What? Did you think those golden curls he sports at formal functions were *natural*?"

She curled her lip and followed me. "Mine are."

I rolled my eyes and followed my prince out into the hall. "Must be nice." I didn't have big romantic curls either, merely black waves.

Alberic marched up the hall at a quick pace, waving his hand imperiously. "Come, peon! I expect perfection from you tonight! Perfection!"

I trotted after him. "Yes, my prince. Of course, my prince."

The ride through the forest back to my prince's hotel

lathered our horses and us. I paced the entire ride up the elevator going over everything I'd need to get my prince ready. He watched me with a small smile on his lips.

As soon as his door was unlocked, I ran right past him to start the bath for my prince. When I came back out, I dropped my coat and my knife harness on one of the lounges and rolled up my sleeves. Moving swiftly from long practice, I scurried around to gather everything he'd need for the ball. Once I had everything set out, I stoked a small fire in the fireplace to heat the pair of curling irons and the flatiron for his silks.

I then turned to my prince with a glint in my eye. "Strip now!"

He blinked, but rose from his chair and got undressed, draping his clothes on the lounge behind him.

Keeping my gaze firmly trained above the waist, I practically shoved him into the bathroom, then into the bubble-filled tub. I tossed a sponge into the water. "Scrub everything!" I turned at the bathroom door and pointed at him. "Use the chamomile shampoo for your hair." It made extra highlights. "And don't forget the pot of conditioner afterward!" That kept his hair from frizzing from the curling irons. I bolted out the door and into the bedroom.

Once I had brushed his velvet coat, waistcoat, and knee-breeches, pressed his shirt and neckcloth, and dry-starched his lace collar and cuffs, I spread everything out on his bed. Nodding at my accomplishments, I hunted through his valise for his good folding razor and the pot of bay rum soap powder.

Dragging the footstool behind me, I strode into the bathroom to find my prince with his back to me, completely nude with his arms upraised, scrubbing a white towel over his damp hair. Droplets of water trickled down the muscles of his back to a rather shapely butt, round, firm and dimpled at the top and the sides…

Alberic turned around to smile from under his towel. "See something you like?"

I was so annoyed at myself for staring and actually enjoying the view that my temper flared hot. At my side, I flicked open the straight razor, and I swear, my voice dropped to a lower register. "I'm sorry. What was that?"

My prince's eyes widened. He dropped the towel from his hair to cover his crotch. "Um, nothing!"

I smiled, showing all of my teeth. "Good." I kicked the footstool toward him and brandished the razor. "Sit."

It took a good four hours to get my prince, shaved, curled, styled, dressed, buttoned, and bowed for his ball, but the results were worth it.

His hair was a cascade of gleaming golden curls that tumbled unbound to the middle of his back. The rich cream silk shirt and the neckcloth tied at his throat were trimmed in gold-embroidered lace, matching the gold-embroidered leaves and vines that practically encrusted his forest green velvet waistcoat and the lapels, cuffs, and collar of his frock coat. A black satin sash, also embroidered in gold, was bow-tied at his back, matching the spit-polished gleaming black knee boots with their gold tassels and spurs.

I sat him on the stool before the tiny vanity to give him the finishing touches. There were jet drops for his pierced ears, a smidgeon of rouge on his lips, then I brushed a whisper of black kohl on his lashes to show exactly how long they truly were.

I stood back. "Finished."

Alberic smiled at my reflection in the glass. "Will I do?"

In the glass, I looked more than a bit frazzled, with curling tendrils of my black hair falling loose from its bow and my shirt wrinkled beyond recognition, but he looked magnificent. I nodded and smiled. "You will definitely break hearts tonight."

He looked down to tuck a lace-trimmed handkerchief into the wide cuff of his sleeve. "Well, hurry up and go take your bath."

I blinked at him. "Huh?"

Alberic scowled at me. "Julian, my personal valet cannot walk into a grand ball looking like that!"

"What..." My mouth fell open, then snapped closed. I didn't want to go. I didn't feel like seeing him in all his magnificent glory dancing and flirting with those equally glorious princesses under the crystal chandeliers. Merely being one more servant standing by the wall had never bothered me before, but for some reason, at that moment, it did. I looked away, folded my arms across my chest, and lifted my chin. Luckily, I had an excellent excuse. "Bath or not, my clothes are all at my campsite, and what I have isn't suitable."

Alberic lips curled into a sadistic smile. "That midnight blue coat, waistcoat, and breeches should not only be suitable but should fit you perfectly. In fact, I know they will."

I frowned. I had noticed that outfit when I'd unpacked it and hung it in the hotel wardrobe, but I hadn't thought twice about it. My prince had new clothes delivered almost daily. "You had it made...for *me*?"

Alberic lifted one golden brow. "Does anyone *else* provide you with clothes?"

He had a point. If it weren't for him, I'd be running around in gleanings from the castle attics. It was rare that he had something *that* extravagant made for me, but he did on occasion. "But I'll make you late!"

Alberic rose from the stool. "Only fashionably late." He pulled his riding crop from the back of his sash.

I blinked. *When did he put that there?*

My prince pointed the crop toward the bathroom and lifted his chin, his eyes narrowing to icy emerald slits. "Bath. Now." He swatted his gloved palm with his crop. It made a sharp thwack. The threat was obvious.

I swallowed and went to the bathroom. My prince never made a threat he wouldn't carry out, and I had no interest in riding all the way to the castle with a sore butt.

Rather than fill the whole tub, I merely ran the water and scrubbed my hair, then myself. Since it was his idea for me to bathe, I didn't feel the least bit guilty using his bar of sandalwood soap or his lavender shampoo. I came back out with a towel around my dripping hair, my breasts rebound in the cotton strapping and wearing my plain white cotton undershorts.

He stared down at my bare legs and curled his lip. He swept his crop out and pointed it at my legs. "Shave those, and your armpits."

I stiffened. "What? Only girls shave like that." Oh wait, he did, too. "I meant, why? No one will see it."

My prince folded his arms across his chest and lifted his chin. "I *could* make you shave your pubic hair too."

I bolted back into the bathroom to shave. It's not easy to shave one's legs or other intimate parts with a straight razor, but I'd had plenty of practice on myself back when I was learning to shave my prince. I just didn't like all the itching from when it grew back. Almost thirty minutes later, I left the bathroom annoyed, but nick-free.

My prince sat on the bed. Beside him was the midnight blue outfit along with a cream silk shirt, a matching neckcloth trimmed in snowy white lace to go with it, and a pair of cream silk stockings. He twirled a scrap of cream silk and lace on his

132

finger. He turned to me and his bottom lip protruded in a pout. "Those under-shorts do not go with this outfit."

I set my hands on my hips. "They're all I have."

He tossed the scrap of silk he'd been twirling at me. "Wear those."

I caught the scrap and discovered that they were a very tiny pair of silk shorts trimmed in very expensive lace. I stared at it wide-eyed. It was very...*feminine*.

My prince smiled. "You'd better hurry and get dressed."

"First things first." I tossed the shorts back at him, grabbed the shirt and neckcloth from the bed, and moved them to the desk, where I'd set up a damp towel for ironing his silks. The flat iron was still hot by the coals, so I was able to press the shirt and neckcloth quickly. I then brushed out the velvet on the breeches, waistcoat, and frockcoat.

I admit I rushed both the ironing and the brushing a bit, but then, I wasn't a prince, merely the servant of one. I did, however, linger over the embroidery on the midnight blue coat's cuffs, collar, and hem. Although the silk thread was a bright cobalt blue rather than gold, the leaf pattern was identical to the embroidery on my prince's coat. There would be no mistaking to whom I belonged.

However, before I could dress, I had to do something about my still-dripping hair. I walked over to the small vanity and pulled off the towel wrapped around my head. My damp hair tumbled in a semi-snarled mess over my shoulders to the middle of my back. I picked up the wide brush to begin the task of taming it.

My prince stepped up behind me and tugged the brush from my hand. "It will be faster if I do it." He swept the brush through my hair.

The tingle of magic spilled down my back, and I could feel hot air swirling around the brush. With each sweep, the brush dried my hair into sleek shiny waves. My eyes widened.

133

"That's a neat trick."

He slid his fingers into my hair, creating even more tingles, though not from magic. "I can dry it, but I can't make it curl." He twirled a tendril around his finger and frowned slightly. "Such a pity…"

I swallowed, somewhat dazed over the strange intimacy of having him brush my hair. "Drying is good enough for me."

Alberic set one hand on my bare shoulders and smiled. "Alright, let's get you dressed, starting with these." He held up the scrap of silk meant to be under-shorts.

I snatched them from his hand and got up from the stool to stomp over to the bed where my clothes were laid out. "Pain in my ass…"

My prince snickered. "I sincerely doubt you're ready for that just yet."

I turned to face him. "What?"

He shook his head and smiled. "Never mind." He waved his hand toward me. "Hurry up and change."

Despite the fact that he'd already seen me naked, I didn't want to drop my shorts right there in front of him. I looked over at the bathroom door. *Maybe?*

My prince took two quick long strides to stand between me and the bathroom. "Don't even think about it."

I ground my teeth. *Bastard!* Having no other choice, I turned my back, dropped my cotton shorts, and slid into the silk. They were surprisingly comfortable, though they did sit a little high on my butt.

My prince whistled softly. "Those suit you *very* well indeed."

I grabbed the silk stockings and sat down on the bed to roll them on. "Gee, thanks."

My prince grinned. "I'm having a dozen more made."

"Don't go out of your way on my account!" I grabbed the knee-breeches and pulled them on.

134

My prince chuckled. "Oh, I'm not. I've always preferred silk over cotton."

I stood up and turned my back to my prince to button the nine-button flap in the front. "Yes, I know, but you're not wearing them."

His voice dropped to a whisper. "No, but I will be the one removing them."

I turned to face him. "What?"

Alberic walked over to the end of the bed. "That binding you wear over your breasts..." He waved his hand in my general direction. "It needs to be replaced with something a bit more...elegant."

I rolled my eyes and slid my shirt into my waistcoat, then both into my coat. I lifted the whole thing and shrugged into all three together. Doing it that way kept the lace from getting crushed. "If you have anyone make something like that, they'll know that I'm female." I whisked through the shirt's lacings and bow-tied the cuffs.

He shrugged. "Only if they know who will be wearing it."

I turned my back to tuck my shirt into my pants. "Kind of hard to avoid when I go in for a fitting."

He snorted. "I'm sure my tailors can make something if I give them the proper measurements."

I buttoned my waistcoat from bottom to top with haste. "Anything will be more comfortable than cotton strapping." I reached for the neckcloth.

My prince plucked the silk from my fingers and stepped close to loop it around my shirt collar. "You wouldn't mind if I had something made?" My prince began tying my neckcloth into an elegant bow under my chin.

I scooped my hair out from under the silk. "Nope. Whatever they make will probably be a whole lot easier and faster to put on."

His voice dropped to a whisper. "Easier to take off, too."

I stiffened. "What?"

He turned away and waved a hand. "Nothing for you to be concerned with."

"Fine, whatever…" I walked back over to the lounge to grab my knife harness and unbuckled it at the shoulders to get it on under the coat.

He frowned. "You're going armed?"

I rolled my eyes at him. "As your valet, it is my duty to protect you."

Alberic lifted a black sash that matched his and walked over to me. "I'm not helpless." He looped it over the coat and around my waist, then turned me around to make a bow in the back. "I can handle myself in a duel of swords or pistols."

"I have no intention of interfering in any of your duels." I reached under my coat to check the set of my knives. "It's the brigands hired by the sore losers that concern me." I looked over my shoulder at him. "You did take your poison antidote, right?"

Alberic curled his lip. "Of course. I'm not an idiot." He walked over to the table by the lounges and picked up a very extravagant black velvet tricorn hat festooned with iridescent green and black feathers. "Your hat is over here on the table along with a pair of gloves." He headed out the door. "Don't dawdle, peon!"

I stomped into my riding boots with all due haste. I still didn't want to go, but what choice did I have? He was my prince, and I was his servant. I rushed over to the table to grab a smaller black felt tricorn hat with three blue-black feathers and the pair of black leather gloves beside it, then bolted out the door after him.

Eleven

Leaning on the polished golden oak banister of the balcony overlooking the grand gala, I thumbed a long tendril of my black hair behind my ear and smiled sourly at the scene of fairytale perfection one story below me.

Flecks of rainbow-tinted light from the massive lead-crystal chandelier suspended from the domed ceiling high overhead sparkled on the slender two-story mirrors that lined the curved white marble walls. Only a few long strides from the walls, gold-flecked marble columns supported the balcony that encircled the entire ballroom. At the head of the room, a full orchestra played before tall windows draped with sheer gold silk.

The dance floor was made of extravagant black and golden oak parquet designed to look like a compass rose. However, it was near impossible to see under the swirl of brilliantly bedecked lords and ladies dancing upon it.

In the very center of the crush of dancers, my prince smiled while promenading with the Rose Red princess. The deep green velvet of his coat set off her emerald and ruby drop necklace and brought the deep garnet roses on her cream and gold gown to life. Emeralds and diamonds glittered among the curls of her titian red hair.

From the frowns and scowls of the bystanders, a goodly number of the other princes and quite a few of the lesser nobles were less than pleased. My prince had already danced with Rose Red twice and Snow White three times. My prince would undoubtedly be involved in more than a few duels over the next few days.

A deep masculine voice whispered just behind me. "They live in a far and distant world from the rest of us, yes?"

I nodded absently, then frowned. *Who...?* I turned around.

Directly behind me, Death's coachman looked past my shoulder at the throng below. He was dressed in his full coachman's coat, cape, and feathered tricorn hat. Blue eldritch light glittered among the folds of his cape and long coat.

I blinked. "Master Corwin?"

He turned to me and smiled. "Well met, Juliann—"

I moved swiftly, pressing my gloved fingers to his lips and whispering a tad hoarsely, "Julian, if you please." I glanced at the other valets and servants that occupied the balcony.

He rolled his eyes and nodded.

I removed my fingers with a relieved sigh.

Corwin moved to stand next to me and set his elbows on the railing. "This masquerade of yours..."

I clenched my jaw and spoke through my teeth. "Is necessary."

He narrowed his golden eyes. "It's annoying. I don't see how anyone could mistake you for..." He cleared his throat and lowered his voice. "Anything but what you are."

I shrugged and smiled sourly. "People see what they want to see."

Corwin nodded at the crowd below. "And I see a prince who may have need of a valet but has no understanding of your true nature."

I lifted my brow and poked out my bottom lip. "I happen to be an excellent valet."

He frowned and leaned close to whisper. "What about what you truly are?"

I looked away and set my elbows on the railing and stared

over the crowd and out the distant window at the night sky. "I've been at the prince's side since I was a child. We had the same tutors and dueling masters. I'm a fair shot with a pistol and a better swordsman. I can read, write, and cipher mathematics and maps…" I shook my head. "I simply don't know how to be anything else."

Corwin leaned against my shoulder and spoke softly. "Do you regret it? Do you regret not getting the chance to be…yourself?"

I frowned slightly. *Did* I regret it? Honestly, I wasn't sure. Every day of my life had been so filled with anticipating my prince's next requirements or avoiding his wrath, there hadn't been any time to contemplate regrets. I shrugged. "I can't regret what I've never known."

Master Corwin set his hand over mine and took a step back, pulling me away from the railing. "Then allow me to give you a taste of what you could be." He pressed his other hand over our joined hands. Blue-white foxfire blazed around him in a corona. It slid down his arms and spilled over onto me.

It happened so fast that I didn't have time to blink. For an entire breath, I was blinded by the brightness. Once my sight returned, the first thing I noticed was that my arm looked wrong. Instead of seeing my cuffed coat sleeve, a long white satin glove covered my arm and rose up above my elbows. Then I noticed the rest.

I was in a floor-length gown of shimmering rainbow-cream silk with full belled skirts. Though simple in design, not a single flounce or ruffle anywhere, the whole thing shimmered with iridescent pearls and leaded crystal brilliants. "What is *this*?"

He turned me to face one of the wall mirrors. "You don't like it?"

To my complete shock, my hair was stark white and held

back from my brow by a tiny tricorn hat set with curling iridescent feathers. Hundreds of tiny crystal brilliants winked among the snowy curls that spilled down my back to an impossibly small waist. However, I couldn't feel the restriction of a corset at all.

It was also very, *very* low-cut, showing off more cleavage than I thought was possible without falling out. Seriously, it was on par with one of Gabriella's necklines, yet even though I could still feel the constriction of my breast bindings around my chest, they were nowhere to be seen. I frowned. "An illusion?"

Master Corwin smiled. "It doesn't have to be. You are so much more than a—" His lips curled disdainfully. "—Valet." He tugged to pull me close, then lifted my hand to his shoulder and set his other hand on my waist. With a tug and a gentle push, he drew me into a slow twirl that became the steps of the dance occurring below.

My skirts belled out with my movements. I could even hear the whisper of silk, yet I could feel only the skirts of my coat moving around me and the riding boots on my feet. Still, something about his illusion bothered me. "Why…white?"

Corwin smiled. "It suits you."

I'll have you know that I did *not* step on Corwin's feet. I had been thoroughly trained in the art of dance. My prince had needed a partner during his lessons. Guess who was volunteered for that position?

Anyway…

Despite the fact that it was only an illusion, it was fun. For a brief bittersweet moment, I wondered what it would have been like to actually be in that gown and on the receiving end of a gentleman's favor.

However, like all good things, someone had to ruin it for me.

Gabriella's unmistakable voice came from behind me.

140

"Mind if I cut in?" She caught my elbow and tugged hard enough to not only pull me from Corwin's grasp but also knock me into a twirl that took me several steps away.

Instantaneously, she took my place, grasping his hand while pressing her massive bosom against his chest. "My, my, my, what an incredible man you are! I simply could not resist having a taste for myself."

Corwin was whirled away and out onto the balcony, his eyes wide...and pinned to her cleavage.

I stood there in shock, the illusion dissolving around me, wondering if I should go to Corwin's rescue, or Gabriella's. Did she even know that she had just cut in on and practically manhandled Death's Coachman?

From behind, a hand covered my mouth and pulled me back against a hard chest.

I stiffened. *What the hell?*

The harsh whisper of my prince's voice lashed against my ear. "Can't leave you alone for a second!"

I was hauled backward into a curtained alcove by one of the mirrors. I hadn't even known it was there. The candlelit space was small, barely large enough for the small, round table draped in white damask and the two elegant wooden chairs with red velvet seat cushions. The prince practically ripped the gold drapery closed, hiding the doorway, and us.

Bathed in shadows cast by the candles in the wall sconces, my prince turned me around and grabbed me by my upper arms to slam me back against the wall. He glared at me ferociously from only inches away. "Are you *trying* to get yourself kidnapped?"

I blinked. "Kidnapped?" I shoved against my prince's chest to make some breathing space. "By who? Master Corwin?"

My prince was unmovable. "Yes, Master Corwin, you imbecile. It's traditional, in fact." His lips curled in a scowl. "I

141

knew I should have kept you down on the ballroom floor where I could keep an eye on you." His fingers tightened on my upper arms.

I winced. I was definitely going to have bruises by morning. "What's traditional? Kidnapping people?"

Alberic's eyes narrowed to green slits. "Death's Coachmen always kidnap their women to bear their children, you little idiot. All he needs to do is kiss you, and he owns your soul."

What...? I blinked up at him. "So you tossed Gabriella his way instead?" Good lord, what was he thinking?

He rolled his eyes. "Gabriella is a sorceress. Even as inept as she is, she's still his equal." His gaze focused on me. "You are not."

Not his equal... Shock hit me like a punch in the gut. Gabriella was a sorceress, Corwin was Death's Coachman, Alberic was a prince, and I...? I was the lowly human among them, a servant who had clearly overstepped their bounds. I had reached too high for my station. I looked away to hide the suspicious burning in my eyes. "I see."

Alberic's whisper was soft but edged. "No, I don't think you do." He grabbed me by the shoulder and shoved me, turning me around to face the wall.

I put up my hands barely in time to save my face from smacking into the marble. I pushed away from the wall. "Prince? What...?"

His harsh whisper rasped against my ear. "Keep quiet, unless you want an audience for this." His hands tugged at the bow of the sash on my back. He yanked it free, tossing it onto one of the chairs behind us. His arms slid around me to undo my coat buttons inhumanly fast, then my waistcoat buttons.

Icy cold alarm washed through me. "What are you doing?"

My coat and waistcoat were jerked from my shoulders and tossed the way of my sash. "What I should have done before

142

we left the kingdom."

I did not like the sound of *that* one bit. "No!" With the flat of my hands, I shoved against the wall hard, pushing him back a step, then twisted out of his hold to grab for my coat.

"Oh, no, you don't!" He grabbed my arm and shoved my back against the wall.

"I'm not doing this!" I pulled back a fist to punch him. It *was* a crime to hit my prince, but I was too desperate to care.

I'm quite proud to say that his eyes actually widened, though he still caught my fist before it could make contact with his face. However, he did wince.

"That would have actually hurt."

"It was supposed to!" I swung with the other fist.

He grabbed my other fist and then slammed both against the wall to either side of my head. "Damn it, Julian, this is for your own good!"

The back of my hands impacting the wall should have hurt a lot. In fact, the wall was marble, but I was too damned pissed off to feel a thing. "Says you!" I lashed out with my boot heel, aiming for his instep. I wasn't about to hit his knee. I didn't want to cripple him for life, just make him back off.

Growling, he stepped in to jam his hip against mine, pinning me against the wall with his body. "Stubborn wench!" He shoved his knee between my legs, then up intimately high against me.

I gasped, reeling under an all-too-sudden rush of carnal excitement that weakened my knees.

He took that moment to yank both of my wrists up over my head and trapped them with one hand against the wall. "Brat!" His whisper was just a tad breathless against my ear. With his free hand, he tugged on my neckcloth, loosening the bow, then pulled it from my neck. "Why do I put up with your insubordination?"

The breath from his words scalded my bared throat,

shocking me from my stupor. Just how far did he intend to undress me? I twisted in his hold and whispered back, "Let me go, and you won't have to ever again!"

"Never!" One-handed, the neckcloth dangling from his fingers, he tugged at the buckles of my knife harness. "What's mine...*stays* mine." The harness dropped to my feet with a thud and a clatter. He kicked it. The harness with all my precious knives slid under one of the chairs.

Once again, I was turned to face the wall, only this time my prince yanked my hands down to the small of my back and began to wind my neckcloth around my wrists.

The bastard was tying my hands!

He was fast too, and thorough. In less than a breath, my wrists were very securely bound, though not so tight as to make my hands go numb. However, the knot my fingers encountered was small and very tight. *Damned silk!* It was going to take a knife to free my wrists. "Prince, is this really necessary?"

He hauled me back around to face him. "Yes, it is." He jerked my shirt free of my pants. "Master Corwin's only interest in you is your virginity." He lifted the hem and tucked a fold of it into my collar, exposing the cloth wrapping that bound my breasts. "Once that's gone..."

"What?" My mouth fell open in shock "You can't! I still have more than a week to go!"

"I can." Alberic smiled and held up a small shiny paper envelope. "I have a condom."

I knew exactly what that was. I fetched his supply from Theo regularly. Most nobles used something similar, but my prince's weren't made of sheep-gut.

Apparently, my prince was dead serious. My blood ran cold.

TWELVE

Alberic tucked the condom into his wide coat cuff and pulled out one of his slender and insanely sharp throwing knives. "Hold still, I don't want to cut you." His smile widened. "Accidentally." He gripped the front of my breast bindings and set the knife's point, edge outward, against the top.

Icy terror froze me for an entire heartbeat, but not because of the knife. He really meant to do...*that* with me? Here? *Now?* "Prince, we're in a foreign country's palace!"

"Which is why you need to keep quiet!" He slashed down and outward.

My breasts practically burst free and the cotton strapping that had bound them dropped to land on my boots. I couldn't quite hold back a small yelp of surprise. The blood returned in a rush of itching. My nipples rose to swift aching erection. I hissed and flinched.

His gaze entirely focused on my chest, my prince tucked the knife back into his sleeve and smiled. "Oh look, your nipples are happy to see me!"

I scowled at him. "They're...like that because the binding cuts off the blood flow, and now it's returning, you pervert."

Alberic peeled the black leather gloves from his hands with quick efficiency and cupped my breasts. "I prefer to think otherwise." His fingers closed on my sensitive nipples, pinching them lightly.

The feeling was almost too intense to be enjoyable, yet

145

somehow it still made my knees go weak. I couldn't quite hold back my moan.

Alberic's brows lifted. "Liked that, did you? Let's see how you like this..." Mouth open, he leaned down to engulf my right nipple. His hot, wet tongue swirled around the sensitive nub, then he sucked, hard. At the same time, his fingers tugged on my other nipple.

Erotic fire speared straight down to blaze in the nub at the apex of my core as though his mouth was there, instead of on my nipple. Something deep in my belly clenched hungrily. I gasped in a deep breath to conceal the moan that wanted to escape, but a small, shameful whimper slipped from my throat anyway.

His mouth switched to my other nipple to torture it with teeth and tongue, accompanied by loud sucking noises. At the same time, his other hand palmed my other saliva-wet breast.

I wanted to struggle. Really, I did, but my body had other ideas. It wanted more of the heavenly sensations my prince was propagating. My back arched to press my breasts harder against his sinful mouth and enticing fingers.

Alberic moaned in open enjoyment, but his sharp green gaze was on mine. His fingers released my nipple to reach down to the front of my pants, where he began undoing the nine buttons of the front flap.

My gaze wandered over to the curtain, the only thing between us and that whole ballroom full of people. Ice-cold paranoia woke me somewhat from my sensual daze. "Prince, this is insane!"

He looked up at me with narrowed green eyes. His teeth clamped down on my nipple, delivering an erotic shock that stabbed straight down.

I gasped and writhed against the wall, but fear kept me from sinking back under the beckoning erotic haze. "If someone catches us like this, I'll be exposed! A woman cross-dressing as a man is a crime in some countries!"

He lifted his head and paused in unbuttoning my pants. "Easily solved." A quick jerk tugged the hem of my shirt back down around my hips. He grabbed my shoulder and turned me to face the wall, the palm of his hand pressing between my shoulder blades.

My swollen and wet nipples were pressed tight against the cold marble wall. The chill made them ache. My silk shirt was far too thin for any kind of insulation. An echoing throb pulsed low and deep in my core. I sucked in a breath and trembled. "What are you doing?"

"Now they can't see your breasts. Not that I want anyone to see them anyway." He opened the last button on my pants and yanked them down around my knees, taking the silky, frilly undershorts with them. "This way, if anyone finds us, they'll just assume I'm ass-fucking my valet."

I stiffened. "And that's supposed to be *better*?"

"They don't burn catamites at the stake here." He cupped my ass with both hands and sank his fingers into the cheeks. He groaned in open appreciation. "On second thought, ass-fucking my valet doesn't sound like a bad idea. Your ass was made for cock."

An illicit little thrill raced through me, and I shuddered. "That's *not* making me feel any better!"

Alberic leaned close to set his chin on my shoulder. "No? How about this...?" He reached around my right hip and cupped my mound.

I gasped, and my flesh shuddered.

He purred against my ear. "Hmm... Maybe I should have had you shave there, too." His fingers slid lightly down the plump lips guarding my core then under to slide among the sensitive folds. "Oh, nice and wet."

Reeling under a strange combination of shock, mortification, and excitement, another small whimper escaped.

"Nothing to say?" His longest finger slid into me, and his thumb caressed the nub at the apex.

I felt both a lightning strike and a hard clench inside. I gasped, and my hips bucked back all by themselves. I had no idea if I was trying to shake him off or encourage him to go deeper.

"Is that impatience?" Two of his fingers slid deep and wriggled, making obscenely loud wet sounds. He pressed against something inside that triggered a deep ache.

I flinched. "Ow…"

"That's your maidenhead." He eased the pressure but continued with his explorations. "Hmm… What to do about that?"

"How about leaving it alone?" Fear had a nasty habit of making me more than a little sarcastic.

He snorted. "Despite my reputation, I prefer delivering pain with something *other* than my dick." His fingers pulled out to swirl around the sensitive pearl.

The kick of raw lust forced a choked gasp from my throat. My body arched away from the wall, shoving my butt right up against his crotch, yet hope rose in my heart. "You're going to let me stay…?"

"No." His tone was cold, hard, and final. His other hand left my butt, slid up under my shirt to cup my breast. "I'll just have to get you too excited to notice." He pinched the nipple between his fingers while tapping his other fingers against my pearl.

Even as my body shuddered uncontrollably under his dancing fingertips, I scoured my brain for something, anything to stop my prince from his course. Up against a wall in a ballroom alcove was *not* how I'd planned to lose my virginity! Inspiration struck like lightning. "Prince, I have to be a virgin to catch that unicorn, remember?"

148

Alberic stilled and then delivered a low, deep, and sinister chuckle. He leaned in close to whisper against my ear. "Julian, we don't need to catch one, Gabriella is *making* one. Did you forget?"

I *had* forgotten. Disappointment crushed me. I pressed my brow to the marble wall and seriously considered knocking my head against it a few times. "Shit."

"Julian..." He gently pinched the plump lips of my mons together and rubbed the sensitive pearl between them. "When your prince is trying to seduce you..." The fingers of his other hand twisted my sensitive nipple. "Pay attention!"

A spike of erotic fire flashed straight from my nipple to my clit, causing something low and deep inside my belly to clench hard. I gasped, and my entire body shuddered. "I couldn't ignore you if I tried!" Moisture seeped down my thighs.

"Oh, for that, you definitely deserve a reward." His longest finger pressed against the swollen little pearl while the fingers to either side slid between my lips and pushed inside.

I shivered hard. "What are you doing?"

He chuckled against my ear. "Rewarding you, of course." His hand moved forward and back, the one long finger rubbing my pearl while the other two rubbed within. His other palm tightened on my breast, squeezing my nipple between his fingers.

The multiple sensations combined into a hungry coiling deep in my belly. Sticky wetness slithered down his fingers and my thighs. I clamped my teeth together to keep quiet, but small whimpers and moans escaped from my throat. Even worse, my hips began to move all by themselves.

His fingers sped up, pressing, rubbing, tugging... His voice rumbled low and deep against my ear, "That's it. Dance for me, Julian. Dance on my fingers."

His deep hoarse whispers went straight to my core. My

head went light. The things I had done in my own bed late at night, the pleasure I'd brought to myself with my own fingers, were nothing compared to *this*. This was frightening and humiliating, but most of all, it was obscenely delicious.

I couldn't think beyond the fact that I was going to cum; that *my prince,* the only man who had ever occupied my dreams, was going to make me cum...and I wanted it. I wanted it with every fiber of my being. I began to rock back onto his hand with enthusiasm, pushing into his strokes and openly writhed for more.

"That's it. Good girl." His hot breath caressed the side of my neck. "Cum for me, Julian. Cum in my hand. Cum *now.*"

My entire body clenched tight, and my breath stilled. Perhaps it was his voice or his skillful flick on my pearl, but most likely, it was his order. Since early childhood, I had obeyed his commands no matter how stupid or even life-threatening. It was practically a reflex. Whatever it was, the tightness in my belly released, exploding in a pulse of carnal ecstasy that made me see stars. I threw my head back and gave out a loud choking cry.

His hand flew up to cover my mouth, stifling my cries. He chuckled against my ear. "I forgot you're a shouter."

Writhing under the onslaught of raw delight, I barely noticed when his hand left my breast. I barely heard the sound of buttons being released, accompanied by soft grunts of effort. I did, however, feel the heated brand of his shaft sliding down the cleft of my butt. Unfortunately, I was far too under the influence of passing ecstasy to consider what all of it meant.

The broad head of his cock nudged past the plump outer lips of my entrance and nosed among the dripping folds. He grabbed me around the waist and his other hand tightened on my mouth. "Try not to scream."

That's when I snapped out of my pleasure-induced stupor.

He's going to…!

He thrust hard, straight up into me, and lodged himself deep.

I was sundered. I felt it, something inside me giving way and a slight burning sensation, but it was fleeting. Rather than scream, I frowned in confusion. *That's it?* I'd expected so much worse. I'd been told by numerous chambermaids that *this* was supposed to be painful enough to make one scream and blood. There was supposed to be blood. Of far more immediacy was the fact that a hot iron bar was lodged within me, stretching me to the point of aching, but even that wasn't so bad, merely…uncomfortable.

It was almost a disappointment.

Alberic moaned in my ear. "Gods, you feel good around my cock." He rolled his hips.

The cock inside me rubbed against something that delivered a rather riveting pang of mild pleasure that vibrated inside my belly. It was similar enough to that clenching feeling right before a hard climax that I rolled my hips the opposite way just to feel it again. The pang returned, a bit more strongly. Not anywhere near enough to make me cum, but the possibility was definitely there. A soft moan sounded deep in my throat.

I suddenly had a very good idea as to why everyone seemed to like sex so much, and I felt vaguely annoyed that it had taken me this long to find out.

Alberic shuddered, then groaned long and hard. "Julian, if you keep that up, I'm not going to be able to control myself."

That spark of annoyance suddenly burned hot. I turned my head just enough to whisper past his hand. "Just hurry up and finish what you started!"

He purred against my ear. "Hmm… That sounds like impatience. Does my cock really feel that good?"

As if I would actually admit something like that to my

narcissistic prince? I rolled my hips and shoved back against him "Hurry up! Are you *trying* to get caught doing this?"

His hands slid up my body to squeeze my breasts, and his chuckle was decidedly malevolent. "Maybe."

"What?"

He pressed his face into my hair to smother another set of chuckles. Not that it did much good. It did, however, smother most of his words. "I swear, no one is as entertaining as you."

My breath caught. However, it wasn't something he hadn't said before. Just not under *these* circumstances. "What?"

His hands slid down my arms to grasp the cloth that bound them. "If you want me to hurry, you're going to have to help me a bit."

The cloth binding my wrists pulled taut, then fell away completely. To my utter surprise, he pulled out of me.

Confused, I had half a second to look over my shoulder. Was he done already?

He grabbed me by the arm and turned me around to face him. He stepped over my pants, which had slid down to my ankles, then caught me under the thighs and lifted me against the wall with disgusting ease. Even so, he grunted.

I clutched his shoulders for balance and whispered hoarsely. "What are you doing now?"

He gave me a cocky narrow-eyed grin. "This." He let me slide downward against the wall until my butt met with hot, rigid flesh. He was definitely *not* done yet.

My legs locked around his hips in an attempt to stave off…the inevitable. "Wait!"

His gaze locked on mine and his smile evaporated. "I'm done with waiting." He shifted his hips only slightly and slid right into my body.

I stiffened automatically, my eyes opening wide, but there wasn't a trace of that sharp pain this time, only a mild muscle ache from being stretched so suddenly. I then noticed that although he filled me completely and utterly, he didn't quite make contact with whatever it was he'd touched before. That delicious pang was missing. Acting completely on their own, my legs tightened around him, and my back arched against the wall. Then I felt it, contact with…that place, that utterly delicious place inside me. I rolled my hips and was rewarded with that deliciously sweet feeling from before. A small moan escaped me.

Alberic's lips parted on a gasp, and the pupils of his eyes widened. His legs seemed to shake under us, and one of his hands released my butt to slap against the wall by my shoulder. He leaned against me to rest his head against my shoulder and groaned long and loud. "Oh… Yes, that's *much* better." Then he rolled his hips and pushed upward with his legs, surging up into me.

That pang inside me wasn't sweet this time. It was hot, thick, and raw in its intensity. My fingers tightened on his shoulders, and I choked out a gasp. Without conscious thought, I squeezed my legs around him and undulated, my hips rolling in a way they never had before, for more.

Alberic replied with an upward thrust hard enough to force a grunt from his lips, then another, and another…

As though possessed, I ground into his strokes.

The stories whispered between the maids and valets of the castle all described lovemaking as tender and sweet, kisses in the garden, caresses under the moonlight, the joining of hearts among blooming flowers.

Lies. They were all lies.

What we were doing wasn't tender or sweet at all. It was an animalistic, near violent and sweaty struggle to chase after the carnal pleasure that was building deep inside me, inside us. The sounds of wet flesh smacking wet flesh, the scent of pungent sweat and lust, his and mine, the moans, the grunts, the bruising strength we used to writhe against each other…

It was sheer carnal madness.

In that moment, in that dark corner, I no longer cared that discovery could happen at any moment, or what price I would ultimately pay for allowing this to happen. With every fiber of my being, I wanted the exquisite release I could feel rising inside me.

The soft sounds of flesh against flesh punctuated by desperate choked-off moans escalated between us.

Release came in a thunderbolt that imploded deep within me. A pleasure so raw it bordered on pain bleached my mind white. A howl burst from my throat.

I barely felt the hand Alberic clapped over my mouth to stop the sound. He abruptly shoved deep into me, impaling me against the wall, then froze. A moan erupted from him, muffled against my throat. Deep within me, his cock pulsed. He bucked shallowly and erratically, his entire body rigid, yet trembling against mine. A long sigh escaped him, and his body seemed to melt, taking me with him.

The two of us slid down the wall to sit on the carpet, panting and trembling against each other.

Thirteen

Hidden away in that alcove lit by only a single candle, the two of us sat on the scratchy carpet, leaning against each other, utterly exhausted. Alberic's panting breath was hot against my neck.

My legs were splayed across Alberic's lap, my pants still around my ankles, and my shirt was wide open. I rested my head on his shoulder breathing in the unique scent of his warm flesh and sandalwood soap. My body ached in ways it had never ached before, but it would pass. Pain always passed eventually.

What wouldn't pass was what I had lost.

I waited for remorse and embarrassment to strike, but those feelings were strangely absent. Instead, I felt an odd excitement, as though we were children again and my prince and I had just got away with some naughty prank. It felt like we were once again the troublemaking co-conspirators we had once been back before rank and responsibility had come between us when we had been more than merely master and servant.

Alberic abruptly lifted his head and grasped my arms. "We have to get you dressed."

"Yes, my prince." I leaned back against the wall and struggled to my feet so I could pull up my pants.

My prince had his pants buttoned, his waistcoat and long coat fully back in order and his gloves back on in a matter of seconds.

My attire was…beyond recovery. My white stockings were smudged, my breeches were wrinkled, and my silk shirt was missing buttons. Worst of all, the cotton binding for my breasts was in pieces on the floor. Thoroughly annoyed, I buttoned my waistcoat to the throat. It was snug enough to do the job, as long as no one looked closely. After retrieving my knife harness from under the chair, I strapped it on over my waistcoat, then shrugged into my coat. Despite my shaking hands, I got the coat buttoned halfway to leave easy access to my knives and the sash tied. However, my neck remained bare, because my neckcloth was also in pieces.

Alberic snorted and pulled a comb from his pocket. He tugged me close then turned me to face away from him and yanked the ribbon from my bedraggled tail. "What am I going to do with you?" He began dragging the comb through my hair. "You're a complete mess."

I turned to snarl at him. "And whose fault is that?"

Alberic shoved my head back the other way and continued to comb my hair. "Can you make it down to the stable without any of the guests seeing you?"

I sighed. I knew a dismissal when I heard it, but he was right. There was no way I could appear in public the way I was. "Yes, my prince."

"Go." He gave me a small shove between the shoulders. "I'll see you at noon."

I turned to look back at him. "You don't need me to escort you back to the hotel?"

Alberic lifted a brow, but his smile was a trifle…subdued. "Is that a request to spend the night in my bed?"

I flinched back. "No!"

His smile curled into an open smirk. "Then I suggest you

escape while you can."

With a short bow and a strange mix of both embarrassment and disappointment, I turned on my heel and left the alcove.

Neither the coachman nor the sorceress was anywhere in sight. Truthfully, I was glad. They would no doubt realize what had just happened from my appearance, and unbound hair. I was not in the mood to make excuses.

I made haste to the servant's stairs behind the dark curtain in the far corner. In the plain narrow stairwell, the passing servants briefly turned my way, then looked sharply away.

That brought me up short. Was what I had just done *that* obvious?

Head down to avoid looking any of the other servants in the eye, I trotted down to the kitchen level. The main hall of the kitchens was crammed with rushing servants carrying trays of food and wine bottles. I strode past them and out the well-room door to the stable yard without saying a word to anyone.

Within the cavernous palace stable, the stable hands were busy dealing with one incoming royal coach after another.

Rather than bother any of the scurrying stable hands, I saddled my brown gelding and pulled my pistols from my saddlebags to tuck them into my belt. One did not wear pistols in a ballroom, but one did not travel at night without one. I led my gelding out of the stable, mounted in the yard, and left the stable area at a lazy posting trot. The torch-lit palace bridge was crammed with a long line of incoming coaches. The dozen half-a-dozen posted guards were so busy checking them that they didn't even glance my way.

Just out of sight of the castle bridge, I turned right and off the road into the woods and onto a deer path. Screened by the trees and underbrush from the torch lights along the castle road, I turned my mount on the path to face the road. There was one thing more I had to do before I could seek my tent;

wait for my prince to pass by, then pick off any strays that might be trailing him.

I had absolute faith in his dueling skills, should any of the petty nobles be foolish enough to challenge him. Assassins hired by jealous courtiers and opportunistic brigands, however, were something else entirely.

After unbuttoning my coat completely, I tugged the ties from the handles of my throwing knives on my shoulder harness, freeing them for quick access with the speed of long practice. The two sheathed in each boot were already free. I then pulled out both pistols and checked them too. They were primed and ready. However, the pistols were only a last resort. Pistol shots drew far too much attention.

Fully prepared, there was nothing left to do but wait. Surrounded by darkness, with the wind whispering amongst the leaves and the faint strains of music from the palace carrying on the wind, the full weight of what had happened finally set in.

I had lost my virginity to my prince. My resistance had been utterly futile. Even worse, I strongly suspected that any further resistance might not even be possible because I might not *want* to resist. I felt so…*stupid*, and powerless…and angry.

Unfortunately, taking my temper out on the cause of my anger — my prince — had dangerous repercussions. Therefore, I was hoping someone would be kind enough to send assassins after my prince so I could safely take my anger out on them instead.

Who would possibly miss a few low-life criminals, right?

After seething in the dark for one full hour, my prince trotted past me on his white palfrey with a pair of what appeared to be royal guards at his heels. Apparently, the princesses Snow White and Rose Red were being rather attentive to his safety.

For some reason, that annoyed me all the more.

To my great delight, three assassins dressed in dingy brown battered leather armor were indeed following in their shadows on foot. Unfortunately, for them, all three trotted one by one right across the path I was on.

I barely had to move my arm to toss a knife into the unprotected throats of the first two. They gave a small choke and went down in a puff of road dust.

The third, however, happened to be wearing a gorget, a band of leather that protected the throat. He was also wearing a sword. He pulled the sword free of its scabbard and a long parrying knife from the small of his back and charged my horse.

I actually had a fight on my hands. Lucky me!

With a wide grin, I tossed myself off my horse and onto the path to meet his bulky battered sword with my far more slender and much sharper blade, scoring a cut on his upper arm with my parry.

I didn't have an actual parrying knife, but I did have a rather long boot knife that did the job of turning his dull parrying blade from its target, my face, and ducked for good measure. I extended my reach to get my sword behind his leg and yanked it back to score a slash across the hamstring on the back of his thigh. Yes, it was a dirty trick, and no, I didn't care. It was my prince's job to fight fair. Not mine.

The man howled in surprise and dropped on his face in the dirt.

If he was hoping for mercy, I was fresh out. I turned my blade to pass between his ribs and gripped my sword with both hands. With a small grunt of effort, I stabbed downward, right through the leather jerkin he wore for armor, and into his heart.

The whole thing lasted maybe five minutes.

I straightened and blew out a long sigh. The fight hadn't been enough to defuse all of my temper, but it was enough to take the edge off.

After wiping off the blood on my sword on the corpse's dirty sleeve, I sheathed my sword and boot knife, then went to pull my two thrown knives from the throats of the other assassins. I wiped them clean on their sleeves, sheathed them, and mounted my horse, who had been kind enough to not wander all that far off.

I left the area at a quick trot, leaving the corpses where they lay on the path. The royal guards would most likely clear them away in the morning.

I dismounted in my campsite with a pained hiss. My body felt like it had been beaten and certain parts were still quite…tender. I wanted a bath, and I wanted my bed, in that order. However, seeing to the horse had to come first. So, with flint and steel, I started a fire in the fire pit, set a kettle of water on to heat for a bath then unsaddled the gelding and saw to his feed.

While the water heated, I stepped into my tent, lit the hanging candle lantern, then stripped down to the skin to find that the air was nippier than I thought. I threw on my scratchy camp robe and stepped back out to rush over to the fire, soap and towel in hand.

I stared at the steaming kettle and wondered if stripping down naked in front of the fire was a good idea. I'd be visible to anyone lurking in the trees. Unfortunately, I didn't have much choice.

With my knives within easy reach, I poured the boiling water into the bucket with fresh stream water, dropped my camp robe, and started scrubbing myself down as much as one bucket of fairly hot water, a rag, and a cake of soap would allow. Sadly, with the night getting chillier by the moment, it didn't allow for much. Still, I got the job done reasonably well. Even so, I would have to wait until morning to wash my hair.

After shrugging back into my robe, I dumped the dirty water in some weeds. By then my fire had died down to coals. Shoving the rocks around the fire pit closer to the edge, I banked the fire for the night and then went back to my tent. I dropped the robe and slipped into my flannel nightshirt with haste, then crawled among my blankets on my straw mattress. Finally, I could sleep.

If I could sleep.

Staring up at the darkness with my arms folded behind my head, I seriously considered simply packing up and leaving in the morning. This was a different kingdom. My prince had no guards at his beck and call to drag me back. He had no one at all, other than Gabriella and me.

However, if Gabriella had been carried off by Master Corwin, could I really leave my prince alone and defenseless?

What was I saying? My prince was not only fiendishly clever, he was also the crown prince of a politically powerful kingdom. My prince was far from defenseless. If I took off in the morning for parts unknown, he'd be just fine. In fact, it served him right.

I crossed both arms over my face, using my sleeves to blot my watering eyes. Damned pollen from the blooming dogwood tree overhanging the tent was getting in my eyes again.

To my absolute surprise, sleep fell upon me almost instantly.

The dreams that took me were filled with thick pillows and phantom hands I couldn't see or escape. They slid across my skin, exploring me rudely while accompanied by low whisky-potent chuckling.

And galloping hoofbeats.

The sound of hoofs was so odd that it literally pulled me from the madness of pillows and hands into a place of mist with no sky or visible ground. Standing there in my flannel nightshirt, my feet invisible in the ground mist, I could hear a horse rushing toward me but saw nothing but silver-gray mist.

The sound of galloping hooves circled around me.

I turned but still saw nothing. "Who's there!"

The hooves stopped directly in front of me, yet there was nothing before me but churning mist. A horse's snort came from the mist, then the sound of a scraping hoof. There was a clatter of fast-approaching hooves.

Something stabbed me directly through the heart.

The pain was immediate and horrific, like a sword thrust. My breath was literally punched out of me. I grabbed my chest and choked for a breath I couldn't catch, then sat bolt upright in my bedding, eyes wide. The tent was bright with sunlight. I jerked at my nightshirt, looking for the hole that should have been in my chest.

I found nothing. My chest was whole and untouched, not even a bruise.

Yet, I could still feel it, the large and gaping hole in my heart.

Completely shaken, I crawled out of the bed and grabbed for my camp robe. On shaking legs, I stepped out of the tent and into the warm spring sunlight.

One would think that under direct sunlight, with my bare feet nestled in soft grass, the dream would fade. It did, and it didn't. After a few moments of standing awake and staring at a robin's egg blue sky filled with fluffy white clouds, the pain in my heart did fade, but to a bruised ache. It did not go away.

Hours later, after completing my morning camp duties of chopping dead wood for the night's fire and feeding the gelding, the ache in my heart remained. In fact, it remained when I bathed and washed my hair. I dressed in my oldest and most comfortable gray leather breeches and coat, and it still remained, a fist around my heart not quite squeezing. It was still there two hours later when I set my plain black tricorn hat on my head and mounted my horse to go meet my prince at the back of the palace's formal gardens.

I couldn't help but feel that something was about to go terribly wrong.

Fourteen

The elegant little copse of birch trees at the very back of the formal gardens was the perfect place to do something nefarious. One could see anyone approaching while remaining perfectly concealed. Pleased with my prince's choice of meeting place, I dismounted and strode under the birches leading my gelding.

A dulcet, feminine voice spoke from within the green shadows. "Hello, Julian."

I started rather badly. I dropped the reins to my gelding and had a knife in one hand and a pistol in the other before I realized that it was Gabriella standing under the birches. She was dressed in a knee-length gown striped in ash gray and black, with tall black boots that had buckles climbing all the way up the sides. Oddly enough, the multitude of white ruffles among the gray and black stripes of her belled skirt, the extravagantly puffed sleeves, and dangerously low bodice actually helped her blend into the black and white tree trunks.

Her presence gave me rather mixed feelings. Considering her jealous threats yesterday, then how she'd thrown herself at Master Corwin last night by shoving me out of the way, I was kind of relieved to see her and kind of…not.

Gabriella eyed my bared weapons and openly sneered. "Make up your mind. Are you going to stab me or shoot me?"

Annoyance soured in my stomach, adding to the ache still lodged in my chest. "You're welcome to take your pick."

One of her brows arched up and she tilted her head, her red curls sliding to one side. "Goodness, Julian, I actually think you mean that."

I didn't reply. I wasn't inclined to disagree.

"Julian, don't tease Gabriella."

My prince's voice made my heart soar with happiness — which was totally uncalled for. Ruthlessly stomping down my feelings, I put my weapons away and turned to face Alberic with a short bow. "Good morning, my prince."

Prince Alberic dismounted from his white mare with easy grace and turned to face us. Despite the fact that I had not been there to care for him or his clothes, my prince appeared perfectly dressed in a royal blue velvet coat trimmed in gold lace. His golden hair was well groomed and tamed into a long tail held back with a blue bow. There wasn't a curl or ruffle out of place.

It was somewhat disappointing.

My prince looped the reins of his horse over a low-hanging branch and frowned at me. "Did something happen last night?"

I blinked at him and scowled. "Beyond the obvious?" *Beyond taking my virginity?* I absently rubbed at my aching chest.

My prince lifted one golden brow and smiled. "You're going to have to learn to let the little things go, Julian." He brushed past me to face Gabriella.

My eyes widened and my mouth fell open. *"Little...?"*

Gabriella was frowning. "Did I miss something?"

The prince waved a gloved hand awash in gold lace. "Nothing important."

Oh, so now my virginity was not only little, it was nothing important? I bit my tongue to hold back what I truly wanted to say on the matter, but there was no erasing the ferocious scowl on my face.

165

"So!" My prince folded his hand behind him. "About this spell, Gabriella?"

"Yes!" Gabriella stepped forward with an enthusiastic smile. "As I was saying before, we don't need to hunt for the unicorn because I can make one." Her gaze slid to me, and her smile turned more than a little sly.

My eyes narrowed. She was definitely up to something.

My prince lifted his chin. "The spell is ready, I presume?"

Gabriella nodded. "It's right here." She reached into a velvet bag tied to her waist, one I hadn't noticed, and pulled out a softly glowing sphere the size of her fist of boiling blue-silver mist. Then she threw it…at me.

The ball of mist whizzed toward me and quite literally bounced away before it even made contact.

I yelped in surprise and dodged away from it.

My prince dodged in the opposite direction. "Ho!"

The sphere whizzed through the trees, bouncing against trunks like a ricocheting bullet. It came shooting back like a comet, flying for my prince.

I rushed in front of him without thought. The ball of mist hit me right between the eyes and exploded all over me, wrapping me in sticky silver-blue gossamer. I gasped in shock.

Gabriella jumped up and clapped. "Yes!"

There was a loud electrical crack, and the gossamer evaporated. I stared as it melted off me.

Gabriella moaned in open defeat. "No!"

My prince chuckled. "I told you before, Gabriella, enchanting Julian doesn't work. It always falls apart on him."

I looked over at my prince. "It does?"

My prince blinked at me. "You mean you never noticed?"

I frowned. "Noticed what?"

Alberic's brow lifted. "That neither curses nor charms have ever worked properly on you."

My eyes widened. "I've been cursed?"

My prince blew out a weary sigh and rolled his eyes. "Only once or twice a week since the day you arrived."

"Are you serious?" I meant to ask for an example. However, my heart suddenly gave a violently hard lurch, and I was too busy gripping my chest and gasping from the pain to pay attention to anything else. The world tilted around me. My knees hit the ground hard.

My prince grabbed me by the upper arms. "Julian!"

My hair fell from its bow to curtain my face, and right before my eyes, it turned silver-white. Then the front of my skull decided it wanted to split in half, and I saw no more.

Far, far away, there was a ripping sound and screaming; a woman was screaming.

In the distance, another woman shouted. "That's not supposed to happen! It's supposed to wrap around the subject, not...not do *that*!"

I blacked out completely for a while. I have no idea how long. I awoke to someone slapping my jaw and a masculine voice shouting in my ear, "Julian! Julian, are you in there?"

I opened my eyes, and the world was very strange. Although I was lying on the ground, I could see almost all the way around me, and what I saw didn't make sense. There were gray rags on the grass around me, and my knife harness was in pieces. Stranger still, there appeared to be a white horse lying on the ground directly behind me. I lifted my head to get a better look and gasped in shock. Or rather, I meant to gasp, but what came out of my mouth was a deep-throated wicker.

That horse was *me*.

I lunged to my feet, all four of them, and they were not at all steady. My balance was completely off. I was not used to walking on my hands. I was definitely not used to my head being so heavy. My line of sight was where it normally was

167

until I lifted my head on my extraordinarily long and mobile neck. The ground didn't seem any further way, just...smaller. *Everything* was smaller. My prince, who was by no means a small man, looked positively childlike, and Gabriella, huddled against the trunks of the trees, looked like a doll.

Even more alarming, the gray rags on the ground appeared to be the remains of my clothes.

My prince dodged away from me with speed. "Watch where you are pointing that thing!"

I meant to frown but quite literally felt my ears turn back instead. "What thing?" Well, that was what I meant to say, but what actually came out of my mouth was a low whicker.

My prince pointed to my head. "*That* thing. In case you haven't noticed, you have a rather long horn on your head."

I looked for it, but I couldn't see it. Oh wait, I *could*, the end of it, or rather, the last foot of it. I lifted my head and found that the spear attached to my head stayed exactly perfect with my line of sight; no wiggle at all. *I have a...horn?* Curious as to just how firmly it was attached, I dropped my head to stab it into the ground.

The impact was impressively *solid*, like I'd used a solid iron spear. The horn sank into the ground a good foot. It was *very* firmly attached. In fact, it was clearly part of my skull. I lifted my head, and the dirt fell away from it as though repelled.

Abruptly, something itched on my...flank. Then something *else* whipped at the itch. The sudden strike startled me into jolting forward into a half rear.

Alberic dodged away from me again, his arms flung upward to protect his head. "Julian, what the hell are you doing?"

"Something hit me!" I turned to look and discovered my tail. It was not a horse's tail. It was long, very long, and slender. The very end curled upward and over with a thick tuft of silver curls at the end and an occasional small tuft of curls along the underside.

Alberic snorted, then threw his head back and laughed. "You're scared of your own tail?" He shook his head. "Are you going to be afraid of your feet next?"

That's when I finally decided to actually look at my feet. My hooves were split like a deer or a goat. My brain blanked for more than a few breaths before I could accept what I was seeing. I was *not* a horse.

I had been transformed into a unicorn, the one creature every single noble on the palace grounds was looking for.

I turned to face Gabriella with my ears flat back, and my long teeth bared. "What the hell did you *do* to me?!" Of course, what actually came out was a squeal that didn't sound like it belonged to either a horse or a deer.

Gabriella raised a shaking hand to point a trembling finger at me. "Don't look at me! I didn't do that! My spell broke before... Before *that* happened!"

Alberic's amusement evaporated at once. "You *can* turn Julian back, right?"

Gabriella shook her head hard, her red curls flying. "I just told you; that's not my spell! I didn't do that! My spell certainly wasn't designed to change Julian's...gender."

That froze me in my tracks. *Of course* there was no disguising my true gender. I was an unclothed beast.

Gabriella bit her bottom lip and wrung her hands. "I have no idea how *that* happened, or..." Her voice dropped to barely a whisper. "Or how to undo it."

I blinked in shock. "You mean I'm stuck this way?"

Alberic scowled at me. "You'd better *not* be stuck this way!"

Gabriella frowned. "Wait, you can understand what he...*she's* saying?"

Alberic looked sharply at me, then back at Gabriella. "Of course." He blinked. "You mean you can't?"

169

Gabriella shook her head. "I hear an animal, that's all."

Alberic turned away from both of us and wiped a gloved hand across his jaw. "Fuck... This complicates things."

Gabriella took a tentative step away from the trees. "Do you know something I don't?"

Alberic laughed bitterly. "I know many things you don't, but..." From his sleeve, he pulled out a small, slender knife. "Only one way to find out." He slashed his palm. Blood welled, rich and scarlet.

I snorted in surprise. What the hell was he doing?

Alberic turned to me. "Julian, hold still." He reached out with his wounded hand and took hold of the end of my horn.

I held very still. I didn't want to stab him accidentally. Even so, something tingled inside my head, right between my eyes. My horn, or rather, what I could see of it, suddenly emitted a blue glow.

Alberic winced and pulled his hand away. He looked at his palm and whistled softly. He looked at me, then turned his hand toward me. The cut was gone, though not completely; a pale, white scar had taken its place.

My horn had healed it like a *real* unicorn.

Alberic's eyes narrowed on me. "It seems that Julian, at this very moment, is in fact, an *actual* unicorn."

Gabriella frowned and tilted her head. "But isn't that...impossible? According to the laws of magic, even if you give something the shape of something else, you can't actually change their true nature. A human shaped like a unicorn, is still a human. They can't do...unicorn things."

Alberic's frown deepened. "Such as healing..."

"Unless..." A deep gruff voice interrupted, and Master Corwin emerged from the deeper shadows. "That human was actually a unicorn to begin with."

All three of us stared at Master Corwin. Had the man lost his mind?

170

Master Corwin smiled. "I can't believe you didn't see it, halfling Prince."

Alberic scowled. "Don't call me that."

I eyed my prince. *Halfling...?*

"Julian's a unicorn? *For real?*" Gabriella's head tilted to the side, and her mouth fell open. "Is *that* why my magic never worked right around him?"

Master Corwin snorted. "Magic warps the natural order of things. Unicorns purify everything around them. They restore the natural order simply by being there. No spell can last in their presence."

I snorted, and one ear tilted back. "And here I just thought she was a screwup."

Both Alberic and Master Corwin choked back a laugh.

Gabriella scowled. "What did he-*she* say?"

Alberic wiped the smile off his face and waved a gloved hand. "Nothing important." He turned to Master Corwin. "So, how do we turn Julian back?"

"Turn her *back?*" Master Corwin broke out into deep loud laughter. "My prince, you just did! *This* is Julianna's true form!"

Alberic tilted his head to the side. "Her wh...?"

Gabriella's mouth fell open again. "Juli-*anna?*"

"No!" I stomped a cloven hoof on the grass and tossed my head. "I was born of *human* parents!"

Corwin's laughter died and his eyes narrowed on me. "One can change the shape of a thing, but not its true nature. That *is* a law of magic. Your nature is that of a unicorn. I saw it the moment I laid eyes on you."

I shook my head in confusion. "How the hell did *that* happen?"

Master Corwin rolled his eyes. "Well, obviously, one of your parents, or possibly grandparents, was a unicorn in human form; how else?"

171

I stepped backward, and it was not an easy thing with four legs. "Not possible."

"Sure it is." Corwin folded his massive arms across his chest. "Unicorns *are* known to be shape-changers."

Alberic blinked. "They are?"

Corwin rolled his eyes. "Of course they are. Why do you think they're so difficult to find?"

Unicorns were shape-changers? Did that mean I was too? I took a step toward Master Corwin. "I can get my human body back?"

Corwin shrugged. "I don't see why not."

Alberic and I both spoke at the same time. "How?"

Corwin set his hands on his hips and snorted. "Don't ask me, I'm not a unicorn."

Alberic scowled. "So we need a unicorn."

And there just happened to be one in this kingdom.

Both Alberic and I looked at Gabriella.

Gabriella blinked. "What?"

Alberic pointed at her. "Where is that unicorn?"

Gabriella scowled and folded her arms under her more than ample bosom. "What for? We already have one." She stared pointedly at me.

Alberic's scowl deepened. "I am *not* leaving Julian this way."

Gabriella scowled right back. "Don't you mean Juli*anna*?" She curled her lip in a sneer. "I'm perfectly fine with Juli*anna* being this way. It's her true form, isn't it?" She turned her back on me. "Let her keep it!"

Alberic's face went white, his hands fisting at his sides. "Obey me, witch!"

Gabriella stepped back from him, but her eyes narrowed, and she bared her teeth. "I refuse! I refuse to help you with that...*animal*!"

Alberic's face went red with anger. "Julian is not an

172

animal!"

Master Corwin shook his head and tisked. "Jealousy is such an ugly thing."

Gabriella balled her fists and screeched at the top of her lungs. "I don't give a fuck! Why should I help him with that *thing –* !" She pointed at me. "When he already has me?" Angry tears began to streak down her cheeks. "I'm more than enough woman for any man, and I'm perfectly human!"

Corwin smiled. "Ah, but the prince isn't – "

"Stop!" Lightning fast, Alberic drew his sword and pointed it at Master Corwin's throat. "Don't say it, coachman. Don't you dare."

Corwin eyed the blade at his throat and stepped back. "As you wish, Your Highness." He bowed and melted into the shadows.

Gabriella backed into the trees; her lips curled in a snarl. "If you want help with that...*creature,* don't come looking for me!" There was a poof of sulfurous smoke, and she was gone, too.

Alberic sheathed his sword with a hard snap and set his hands on his hips. "Shit."

I heartily agreed.

There was a crunch of boots and a jingle of buckles then a pair of palace guards in blue and white dress uniforms stepped through the trees with their long bayonet-tipped muskets at the ready.

One of them looked at my prince. "I heard a woman screaming."

The other looked at me, his eyes going wide. "Holy shit!"

I freely admit I panicked. I turned tail and bolted deeper into the trees.

My prince shouted after me, "Damn it, Julian, get back here!"

FIFTEEN

Don't ask me how I managed to gallop through a small forest of closely seated trees without ramming right into one or tangling my horn in their low branches even once. I have no clue. Rather, it seemed as though the branches and even the trees themselves moved out of the way, parting to make room for me. An illusion? A form of enchantment? I had no idea. What I did know is that I had no problem passing through spaces I wouldn't have been able to fit as a far smaller human.

Not even my gelding was able to follow me very far, and he *did* try. I clearly heard him neighing for me to wait for him. A certain flock, or unkindness, of ravens, however, had no problems following me. I could hear them laughing over the treetops.

In what seemed only minutes, I was once again in my own campsite, not that it was much of an improvement. Completely at loose ends, I wandered about the tree line of my campsite, confused as to what I should do. In the body I currently wore, I couldn't very well sit down and have a cup of tea.

I had to find that unicorn, preferably before some random noble found me. Obviously, the unicorn wasn't on the palace grounds, or someone would already have found it. I would have to search the wider countryside. I had plenty of travel notes and maps for this country in my notebook.

However, that notebook was most likely still on the ground by my torn clothing and knife belt.

Crap! I turned to face the way I had come. The knives I could live without could be forged again, but the information that notebook held was irreplaceable. I needed that notebook, or rather, if I returned to human form, I would need it. I shook my head hard, my white mane flying against my arched neck. I *would* return to human form. How soon that would be was anyone's guess, but I would definitely return to my own body. I had duties to perform, damn it!

Pacing back and forth at the tree line of the campsite, I knew exactly where I wanted to go and even how to get there without stepping one foot...err, hoof out of the trees. Although, *how* I knew such a thing was beyond me. However, I wasn't sure that going back to the birch copse was a good idea. Who knew how many people would be tramping through that very spot once the guards reported that a unicorn had been there? Did I really want to take that chance?

There was faint hope my prince would pick up the book for me. Doing things for the convenience of others was not among his habits. If I wanted my knives and notebook, I would have to go back and get them. I scraped a cloven hoof in the dirt in indecision. My tail, however, snaked back and forth at its own discretion.

A sparrow suddenly flew down from the dogwood tree I stood under to land on my horn and promptly screamed in my face. "Behind you, stupid!"

Shocked by the absolutely clear meaning in the bird's shriek, I turned to look behind me.

Leaning casually against the trunk of one of the flowering dogwoods with his arms folded across his chest was a man. He wore no coat or waistcoat, and his white, lace-trimmed shirt hung open from neck to waist, the tails only casually tucked into his pale silver-gray breeches. He looked as though he'd just stepped out of bed. Half his face and one eye was obscured by the long waves of his unbound silvery white hair. The other eye was deep blue-green and narrowed, though his pale pink lips curved upward on one side. "So, you *can* understand animal speak."

I was so surprised to see him there I reared up on my hind legs and wheeled about to point my long horn at him with my ears flat back. "Who the hell are you?"

The white-haired man snorted, and his lip curled in sour amusement. "It was a given that a few of these noble idiots would enchant something into the form of a unicorn, but I didn't expect one of them to actually bring a real one with him." His gaze narrowed even further. "Certainly not a doe."

Doe? I shook my head and lifted my chin. "I'm not really a unicorn."

Every bird in the trees overhead started flapping their wings and screaming, "Liar! Liar! Liar!"

I flinched in shock and looked up at the trees. "What the...?"

The white-haired man burst out in laughter. "Great Mother, are you a newborn fawn?"

Several small yellow and black chickadees fluttered down to land on the flowering branches directly over the man's head. "Yes! Yes! Yes! Just hatched!"

A chubby raccoon waddled out from the underbrush to sit by the man's boot. "Approximately twenty-eight minutes old, Your Highness."

I tilted my head to the side. "You're a highness? Are you a prince?"

The man's chin lifted, but his odd, sourly amused smile remained. "King, actually, of this entire island."

King? Both of my ears turned forward. "What happened? Were you enchanted?"

The man rolled his blue-green eyes. "Newborn indeed."

176

My ears laid flat, and I stomped a hoof. "What?"

The man blew out a breath. "In brief, the humans took over this land without ever realizing that we already ruled here."

I blinked in confusion and tilted one ear to the side. "I don't understand. Who are 'we'?"

The man straightened to stand with his shoulders back. A chime seemed to ring in my inner ear, and the world seemed to vibrate around me. The white-haired man blazed with blinding light and stretched upward, and then he was gone. In his place stood a silver-white unicorn far larger than I was in both height and breadth.

This was no enchantment; he was real. I could feel it vibrating in my bones. If I had still been in my human form, my mouth would have fallen open.

The unicorn that stood before me scraped a split hoof in the grass. "Our kind ruled in all the kingdoms of this land long before the humans ever found it."

There was another chime in my inner ear and another flash of light. The man was once again leaning against the gnarled dogwood, the waves of his silver hair wafting gently in the breeze, his lips curled in a sour smile. "However, humans do not have the eyes to see or the ears to hear us. To them, we are merely just another type of beast." He waved an elegant hand. "So... Rather than attempt to wipe out the human infestation, an impossible task since they breed so damned rapidly, we have taken it upon ourselves to combine our blood with their ruling classes."

I nodded thoughtfully. "Winning the war from the inside, so to speak."

The white-haired man smiled sourly. "Exactly." His eyes narrowed and his lips twisted in a snarl. "And I had very nearly succeeded when this idiot human ruler decided to interfere!"

I flinched back. "What did he do?"

The man began to pace between the dogwoods. "I was well on my way to seducing both princesses when their idiot of a father tried to push one of them into marriage with a foreign ruler."

"Seducing?"

The man nodded. "Once one of them became pregnant, it would be a simple matter of stepping forward as the father of the child."

I flicked an ear back in annoyance. Apparently, this kingdom had the same law as ours; a pregnant woman *had* to marry the father of her child. However... "This is a royal house. What's to stop the king from declaring someone else as the father of her child, someone he chooses?"

The man smiled bitterly. "My fate is unimportant as long as my child, my bloodline, becomes acknowledged ruler of this land."

I tilted my head and one ear to the side. "That doesn't seem very fair to you, Your Highness."

One silver brow rose. "Oh?" He took a casual step toward me. "Then you're willing to assist me in my quest to become prince consort and heir to my own kingdom?"

I stiffened where I stood, but my long, curling tail lashed from side to side. I could smell a trap in this somewhere. "Err..."

He set his hands on his narrow hips and smiled with narrowed blue-green eyes. "Considering your physical maturity, fawn, I'm willing to bet that you had no idea what you were before you transformed."

Both my ears laid flat back, and my head lowered. I couldn't lie, though I wanted to. The birds and animals sitting in the branches around us had already proven how quickly they were to tattle on me. "Yeah, so? What's your point?"

His smile broadened and sharpened. "You have no idea how to assume a human form, do you?"

178

I hid my flinch by looking away, but my tail decided to snake itself shamefully between my legs.

The white-haired man chuckled. "Fear not. You will discover it eventually."

I stomped a hoof. "I don't want to wait for eventually!"

"Is that so? Then how about this, fawn?" He tilted his head to the side. "Allow me to hand you over to the princesses, thereby winning their hand, and I will show you how to return to a human form. After that, you may escape as you please."

I backed away and laid my ears back flat. I didn't like the sound of that one, one little bit, so I changed the subject. "I have a name, you know!"

"Oh, do you now?" His sly smile didn't change one bit.

"It's—!"

"Julian!" The voice that called out was out of breath, masculine, and painfully familiar.

My entire body jolted at the sound. I looked sharply to my right.

At the edge of my campsite was Prince Alberic. One gloved hand was pressed against the trunk of a leaning oak with the reins of his lathered horse, and my equally lathered gelding fisted in his other hand. His coat and sash were utterly disheveled, with leaves and twigs caught in his mussed golden hair. There were scuffs and smudges of dirt on his boots. With his brows low over narrowed green eyes and his mouth tight, the jaw clenched, he glared at me, then nodded at the white-haired man. "We'll take your offer."

The white-haired unicorn smiled. "I was wondering when you would make your appearance, little cousin."

I tilted an ear to the side. *Cousin?*

Alberic smiled bitterly and gave a half-bow. "My apologies for not recognizing you, Your Highness."

He bowed? Both of my ears went up, and one knee lifted in

179

utter surprise. My prince never bowed, not even to his own father. The best he gave anyone was half a nod, and only to those he truly respected. Well, and princesses he was actively courting.

The unicorn nodded. "Imagine my surprise when I saw you paying court to the human princesses with this doe at your side."

I stomped a hoof in annoyance. "Did *everyone* know what I was except me?"

The unicorn turned a narrowed glare on me and bared his teeth. "Who else knows?"

I fully meant to hold my ground, but my body literally had a mind of its own. Despite my best efforts, my skittish body reared back, bumping my butt into a tree in the process.

The birds overhead burst out in twittering laughter.

"That would be me, Your Highness." A large crow flew down from the branches overhead to land on the ground in front of me. It bobbed its black head, then in a burst of shadows and black feathers, abruptly materialized into the kneeling, winged, and masked form of Master Corwin. He rose to his feet and drew the mask from his face. His wings folded back and settled into a tattered black cape.

"Death's coachman." The unicorn's blue-green gaze slid to my prince. "How interesting that yet another fey should be here."

Alberic's mouth tightened into a scowl.

Master Corwin lifted both hands and smiled. "I have no interest in either of the human princesses, Your Highness."

The unicorn king lifted a brow at Prince Alberic. "And you?"

My prince shrugged very casually. "Passing fancy."

Actually, it had been an order from his royal father. However, the birds in the branches above merely tilted their heads, and didn't object. Apparently, his answer was close enough to the truth for them.

The white-haired unicorn in human form nodded. "Very well, then…"

High overhead, a hawk called out with a vibrating whistle, but I clearly heard, "They're coming!"

The unicorn king blew out a shrill whistle of his own. "Understood." The king turned to look at Alberic and Master Corwin. "The palace conservatory, by the orange trees, this sunset." He pointed at me. "You, come with me." There was a flash of light, and the man was once more a silver-white unicorn. He turned toward the trees.

"What?" I felt a powerful urge to follow him, but I didn't want to leave my disheveled prince behind. "Why?"

The unicorn turned his long, elegant head toward me. "There's a large party of nobles on horseback headed this way, with dogs."

I blinked. "Dogs?" That was stupid. They were trying to take the unicorn…err…me *alive*, weren't they? Dogs had a nasty habit of killing the quarry before the hunters even got to it.

The unicorn king lunged into the trees.

Alberic snarled. "Fuck, they followed me!" He turned sharply to face me. "Go!"

"But…"

Alberic swung his riding crop at my butt. "Now!"

Startled by the swinging crop, I jumped and ended up leaping all the way across the campsite. I meant to stop and look back, but my body dashed into the trees after the king as though pulled by a string.

Sixteen

I ran through the trees following the white flash of the unicorn king, but it seemed more like a dream. I didn't feel the least bit tired, and the world around me seemed to be made of mist and shadow. There were trees, but they weren't very distinct. Everything had softened edges, bushes, branches, the ground underfoot — err, hoof — as though they weren't quite there…or *we* weren't.

Only a handful of minutes later, the forest changed around us; the trees became very tall, very slender, and bone white. Not like birches with their white bark and green leaves, but entirely white, trunk, leaf, and stem alike. The leaves didn't rustle, they tinkled like glass chimes. The sky turned entirely gray with low-hanging swirling clouds as though a storm rolled overhead, but I heard no thunder, and it did not rain. Even more alarming, the ground under my hooves disappeared under a thick layer of mist, erasing all remaining traces of natural color.

All of a sudden, we emerged from the trees into a clearing of tall grass and white flowers. The sudden normalcy of green was actually comforting to my eyes. At the very center of the clearing on a gentle hill sat a golden dome upheld by pillars, each intricately carved with fanciful twisting vines. It had no walls. Instead, there were pearl-white sheets hanging between the pillars, wafting gently in the breeze. It looked more like a temple than a building.

The king trotted up the three broad white marble steps and passed between the wafting sheets, out of sight.

Not knowing what else to do, I followed him up the steps and beyond the wafting sheets. Blinded by the shimmering folds, they brushed against my neck and sides. I felt a pull against my flesh, as though some sort of skin was peeling from me. It wasn't uncomfortable. Rather, it was like a weighted cloth was dragged off me.

I blinked to clear my sight and took half a dozen steps beyond the floating cloth. I felt light as a feather. Directly before my eyes only a yard or two away, a tall oval mirror stood suspended in a frame of white branches. For the first time, I could actually see myself after my transformation. However, my reflection did not show a unicorn.

To my absolute astonishment, my body had changed into that of a deer, an almost blindingly white deer with tufts of fur around my hooves and at my elbows, though the snaking tail remained. My single spiral horn, however, had been replaced by a small pair of bladed antlers with a pair of very sharp points jutting out over my brow. I looked very much like one of the snow deer found in the far reaches of the northern wastes.

"Now you know."

I turned from the mirror to look to my left.

Lying atop a large oval cushion of opalescent white silk, one of many cushions scattered about, was a huge stag with a thick ruff of fur covering his throat and a massive set of bladed antlers crowning his head. It was the king. I could feel the hum of his power in my very bones. He spoke, though his mouth did not move. "This is our truest form, the form we wore when our kind first greeted humans."

I stepped lightly toward him. "We're really *deer*?"

A chuckle sounded and his graceful head nodded despite

the enormous rack of antlers it supported. "The weight you felt lift from you when you entered is their collective assumption of our appearance."

Confused, I shook my head. "I don't understand."

"Humans see us as unicorns; therefore, we look like unicorns."

I would have frowned if I could have. Instead, I tilted one large ear back. "You're saying that their *opinion* of us shape the way we look?"

I had the strong impression of a shrug, though his body was clearly incapable of one. "To some degree, yes. We are…" He looked away briefly. "How do I say this simply? Hmm…" He looked back at me. "We are less earthbound than they. Our bodies are more fluid in form, so we are more easily affected by the flow of magic, which is affected by collective human belief. As their beliefs changed with the passing of the centuries, our bodies changed to match their views. In addition, their individual belief in what they consider real and not real also affects what form they see."

I *almost* grasped what he was saying. "So, over time, we shifted from a deer into a unicorn from their beliefs alone?"

The great stag turned his head slightly. "More like they added a shape over top of what was truly there."

"And someone that didn't believe in unicorns wouldn't even see that form?"

I had the strongest impression of a smile. "Correct. Those who cannot accept the existence of even a unicorn might see a common white horse or a white deer."

Curiosity burned in me. "What about dragons? Are they something else too?"

He chuckled. "They are indeed, but what they are has no name because their true forms come from a time long before humans walked the Earth. In fact, they are the oldest of us all, for they were the first to walk upon the Earth."

I tilted my ears back and looked away, trying to imagine a world where only dragons lived. "Wouldn't that mean the world was originally something of a wasteland?"

The stag king laughed, though again, his mouth didn't open. "Not at all! According to the dragon I spoke to, the world was far warmer than it is today and one vast jungle covered in trees, ferns, and flowers."

I turned my head this way and that trying to imagine such a world. "I find that difficult to believe."

"As do I, but then our kind came into being during the great Fimbul Winter, when humans were still new, and nearly all the world was covered in snow and ice."

I turned back to face the king, both ears forward. "Snow and ice?"

The king nodded. "Very much so, which is why we are at our most powerful in the heart of winter, whereas dragons are at their most powerful during the heart of summer."

Something suddenly came to mind. "The princesses said that you only appeared in the winter."

The great deer let out a soft sigh. "Because it is only during the winter, the time of my greatest strength, that I can sustain mortals here."

Sustain...? I swallowed hard. "Is this place...*bad* for humans?"

The king sighed. "This place is not meant for *any* mortal, human or otherwise. Only in winter is my power strong enough to shield mortals from falling into a slumber from which they will not wake."

That was more than a little creepy.

"In fact, the reason why the trees here are white is because they have fallen asleep and turned to crystal."

"Crystal?" I turned to look out past the floating sheets wafting between the pillars. "But the grass isn't white?"

"That is the limit of my influence. Beyond that green circle,

185

any mortal being will fall asleep and turn to crystal."

"But, I--"

"You no longer wear a mortal body."

I looked sharply at the king. "I'm...immortal?"

"Correct. You cannot die."

Well, that was reassuring.

"Should something actually succeed in destroying your body, it will reform in your place of sanctity, and you will awaken as though from a deep sleep. However, all memory of who you once were will be gone."

Suddenly I wasn't so reassured anymore. In fact, a full body shiver overtook me. I did *not* want to lose the memory of who I was—or more specifically, my prince. To counter the sudden terror attempting to turn my bowels to water, I changed the subject. "So where exactly are we?"

"This is my place of sanctity. Yours will be back in your own land."

I blinked in open confusion. "I'll have one, too?"

The king chuckled. "You probably already do. It's the one place you go where no one can find you."

I puzzled over that for a bit. "Well, no one's ever found me in the castle attics..."

The king turned an ear back and spoke very dryly. "It will be outdoors, such as a wood or an unused garden."

I turned away, thinking hard and found myself distracted by what looked like a miniature castle of white wood surrounded by small pale blue cushions. However, miniature wasn't quite the right way to describe it. It was actually a rather large piece of furniture, the size of a lounge. Tiny dolls were scattered on the cushions around it. "Is that a dollhouse?"

The king sighed very softly. "I made it for the princess."

"Princess?" One of my ears turned back all by itself, openly displaying my confusion. "Only one of the two?"

"Originally, there was only one." The king looked away very briefly. "The second princess joined the royal household the following winter."

"Was the second a royal orphan?"

The king tilted his head just a little. "Something like that."

I nodded. Orphans from noble lines were often adopted into other noble families, usually for potential marriage partners, but sometimes simply as companions for solitary children. "The princess must have been happy to have a playmate."

The king turned to gaze upon the massive dollhouse. "Once the two joined hands, they became inseparable."

I walked around the structure, impressed by the detailing on the turrets and windows. "They must have been very young." Truthfully, I hadn't meant to say that out loud.

"When I first brought them here, they were about eight."

I turned to look at the king. "You brought them *here*?"

The king's ears went flat. "An uncle sought to murder them."

Both of my tall ears shot up. "What?"

The king snorted. "One of the hazards of being heir to a kingdom is bloodthirsty relatives." He suddenly gave me the distinct impression of a rather nasty smile. "Worry not. That one and two others are no longer anyone's concern."

Apparently, the king had been protecting the two princesses since childhood. To my mind, he was indeed the best choice for a husband for them. I nodded firmly. "I'll do everything in my power to help you win the princesses."

The king tilted an ear, and his expression seemed troubled, though I couldn't actually see it on his deer's face. "You're very...kind."

I turned my ears back. "Is that bad?"

He looked away. "Not necessarily. However, it could be used against you."

I looked the other way. "I'm not *that* kind." My brother had been that kind, not me. While I was willing to help when I could, the only person I allowed actually to take advantage of me, was my prince.

The memory of last night flashed through me, of the two of us writhing against the wall in carnal ecstasy.

Taken advantage of, indeed.

Annoyed, I stomped a hoof to drive away the memory and the feelings it brought with it.

The stag snorted lightly. "Sunset is still a few hours away. You should take this time to rest." It wasn't quite an order, but it *felt* like one. He was, after all, a king.

I moved to a large cushion and struggled with the process of kneeling down and then lying down without *falling*. It was...awkward.

The stag didn't exactly chuckle, but I could tell he was amused.

When I finally laid myself down with my legs neatly tucked under me, I abruptly remembered that those that fell asleep here didn't wake up. Panic turned my blood to water, and I started to struggle back up onto my feet.

The stag did chuckle then. "Calm down, doe. You are not mortal. This place will cause you no harm."

I allowed myself to flop back down and blew out an annoyed breath. "I never knew that being a magical being was so much work!"

The stag lowered his head to the cushion and seemed to smile at me. "It will get easier with time."

I lowered my head as well, my long neck easily curving around to lay by my knees. "Easy for you to say. You probably have centuries of experience."

"True, with many different lifetimes among them."

I turned my gaze and one ear toward him. "How do you keep from forgetting the important things, the things you don't want to forget between those…lifetimes?"

He chuckled softly. "To ensure that what I need to remember is never lost, I keep a written account."

I turned my head to look at him. "You keep a diary?"

His eyes closed. "Of sorts. The tapestries that hang between the pillars."

I turned my head to look at the closest curtain, the one directly behind me. What I had thought was solid white was in fact subtly shaded in iridescent colors and absolutely covered in intricate knotwork. A form of writing perhaps? There were small images interwoven among the knotwork of deer, people, unicorns, and other magical beings such as winged faeries. Forests, farmhouses, and castles were also among the inter-branching knotwork.

It was absolutely stunning, and there were eight of them wafting in the mild breeze. I stared for quite a while until my eyes grew heavy, and I drifted off, rapt in the wonder of what it was like to live many more than one lifetime.

Seventeen

"It is time."

My eyes opened, and I lifted my head, completely and utterly awake. I had slept but not dreamed at all, which was a peculiar feeling because I always dreamed when I slept.

The stag king stood by a wafting tapestry. "Follow me." He turned and walked toward the fluttering tapestries, his hooves clopping lightly on the marble floor, then beyond and out. I crashed to my knees, then over onto my side, hooves flailing, grass and flowers flying.

I rose to my four hooves utterly refreshed. However, what was truly odd was that I didn't feel hungry or thirsty, even though I hadn't eaten or had even a sip of water since the day before. Unfortunately, I didn't have the luxury of examining that oddness. The king was clearly going to leave me behind if I didn't get out there.

I trotted lightly to the tapestry and leaped past it.

Just beyond the curtains, weight crashed down on me, literally. I suddenly felt so heavy it honestly felt like I'd just come out of a pool of water. So what was meant to be a graceful leap to the grass became a sudden heaviness around me. I rose to my four feet no longer a silver deer but the silver unicorn once again. I shook the grass and flowers from my hide. "Ugh! Why do I feel so heavy?"

The unicorn king turned to look back at me and openly

laughed. "What you feel is the weight of the unicorn overlaying your true form." He turned and began to walk gracefully away. "A human form is an even heavier burden to bear."

I trotted after him. "You could have at least warned me!"

The king laughed again and cantered toward the trees. "And miss the sight of you floundering among the flowers? Hardly!"

I lunged into a gallop after him. "Sadist..."

After a very short gallop, the trees around us turned from white and crystal to shadow and mist. The king abruptly stopped. "We are here."

I looked around, seeing nothing but indistinct trees and undergrowth. "We are?"

The king abruptly rose to his hind legs and assumed the human form I'd seen him in before: a tall, slender man with pure white curling hair that fell to his waist, wearing a silver-gray coat and breeches heavily embroidered in white. His waistcoat was also silver-gray but embroidered in pale blue. His gloves and boots, however, were black. He flicked his wrist and from thin air produced a silver-gray tricorn hat nearly overflowing with curling white feathers. He set the hat atop his head, then turned to me. "Stay right here. I'll return for you momentarily." He turned his back to me and vanished.

That startled me. However, it also made me wonder if I could do the same thing: just vanish into thin air. Of course, creating things out of thin air seemed like a neat trick, too.

I had barely completed that thought when the king returned. His slender white brows were lowered over aqua eyes that were narrowed to slits, and his mouth was a taut line. He held a slender sword in his hand.

I stiffened all over. "What happened?"

His blue gaze narrowed and turned to silvery frost. "Death has come to the palace."

"What?" My first thought was that he was talking about Master Corwin. Then I caught the all-too-familiar scent of copper and iron drifting from him — the scent of spilled blood.

Alarm spilled through me like ice water, but half a heartbeat later, it became fury. My ears laid flat back. "Take me to my prince, now!"

"This way." He turned and stepped away.

At his side, I stepped with him. A mild tingling brushed against me, as though walking through a spider's web, and then golden warmth overtook me. I blinked and found myself standing among potted orange trees and roses, my hooves clicking lightly on polished tiles. High overhead arched a domed roof made entirely of windows set in ornate cast iron.

I was *inside* the palace conservatory. This revelation brought a shiver to my hide. Apparently, that white forest existed outside this world, and that shadowy forest was the bridge between them, a literal case of being neither here nor there. In other words, stone walls would not bar the unicorn king from entry into or out of any place he cared to be.

Unfortunately, I didn't get much time to ponder such thoughts because two things distracted me. The first was that instead of being well-lit as in my last visit, it was deeply shadowed, as though the lights had all been blown out. The second was the *stench* floating in the air.

I could definitely smell the iron and copper scent of blood, but stronger than that was the ammonia reek of an unclean animal. It was vaguely familiar, but it didn't smell anything like a horse, dog, or even cat. It was definitely something I'd smelled before, but I couldn't quite pin my finger on what it

192

was, and whatever it was, it was *big*. The stink was so profound it could only come from something huge, or rather, several of them.

Following the king, I stepped beyond the potted orange trees and recognized the back of a familiar red velvet settee.

Beyond it, I recognized nothing.

Potted trees and rose bushes had been overturned, the roots exposed, and the potting soil scattered across the tiled floor. The plants themselves were smashed and broken as though trampled under something heavy. In addition, however, there were small heaps of what looked like scattered garbage piled literally everywhere; shreds of fabric, broken weapons, broken boots, split gloves, torn and scattered papers, and puddles of clear, thick viscous liquid. Among them were small splatters of blood.

I also noted strange gouges in the floor clearly made by something heavy and sharply pointed. They were grouped in sets of four, like claw marks, but no animal claws I knew of could cut into *stone tile*.

That hideous animal reek floating in the air permeated everything. It practically burned in my nose. However, it didn't quite cover the near-choking scent of spilled blood. It literally stank like a slaughterhouse.

Only hours ago, the palace had been crammed with nobles and servants of every class and distinction. Something horrifically violent had clearly happened, and there were indeed random splatters of blood, but not nearly enough to account for the strength of its scent. According to the smell, I should have been walking hock-deep in it. People—a *lot* of people—had clearly been killed in that very room, so where was the blood, and where were the bodies?

More than a little in shock, I nickered softly to the king, "What the hell happened here?"

"Sorcery." The king at my side stepped forward, the waves

of his snowy hair and the feathers of his hat lifting on a breeze I couldn't feel. His anger, however, I could most definitely feel. In fact, I could see it. A chillingly cold, silvery mist floated from his body. "Sorcery happened here."

"Sorcery?" I'd seen more than a little magic in my life, but... "What kind of sorcery did *this*?"

More importantly, where was Alberic? He was supposed to be waiting in this very place. I raised my head high, one knee lifting with it, looking over the debris scattered about. I didn't see anything I could identify as his, and I knew every single belonging he had. After all, I was the one who cleaned them. "I have to find my prince."

The king stepped further into the room, his bootheels clicking on the tiles. "This way." He strode across the shattered room toward a pair of wide-open glass doors.

Beyond the doors was a soaring hallway, the distant arched ceiling covered in paintings. Hanging crystal chandeliers tinkled overhead, but the candles had all been blown out. The scent of smoking wicks still drifted in the air. The left side was a long row of floor-to-ceiling windows, revealing the encroaching night. The right was solid floor-to-ceiling gold-framed mirrors, many of them cracked from heavy impact.

The floor was polished wood with a long, plush blue and gold floral carpet marred with blood spatters, jagged tears, and more of those puddles of clear, viscous fluid. At the end of the hall was another set of double doors, but they stood wide open, the frosted glass shattered.

The hallway clearly led into the palace.

My split hooves thudded softly on the carpet, my long tail snaking behind me. "So, what kind of sorcerer are we dealing with?"

At my side, the unicorn king strode with stiff shoulders and a tight jaw. "Fear not. Our kind are not affected by enchantments. However, the monsters they create can be *quite* a nuisance."

I looked sharply at the king. *"Monsters?"*

The king stopped to give me a tight smile. "You smelled it did you not, the stench of beasts?"

I snorted. "Is *that* what that stink is?"

It was at that point that something moved just beyond the broken doors at the end of the hall, something *big.*

The king smiled grimly. "I believe you will soon see for yourself."

"Terrific." My ears turned back to lay flat. "So, how do I kill these monsters?"

He shrugged. "They die easily enough with blessed or bespelled silver."

I snorted and rolled my eyes. "Most enchanted beings are weak to bespelled silver." Which is why my prince and I both carried a small pouch of silver shot. I turned sharply to glare at the king. "But, in case you haven't noticed, I'm not currently capable of *holding* a weapon of any kind!" I tucked my chin and stomped all four hooves on the torn carpet. *"Hoofs,* not *hands,* remember?"

The king laughed. "Foolish, doe... Did you forget your horn? It will easily destroy them, for it unravels magic on contact."

I turned my entire head to stare at him. "Wait... Are you telling me to ram head-first into a *monster?"*

The king plucked at the lace of his cuffs. "I suggest getting behind them before you *ram* into one of them, as you so delicately put it. They have rather nasty claws, and teeth too." He patted my shoulder. "And aim for the heart."

I blinked twice. Once because I wasn't quite sure I'd heard him correctly, then a second time when I realized that I *had.* "Aim for the heart, through the *back* of the ribcage?" *Is this guy an idiot?* "Do you have any idea how hard it is to get a sword between the *back* of the ribs, never mind actually reaching the heart from there?"

The king's lips curled up into a wicked smirk. "Speaking from experience?"

I turned one ear back. "Yes, actually." My prince had a habit of making enemies *very* easily, and with enemies came assassins. My temper flaring hot, I abruptly reared up on my hind legs. "But that's not the point here!"

The king abruptly smiled. "Point or not, your first target has arrived." He waved his hand toward the far end of the corridor.

Something huge was plodding down the corridor toward us on two legs, something big and...furry. Rounded ears lifted at the top of its round furry head, and it pointed its short muzzle at us. It looked like a bear, except it didn't have paws; it had hands tipped with long black claws that curved. Scattered about its limbs were shreds of dull gray fabric, almost like clothing. Its eyes suddenly glowed green. The mouth opened, showing long, jagged teeth, and a bass growl rolled from its massive chest.

It wasn't just a monster. It was my childhood nightmare. A monster such as *this* had slaughtered my entire family.

For two whole breaths, I just stared. Honestly, I expected to feel the icy chill of terror freezing me in place. Perhaps it did for a single brief moment, but what came over me was an emotion far colder, and far more powerful than fear.

Rage.

I wanted to kill it with every fiber of my being.

Wrapped in a frigidly cold calm, the world slowed down around me. As though I was in a dream, I leaped the full length of the space between the monster and me in one jump. The floor thundered under my hooves with my landing, and the creature roared, but the sounds came from far, far away. It took all the willpower I possessed not to ram straight into its black heart right then and there. Instead, I ducked under the swings of the clawed hands to slip to the right, along the ornately painted wall of broken mirrors.

In that moment I absolutely regretted my lack of hands. If I'd been able to hold a saber, I could have decapitated it in that one move.

Once past the beast, I reared up behind it. With icy calm, I carefully selected my target and stabbed two feet of spiraling horn into it, between the ribs and into its heart.

It froze, its mouth open and its eyes wide. All sound ceased. Then it slumped heavily to the floor.

The world returned to normal speed and normal sound around me. My knees quivered under me, but a feeling of disappointment washed through me. It had happened so fast, and so easily. *Too* easily. I wanted to kill it again, slower this time so I could enjoy it more.

However, the beast started to *melt*. First went the muzzle, and ears, then it condensed in size at a rather swift rate. Finally, the fur evaporated completely until what lay face-down on the blood-soaked carpet wasn't a beast at all but a half-naked person, a woman with long, tangled blonde hair. The tattered remains of a maid's uniform clung to her limbs. The stab wound I'd made was clearly visible on her back, bleeding freely and profusely.

I reared back in wide-eyed shock. "What the...?" I looked over at the king. "What *is* this?"

The king strode toward me, his gaze cold, his lips curled in open disgust. "I told you, sorcery. I doubt she even knew what she was doing." Then this was an innocent person? I was perfectly fine with killing someone that killed others, but this was just a housemaid. She'd probably never hurt anyone, well...other than cuffing a house boy or two.

An impossible thought stabbed through my heart. *Does this mean...?* Was the monster that killed my family an innocent victim, too?

197

Every drop of rage I'd had spilled out of me.

He looked away, his lips tightened, and eyes narrowing. "And this is only one of a great many who have been cursed into monsters."

What? I stared, horrified. "How many people are we talking about here?"

The king smiled sourly. "How many humans originally occupied this palace?"

"Including the servants and staff?" My eyes widened. "Hundreds, but with the addition of all the visitors for the unicorn hunt and their staff, probably several hundred."

The king nodded. "That is your answer."

I stiffened in alarm. "The entire palace? Are you *serious*?"

The king caught my gaze and nodded. "Only those with an affinity for magic could have repelled this curse. Everyone else will be just as she was, a monster unable to stop themselves from slaughtering anyone in their path."

I winced. Magic wasn't something just anyone could use. Only the rare individual could cast even a small enchantment. Most people, even among the nobility, were generally powerless. In other words, the castle was probably crammed full of monsters.

At the same time, a profound sense of relief came over me. There was no way Alberic was among the cursed. My prince had most definitely been schooled in the use of magic, though I had no idea who might have taught him. I'd never seen even one of those lessons. However, I immediately felt disgusted with myself for feeling so relieved when so many others had been turned into raving monsters. *All those innocent people!*

I lifted my head. "Can we break their curse? Unicorns are good for unraveling enchantments, right?"

The king snorted, but his eyes remained narrowed. He nodded. "Your horn can unravel their curse...temporarily, at least."

Both of my ears tilted forward, hope blooming in my heart. "Then I don't have to kill them? I can just wound them, and they'll go back to normal?"

The king looked at me with cold, narrowed eyes. "Wounding them will only return them *tonight*. The curse will still remain. At the next full moon, they will transform and slaughter any living thing near them."

Disappointment crashed down on me. *Crap.* Then another idea occurred to me. "What about the one who cast it?" I laid my ears back flat and stomped a fore-hoof on the carpeted floor. "If we kill the sorcerer, will that break the curse?"

The king smiled, showing straight white teeth. His eyes blazed with icy blue fire under lowered white brows. "You don't mind putting off finding your prince in favor of hunting down the sorcerer that did this?"

I stiffened. Sure, Alberic was likely safe from being cursed, but how safe was he from those who *weren't*?

My first instinct was to find my prince and just plain escape, but I had no idea *where* in this vast palace to even look for him. That meant fighting my way through the monsters until I found wherever he was hiding, then fighting my way back out.

On the other hand, if I killed the sorcerer, all the monsters would disappear at once, and I could take my time locating my prince.

I turned my head to look past the shattered doors to the palace. "Do you know where to find this sorcerer?"

The king strode past me with a sidelong smile. "If you were an all-powerful sorcerer that just successfully cursed an entire palace of humans into monsters that obeyed your every wish, where would *you* go?"

I blinked then blew out a heavy sigh. The answer was obvious. "The throne room."

The king nodded. "Exactly."

Eighteen

At a flying gallop, my white coat softly glowing in the smoky darkened hallway, I ran alongside the king.

He jumped as nimbly as me over fallen furniture, charging down the halls faster than any human I'd ever seen.

From a doorway on the right, a cursed beast lumbered out across our path.

I lowered my head for a sidelong slash.

"Do not!" The king grabbed onto my mane with one gloved hand with far more strength than his slender human form appeared to have, dragging us both to a sliding, skidding halt.

I reared in confusion. "What…?"

The king gripped my mane tighter, his gaze narrowed, staring hard at the beast before us. "Do you not want those released to survive?"

My ears lifted. "Survive?" I flattened my ears, showing my annoyance, and tilted my head to eye him. "Of course!"

"If you release this one from the curse, what do you think will happen to him? To *any* human surrounded by such beasts?"

They'd get slaughtered. *Crap!* I shook my mane from his hand. "Then what are we supposed to do?"

The king set his hand on his hip and cracked a serene smile. "We run." He took off at a sprint, dodging the beast with

200

disgusting ease.

I dashed after him, ducking under a massive, clawed hand in passing. *Damn it, he could have mentioned that beforehand!*

We bolted down broad galleries with soaring, arched, and buttressed ceilings. Everywhere the floors were cluttered with broken furniture, and shattered glass. The once pristine marble walls were gouged, and the priceless paintings and tapestries were slashed. It was also dark, the air thick with smoke from untended fires set by fallen candles.

Then there were the monsters.

In every room, every hall, everywhere, there were monsters, howling and fighting amongst each other or hunched over and tearing into things I didn't want to see, their fanged muzzles dripping deep red.

Eventually, we reached the broad arching white marble staircase at the palace's center. We climbed floor after floor. While I easily climbed with four legs, I was not looking forward to going back down it.

Somewhere in the middle of the staircase, the king left the stairs to run down a broad gallery lined with gold-flecked marble pillars.

Leaping broken tables and chairs, and dodging past monsters, I pushed into a gallop to keep up with the running king. "Where the hell is the damned throne room?"

The king lifted a hand, pointing dead ahead. "There!"

At the end of the hall were a pair of massive, ornately decorated double doors that appeared to be made of solid brass. Even so, the one on the right had been pushed open and crushed inward by something large, round, and apparently hot. Black scorch marks sprayed outward, and a black smoke stain blighted it in an upward pattern, marking the wall above it as well. At the center was a huge crater that was melted.

It looked as though an immense fireball had struck it.

I slid to an alarmed halt. What the hell kind of sorcerer

were we about to face?

The king stopped to look over his shoulder at me. "Hmm?" He looked back at the door and then rolled his eyes. He leaped to my side and set one hand on his narrow hip. "What? Are you frightened? We purify magic simply by our presence, remember? If it comes in physical contact, it shatters or rebounds."

I nodded toward the blasted door. "Even *that* kind?"

He smiled. "Even that kind." He looked toward the door, and his smile faded. "The problem is those around us."

"Huh?" I tilted an ear toward the king. "Those around us?"

The king stared at the door. "While enchantments do not affect us, stronger spells will still affect the area around us, and anyone that happens to be in that area."

Oh... I laid my ears back. I might be fine, but if there were innocent bystanders...?

"But!" The king smiled and patted my neck with far more strength than necessary. "I doubt that will be a problem here."

I flinched under the king's hand, my neck actually stinging. "Right." Because anyone that had been nearby would have been cursed and likely run off to tear something up. Which brought something else to mind.

I turned to the king. "What about the princesses?" He hadn't mentioned them, not even once. "Do you think they fell under the curse?"

The king didn't even look my way. "No."

Both of my ears lifted. "No?" *The princesses can use magic?*

He strode for the destroyed bronze door. "Come. We have a sorcerer to destroy."

I trotted after him, my hooves clicking on the marble flooring. The carpets that had once graced the floor had been burned completely away, leaving only scorch marks and powdery ash.

The king passed by the door easily.

Being far larger, the size of a full-grown horse, I actually had to shove the door further open with my shoulder to pass. The door moved with a horrific screech. I sighed. *So much for entering quietly.*

The circular throne room had clearly been magnificent. A full wall of delicately arched, soaring windows rose to the left with a view that overlooked the land all the way to the sea that surrounded the island of Lyoness. A nearly full moon glowed among a sea of stars.

However, the window glass, though still intact, was spider-webbed with thousands of fractures and framed with the torn and burned remnants of gold velvet curtains. The once snow-white walls of the room were blackened from multiple blasts. The marble floor was burned bare of carpets, and the furniture was splintered and charred beyond recognition.

The only piece left intact was the marble throne carved into the far wall, the curtains hanging above it still pristine in gold and blue. Sitting, or rather lounging sideways across it and facing the windows was a woman with her legs thrown across one arm and crossed at the ankles. They were encased to the knee in boots that were buckled from toe to knee. Her black gown barely reached the top of her boots, revealing red and black striped stockings. Multiple layers of lacy red petticoats spread the skirt wide with an impossibly narrow, buckled corset that barely contained her impressive bosom. Long gloves encased her arms, nearly to the shoulder. Blood-red barrel-curls tumbled down her back and across her brow, framing a lovely heart-shaped face. Her eyes were closed, her hand pressed to her brow as though in pain.

I stood there blinking at the impossible sight. *Gabriella?*

She lifted a gloved hand negligently. "Whoever you are, go away. I don't have time to play with you." She waved her hand. A white-hot ball of fire the size of a fist bloomed into existence and blazed towards me.

Truthfully, I was far too shocked by the sight of Gabriella to even think to dodge. Something, perhaps instinct, made me rear at the last second to point my horn at the flaming projectile.

The fireball popped like a bubble, leaving a small cloud of black smoke and the smell of burning paper.

I blinked in some surprise. I hadn't even touched it.

The king stepped to my left side and set his palm against my neck with an amused smile. "See what I mean?" He lifted his chin and looked over at the woman lounging comfortably on the throne. "My apologies, miss, but I'm afraid that magic doesn't work against unicorns."

"Unicorns?" Her head lifted, her green eyes opening wide. Her gaze focused on me and narrowed. "You…" She swung her legs off the throne's arm to stand on the dais, booted feet braced wide. She pointed a finger toward me. "You!"

I still couldn't quite believe what was going on. "*She's* the sorcerer?" I turned my head to look at the king. "Gabriella? *She* did this?"

The king crossed his arms. "You know this one?"

I nodded slightly. "Gabriella is my prince's personal spy." No need to be nice about it anymore. "She followed us here, but…" I shook my head in confusion. "But her spells never work right. Are you sure *she's* the sorcerer?"

Gabriella howled in fury. "Don't you *dare* ignore me!" She opened her hand, and a fireball formed, this one the size of a human head. "You bitch!" The flaming sphere came speeding toward me.

I whipped my head around and pointed my horn toward it.

About three feet away from me, the fireball popped into a small cloud of smoke.

With a sour smile, the king tilted his head toward

Gabriella. "Is there any room for doubt?"

I reared up and trumpeted in anger. "Gabriella! What the hell do you think you're doing?"

Gabriella shook a fist at me. "Is that a threat, you... You stupid *animal!*"

The king stepped forward, his hands resting on his hips. "Excuse me, Miss Gabriella, I believe?"

She scowled at the king. "What do *you* want?"

The king tilted his head to the side. "Would you happen to be responsible for this palace being cursed?"

Gabriella crossed her arms. Her gaze narrowed but her lips curved up into a bitter smile. "I notice that the curse hasn't affected *you.*"

The king smiled, but his gaze narrowed, and his eyes ignited into orbs of frosty blue-white. "Yes, well, magic doesn't affect me quite the way it does others." He began to walk toward her with slow casual steps. "May I ask why you did such a thing?"

She turned away with a pronounced pout. "Look, I don't have time for you. I'm waiting for someone."

I tilted an ear back. *Waiting for someone? Who?* But there was only one person Gabriella ever wanted to see. *That idiot!* I tossed my head in annoyance and trotted up to the king's side. "Gabriella! Do you honestly think Prince Alberic would be happy with you cursing a whole palace full of people?"

"Tell that animal to shut the hell up." Gabriella turned to curl her lip in a sneer at me. "All that braying is getting on my nerves."

That's right, she can't understand me. I turned to the king. "Tell me how to get back my human body! I can't talk to her this way!"

The king's gaze slid to me. "No."

"What?" I stiffened, my ears standing straight up. "Why the hell not?"

205

The king's voice dropped to a whisper. "Even if you could reach her, it won't change the outcome."

Outcome? I froze in place, my breath stilling in my chest.

The king's gaze moved back toward Gabriella, and he smiled. "So, Miss Sorceress, would you mind taking off the curse you placed?"

Gabriella's gaze slid to the side. "Why should I?"

I shook my head in disbelief. *Why should she?* I reared up in anger, lashing my hooves. My voice trumpeted out in a loud equine neigh. "Because people are *dying*, you idiot!"

Gabriella's eyes widened and she jumped back. Fury twisted her features, and she pointed a long finger at me. "This is *your fault*, you bitch! I wouldn't have used this stupid spell if *you* hadn't...! If *he* hadn't...!" Tears began to well in the corner of her eyes. She abruptly screeched. "If you had just been the stupid boy you were supposed to be, and the —" Her voice hitched on a sob. She closed her eyes and tears slid down her cheeks. " — And the princesses hadn't been so —" Her pointing hand fell to her side. "So pretty."

Gabriella wiped at her eyes with her hands. "I just couldn't —" She gasped in a small breath. "I just couldn't stand the fact that he was going to take them." She waved a hand toward me. "And you, too —" Her eyes opened, black smears running down her cheeks. " —Over me!" A snarl curled her painted red lips. "I had him first! He should be with *me!*"

I blinked. She did all this out of *jealousy?*

The king snorted. "So you cursed the entire palace?"

Gabriella sniffed and wiped at the black running down her cheeks. "It wasn't supposed to..." She sniffed again. "It wasn't supposed to be the *whole* palace." She folded her arms under her bosom. "It was just supposed to be *this* room and the princesses."

The king stiffened, his jaw visibly tightening.

Gabriella took a deep breath, gaining visible control over herself. "But it turned out to be a much bigger spell than I thought."

The king sighed. "Foolish sorceress, the prince had no intention of marrying the princesses."

Gabriella's mouth dropped open, and her eyes widened. "What?" Her gaze darted to me. "But Julian is Alberic's—"

The king shook his head. "This doe—"

I stomped a hoof and tossed my mane. "*Julian*, my name is Julian!"

The king glanced at me briefly. "Ah, yes, Julian agreed to be presented as *my* unicorn. The princesses were to be mine."

Gabriella blinked, then sniffed and lifted one shoulder in a half-shrug. "Well, too late now." She abruptly smiled. "With everybody gone, it's *my* palace now, which makes me a princess!" She tilted her head to the side, her smile curling into a broad smirk. "And since I'm a princess, Prince Alberic can marry me!"

From behind me, a strong masculine, familiar voice called out. "The princesses were unaffected by your curse. This palace, this land, is theirs, not yours."

Gabriella leaned to the side to look past the king and me. A smile bloomed on her lips. "Ah, you're here!"

I turned my head, arching my neck to look behind me.

Standing just within the broken bronze door was Prince Alberic. His blue frock coat was ripped at the shoulders, ragged at the hem, and stained with random splashes of dark red. The lace at his wrists was filthy. His cravat was missing, leaving his throat bare. His green eyes were narrowed under lowered brows, and there was a scowl on his lips. Alberic was clearly more than a little battered, and not at all happy.

Even so, I was utterly relieved to see him.

Nineteen

Prince Alberic, bedraggled and furious, stomped right past me straight to the very center of Swanstone's fire-blasted throne room.

That's when I noticed that his frock coat had two long and evenly placed rips from the shoulders down to his waist. I tilted my head in confusion. *How did his coat get ripped like that?*

Alberic lifted his right arm, pointed at Gabriella, and spoke firmly and rather quietly. "You are fired." He then turned his back on the red-haired sorceress to face me and the king. "This debacle has been *quite* an inconvenience."

Gabriella looked at the floor, her brows scrunching together, her lip curled. "Fired...?" Her head lifted and a look of shock widened her eyes. *"Fired...?"* She trotted down from the throne's dais, her heels clicking on the marble floor. "What do you mean, *I'm fired?*"

Alberic tugged at his wrist lace and did not turn around. "Would someone kindly explain to the *persona non grata* behind me that I have no interest in employing those who lay curses without my expressed permission?"

The king folded his arms across his chest. "I refuse. She's not my sorceress."

Alberic heaved a dramatic sight. "She's not mine either, anymore."

Under normal circumstances, it would have been my duty.

However, at that particular moment, I was incapable of human speech. I gave a long, loud equine snort instead.

Gabriella began to tremble, her teeth grinding audibly. "Hey! I'm right here, you know!"

"Now then..." Alberic turned to the unicorn king and set his hands on his hips. "If you would kindly return my valet?"

Gabriella sucked in a sharp breath. "What?"

The king smiled at my prince with narrowed eyes. "I'm afraid I have one more task for her if you don't mind?"

I laid my ears back and scraped a hoof. "What is it now?"

The king turned to me and spoke very softly. "Have you forgotten why we entered this room?"

It actually took me a full breath to recall that we were here to *kill* the sorcerer responsible for the curse. I froze in place for half a breath then turned sharply to my prince. "Gabriella needs to take the curse off!"

The king sighed and looked away. "I don't think that's possible at this point."

My prince's brows lowered over narrowed green eyes, his mouth pinching tight.

Not a good sign. He was clearly angry with Gabriella, and never liked following someone else's instructions. However, when all else failed; *beg*. I turned my ears forward. "Please, my prince?"

"Wait..." Gabriella pointed at the king. "Are you saying that you can return that animal to human form?" She pointed toward me.

The king smiled. "Of course!"

"No." Blackened tears began to slip down Gabriella's cheeks. "I won't allow it."

Alberic abruptly turned to face Gabriella. "Do you wish my forgiveness?"

She blinked, clearly startled. "You'll forgive me?" She clasped her hands together, pushing her full bosom higher, and smiled despite the black tears slipping welling in her eyes. "Yes, please, forgive me! I didn't mean to curse the whole palace. Honest!" She shrugged, her smile twisting with chagrin. "The spell was a lot more powerful than I thought."

The prince nodded and clasped his hands behind him. "Remove the curse, and I will forgive you."

Gabriella's eyes widened and her smile crumbled just a little. "Remove the curse?"

Alberic arched one golden brow. "You do wish to be forgiven, don't you?"

Gabriella bounced on her toes while wringing her hands. "Yes! Yes! More than anything!"

My prince smiled. "Then, remove the curse."

Gabriella bit down on her bottom lip and began to tremble. "I— I want to, but..."

Alberic's brows lowered. "But?"

Gabriella hunched her shoulders and glanced away. "I... I can't."

Alberic folded his arms across his chest. "What do you mean, you can't? It's *your* spell, isn't it?"

"Well..." Gabriella lifted a hand to twirl her finger around one of her red curls. "N-not actually."

"*You* cast this curse." Alberic set his hands on his hips and tapped one booted toe. "How can it *not* be yours?"

Gabriella stiffened, then scowled, her hands fisting at her sides. "Because I bought it from a tinker, back home!"

I blinked. Someone was *selling* curses in our kingdom?

Gabriella winced and clasped her hands around her waist. "For two silver coins."

"The price of a ride in my coach." The voice was deep, gruff, and very familiar. From the deep shadows by the windows stepped a tall, broad figure wearing a ragged black cape that swept the floor. A mask with a crow's beak concealed his face under a tricorn hat with black feathers.

I lifted my head, ears up in surprise. *Master Corwen?* What was he doing here?

Alberic curled his lip, his focus entirely on Gabriella. "You *bought* this curse?"

Gabriella crossed her arms under her bosom, a pout on her lips. "I buy a lot of spells. This was just one of them."

Alberic rubbed his brow. "Why did you buy a curse you couldn't remove?"

Gabriella threw up her hands. "I didn't know I couldn't remove it! I thought I could!"

I rolled my eyes. This was going to take a while. Heaving a sigh, I strode over to Master Corwin, my hooves clicking lightly. "So why are you here?"

He sighed. "I have a confession to make."

My ears lifted. "Oh?"

Master Corwin's beaked mask tilted downward. "I did not take a few days off. I'm here because I have an assignment."

"An assignment?" I froze, the hair along my spine rising. He was Death's coachman; his job was to collect the dead. This meant he'd known all along that people would die at the palace. I laid my ears back, my tail lashing behind me. "Why didn't you warn us?"

Master Corwin shrugged and looked away. "I couldn't. It's...not allowed."

"I see." I blew out a sigh, and my ears lifted. "Telling people something like that could...change things."

Master Corwin tilted his head slightly, and I got the distinct impression that he was smiling. "You are very understanding. Are you quite sure you won't be my bride?"

I tilted my head to the side and snorted. "You never give up, do you?"

Master Corwin chuckled, his eyes bright gold behind his beaked mask. "Not when the prize is so worth gaining." He lifted his head to look past me. "However, I think you'd better

211

go back. Your prince is going to need you in a moment."

I turned to look at my prince.

Gabriella stomped her booted foot. "It's not fair! That animal got in my way from the very beginning!"

Alberic lifted his chin in open disdain. "Julian only looks like an animal at the moment, and Julian has nothing to do with *your* curse."

"Julian has everything to do with this curse! I was so used to that stupid bitch warping every spell I cast for you, I put more power into it than it needed. It wasn't supposed to be this big!"

Alberic took a step toward her. "Oh, so you intended to only curse a few people into slavering beasts that killed everything in their wake?"

Apparently the argument had shifted.

I blew out a snort and turned away. "If you'll excuse me, Master Corwin?"

Death's coachman nodded. "Of course. Oh, and one more thing?"

I turned my head to look back at Master Corwin. "Yes?"

Master Corwin lowered his head. "I'm sorry."

I turned an ear his way. "For what?"

Gabriella abruptly shouted. "I only wanted to curse the princesses, okay?"

Master Corwin waved toward the escalating argument behind me. "I think you'd better hurry."

"Curse the princesses...?" Alberic stared wide-eyed at Gabriella. "Why would you do something so stupid?"

Gabriella burst into gasping sobs. "Because I didn't want you to marry them. I want you to marry me!"

This was not going to be pretty. I trotted toward my prince, my tail swinging back and forth in annoyance.

Alberic scowled. "I already told you, I can't marry someone that isn't of royal blood!"

The king shook his head. "He certainly can't marry someone poisoned by a curse."

Gabriella stiffened. "Poisoned? But I'm not cursed."

The king set his ice-blue eyes on Gabriella. "Haven't you noticed? Your tears have turned black. You've been poisoned by the evil inherent in that curse."

Gabriella ripped off a glove. Her nails were as black as pitch. She wiped at her eyes and then stared at the black smears on her fingers. "That's just...makeup. My kohl eyeliner."

The king shook his head. "It's not. Your blood has more than likely already turned black and poisonous as well."

Gabriella shook where she stood. "Impossible... That's impossible!"

I moved to stand by the king and looked at Gabriella's face. Her eyes were solid black orbs, and she looked like she was wearing black lip color. She looked demonic. Startled, I threw up my head and jerked back a few steps.

She scowled at me. "What's with you?"

Alberic sighed. "Your eyes and lips have turned black."

Gabriella set her palms on her cheeks. "No... No! You're lying!" She shoved her hand into her skirts, very likely a pocket, because she pulled out a tiny round mirror. She stared at her reflection for a few seconds, then let out a horrified shriek. "What's happening to me?"

The unicorn king shrugged. "I told you, you've been poisoned by the curse."

She turned to the king. "How do I get rid of it?"

The king smiled sourly. "You can be purified, but you will never wield magic again."

Gabriella's eyes opened wide, and her mouth dropped open. "I'll lose my magic?"

The king nodded. "Your magic is what's poisoning you."

Her eyes narrowed. "Will it kill me?"

The king's brows lifted. "Purification? That will hurt a little, but you'll live."

Gabriella shook her head. "The *poison*. Will it kill me?"

The king smiled slyly. "Not at all. You'll just lose every drop of humanity you have and turn very, very evil."

Gabriella shook her head, then began to back away from us. "I can't... I can't lose my magic. It's all I have. It's all I am!" She shot a glare at the king. "If I lose my magic, the curse will break, won't it?"

The king nodded. "It will."

Gabriella sneered at the king. "I refuse! I am *not* giving up my magic! They can stay cursed for all I care!"

Alberic scowled. "How do we purify her?"

The king tilted his head toward me. "With a unicorn's horn, of course. A small stab to the arm or leg should do."

Alberic strode for Gabriella.

Gabriella backed away. "No! No way in hell!" She lifted her hands, and a fireball bloomed into life, but this time, the flames were blue.

Alberic stopped cold.

I lunged forward to stand before my prince.

Gabriella stared at us with her solid black eyes. "You again... You stupid bitch, why is it always *you!*" She threw the fireball at me.

I reared and pointed my horn at it.

Several feet away, the fireball popped, leaving oily black smoke.

Alberic blinked at me. "You know, that's rather handy."

I laid my ears back and curled my lip, showing my long equine teeth. "Don't get any ideas."

Gabriella bolted for the bronze doors.

Alberic ran to cut her off to the left.

I galloped for the right.

The king leaped to stand before the doors and drew his

sword. "I'm afraid I cannot allow you to leave."

"Out of my way!" Gabriella threw a blue fireball at him.

Three feet from the king, Gabriella's fireball popped, leaving only smoke.

The king smiled. "I told you, magic doesn't work on me." He stepped forward, the long blade of his silver sword pointed at her.

Gabriella fisted her hands at her sides and stepped back. "No, no, no! This is not happening to me!"

Alberic closed in on her left.

With an inhuman screech, Gabriella lifted both hands, palm out, and cast a huge fireball at my prince.

In utter panic, I leaped to reach him, but I was not going to make it in time. Alberic was far too close to her.

Alberic lifted his right arm, palm out. A flash of blinding white light burst in a corona around him, and at his back, a pair of diaphanous golden butterfly wings opened. "Be gone!"

The fireball popped out of existence.

Gabriella stood frozen for an entire breath, her mouth open in astonishment.

I skidded to a halt only a few feet behind Gabriella, astonished myself.

The light disappeared from around Alberic, but his wings remained. He folded them down against his back, and his lip curled in disgust. "Damn it, I hate using that. It takes forever for the stupid wings to disappear."

Gabriella blinked. "You're fey?"

Alberic set his hands on his hips and looked away. "Half-fey. My father was human."

Well, *that* certainly explained a few things.

Gabriella abruptly burst into peals of laughter. "No wonder you prefer that animal over me! You're no more human than she is!"

215

The king snorted and stepped closer, his sword lifted to rest on his shoulder. "At the moment, they are both more human than you, demoness."

Gabriella's laughter cut off completely. "A demon, am I? Fine." She smiled. "I can live with that."

The king lowered his sword. "Perhaps you can, but I'm afraid that I cannot allow it." He lunged at her, his sword aimed at her heart.

Gabriella whirled around to run.

I charged to intercept her.

Gabriella stopped cold only a foot before my nose, her black eyes wide. She coughed thick black liquid. It spattered on the horn that impaled her right through the chest, then turned to smoke.

A body-length away, Alberic froze where he stood.

I stared in horrified shock, then jerked back.

Gabriella slid off my horn, crumpling to the marble floor. The black in her eyes receded, revealing her natural green behind, but they were glassy and unfocused. Her lips turned back to red. The poison was gone from her, but so was her life.

I'd killed her.

The king sheathed his sword. "Well done, doe."

I stared at the king unable to move from where I stood. *Well done?* I'd killed her! It hadn't been on purpose; I didn't actually intend to impale her with my horn. She'd just run right into it before I could think to turn my head.

Master Corwin abruptly strode forward, his boot heels echoing far too loudly in the large oval room. He knelt at Gabriella's side and took her hand. "It's time to go, Gabriella."

Gabriella abruptly sat up, or rather a second Gabriella, one transparent and colorless, separated from the Gabriella that lay on the marble floor. She smiled at Death's coachman and rose to her feet. Silently, she allowed Corwin to draw her away. She stopped briefly and turned to smile at Alberic. "I really did love you."

Alberic nodded. "I know."

Master Corwin led Gabriella into the shadows, and they faded from sight.

If I hadn't had four legs, I would have fallen where I stood.

I turned my head to look at my prince. "I didn't mean to..."

Alberic lifted a hand but looked away. "I know. I saw."

My heart ached as though it was being crushed. I wanted to weep, but as a unicorn, I couldn't.

"Can someone tell me what just happened here?" At the bronze doors was an older man looking more than a little battered, wearing a royal Swanstone guard's blue and white tunic over scale-mail armor. His eyes widened. "Wait, is that a *unicorn?*"

TWENTY

Dawn rose on the smoke-stained spires of the once pristine palace of soaring towers. Light began to fill the huge, circular, and fire-blasted throne room. With the light came people from all over the palace, their bodies battered and their clothes torn; servants, valets, maids, kitchen staff, a few royal guards, the occasional noble... They pressed up against the walls, confused, frightened, more than a few tearful, and all of them staring at the very center of the room—at *us*.

The unicorn king on my right patted my neck and smiled.

Behind us, Alberic knelt by Gabriella's body. He pressed his palm down her face to close her eyes, then set her hands together on her breast. With a soft sigh, he rose, then walked over to stand by my left side, his wings still plainly visible.

Soft whispers broke out in the vicinity of the bronze doors, then the crowd parted, moving back to allow someone entrance—two someones.

The two princesses, pristine and perfect, stepped into the throne room, side by side, and hand in hand. The one on the left had green-gold eyes, fiery red curls that cascaded past her waist and wore a gown of shimmering gold embroidered with red roses. The princess on the right had sky-blue eyes, pale blond hair that flowed straight down to her knees, and wore a gown of shimmering silver embroidered with white snowflakes.

The unicorn king smiled warmly, dropped to one knee, and held out his arms.

The two princesses, Rosette and Blanchette—Snow White and Rose Red—bloomed into rosebud smiles and rushed forward into his embrace.

The king had successfully acquired his princesses and his kingdom.

Calmly, and casually, Alberic and I walked around celebrating monarchs, through the cheering palace folk, toward the broken doors of bronze.

"Stop!" The voice was feminine, and loud.

Every whisper in the throne room stilled utterly.

I stopped, the hairs lifting on my back.

At my side, Alberic also came to a halt, his shimmering wings twitching at his back. He scowled at the bronze doors. "Damn..." Very softly he whispered. "I *knew* this would happen." He smoothly performed an about-face, and smiled, but his golden brows lowered over his green eyes.

I turned my neck to look over Alberic's shoulder.

Princess Rosette stood before the king and princess Blanchette, her red brows lowered, and a frown marring her lovely features. She spoke in a soft and sweet tone. "Where are you going with my unicorn?"

Alberic nodded regally to the princess. "As I have delivered on my promise, it is time for my companion and I to depart."

Rosette tilted her head slightly and blinked. "Depart...?"

I turned my head to look at my prince. "Promise...?"

Alberic looked at me from the corner of his eye and spoke very softly. "I promised I'd find *their* unicorn."

"Then they know that he's...?" I looked toward the king.

Alberic snorted then whispered softly. "*Of course* they know. That's why they set up this whole sham of a hunt. She never intended to marry anyone else."

The unicorn king moved to Rosette's side. "My dear, it is time for the fairy prince and the unicorn to return to their kingdom."

Princess Rosette turned to present a pretty pout to the king. "But you brought the unicorn to me. It's mine, isn't it?"

The king shook his head slowly. "One does not capture a unicorn. One invites them to be one's guest."

The princess turned to stare at me. "I'm afraid that I must disagree." She smiled, but this time it wasn't sweet. "Blanchette?"

The platinum-blonde princess smiled and raised her hands. Silvery mist rose around her, and the smell of midwinter frost became unusually strong.

There was a loud crackle all the way around me and my prince. From the floor all the way around, thorny branches made of solid ice lunged upward and entwined together over our heads to form a cage around us. With soft crystalline tinkles, roses of ice bloomed on the cage's thorny branches at random places. Chilly mist wreathed the entire structure.

Suddenly, I understood perfectly how the princesses had evaded the monsters unscathed. However...

I stepped close to the cage's bars and tapped one of them with my horn.

That branch of the cage and those closest to it hissed and began to evaporate into mist. A hole formed, and swiftly enlarged to a size even I could walk through.

Alberic and I stepped out of the cage.

The king sighed and strode for the swiftly evaporating cage. "I told you before, my dearest princess, magic cannot hold a unicorn because unicorns return all things to their natural state."

The princess frowned. "Unless it is the unicorn that creates the state."

The unicorn king stopped to turn and smile at her. "True.

However, I made a promise to this unicorn, and the fey prince." He turned to face me and winked. "To return to your form, doe, rise on your hind legs and picture your human body as a robe you wrap around yourself." He abruptly turned to Alberic. "Once she is restored, I suggest you make use of those wings, little Prince of Air." He took several steps back.

Alberic's lips tightened into a firm line, but he nodded.

I blinked at the retreating king. "Just picture myself as human? Is it really that simple?"

The king smiled, but one side of his lips curved upward sharply. "Burdening oneself is never *simple*."

Princess Rosette stepped forward to grasp the king's arm and frowned up at him. "What promise did you make to them?"

I ignored them to rear up. Holding my balance on my hind legs was no easy task, but I was able to do it just long enough to picture my body as it used to be; hand, arms, a human torso, legs, feet, a human face…

Something squeezed around me until it became a crushing force around my legs, chest, ribcage, belly, and head. It squeezed the breath from me until I couldn't make more than a pained moan. With it came a horrific weight that pushed me downward and knocked me from my feet.

Gasping for breath, I suddenly realized that rather than sprawling on the marble floor, I was being held in warm, firm arms. I opened my eyes.

Alberic held me, resting on one knee. The warmth and scent of his body were all around me, soaking into my skin. His green eyes were wide.

My heart lurched in my chest, and my cheeks warmed.

Alberic released a breath, and his lips relaxed into just the barest hint of a smile. "Welcome back."

My voice came out in a hoarse whisper, my throat stiff and

dry. "Thank you." I struggled to sit up, but my body felt stiff and unfamiliar. That's when I noticed that I was utterly naked. It shouldn't have surprised me, but I just couldn't help it. Not to mention that it was absolutely mortifying to be stared at by the hundreds of people all the way around us. I crossed my arms over my breasts, not that it did much good. That's when I noticed my hair. Instead of being the silky black waves I was used to, it was a silky *white* mane that draped across my shoulders, arms, and thighs.

To my surprise, Alberic looped his arm under my knees and stood holding me cradled against him, my long white hair draping over his arms.

The king smiled at the princess at his side. "I promised the unicorn a human form so that she might give her love to the Prince of Air."

Princess Rosette blinked again. "Oh...!" She turned to me and smiled very sweetly. "Well, then, of course they may have leave to go. One would not wish to stand in the way of true love."

True love? I opened my mouth to retort that *that* was not why I wanted my human body back.

However, before I could do so, Alberic opened his iridescent wings, a corona of light erupting around him, around us. His wings flapped once, and we rose from the floor like thistledown.

Sucking in a sharp breath, I grabbed onto Alberic's coat.

The crowd around us sighed collectively in wide-eyed awe.

His wings flapped again, and we rose higher. Another flap of his wings had us swooping toward the tall, cracked windows lining the left wall. My prince abruptly shouted. "Make way!"

The window glass closest to us exploded outward.

Alberic carried me beyond the window frame and into the

morning sky, the ground very, *very* far away.

Alberic alighted at the edge of my campsite, his wings folding neatly against his back. The light around him faded away.

My gray gelding was unsaddled and tethered to the blooming dogwood tree by the tent. He contentedly munched on the long grass growing under it. He looked over at us, then, with a switch of his black tail, went back to grazing.

I was so happy to see my tent, my gear, my personal belongings…all the things that identified me as a human, not an animal.

Was I really only gone for half a day and a night?

Rather than set me down, Alberic kicked open the flap to the tent, and hunched over to carry me inside. We fell in a tangle of limbs onto my grass-filled mattress, on top of the blankets.

On my back, I blinked up at the roof of the tent.

Alberic lay heavily on top of me, gasping for breath, his loose hair slid in a gold curtain across his back and shoulders. His legs tangled with mine, his hip pressing intimately against me. His heart thumped almost directly against mine, a warm and disturbing presence. He sighed heavily. "That was…tiring."

All too aware of our intimate positions, languid warmth, and desire began to spread in slow waves through my body. I needed to get him off me. I groaned, then shoved at him. "Are you all right?"

Alberic sighed, his breath warm against my neck. "Flying isn't something I do all that often."

I flopped back on the mattress, too tired to fight. "I didn't know you had wings."

Alberic pushed up with his arms, lifting his chest from mine, and stared down, his leaf green, only inches away. "Of course not." He looked away, his cheeks turning pink. "They're embarrassing." Casually, he began unbuttoning his frock coat.

I blinked. "But they're so pretty!"

"Of course they are." Alberic shifted to pull his sword belt off and tossed it, and the sheathed saber to the far side of the tent. "Fairy wings are always...*pretty*." He sighed, then worked the buttons of his waistcoat open. "They're also a blatant reminder that I'm not completely human."

I smiled sourly. "That makes two of us."

He raised his head, and a small smile lifted his lips. "So it does." Crossing his arms over my breasts, he set his chin on his arm, clearly making himself comfortable on me. "I had no idea that there were unicorns in my kingdom."

"Neither did I." I tried to sit up, but I couldn't get my arms under me properly to lift us both. I flopped back down on the mattress again and realized that I kind of liked his weight pressing down on mine.

Urgent heat stirred and pressed against me. Deep in my belly, interest flared hot. I stiffened. *Uh, oh...* I sucked in a sharp breath and tried to roll out from under Alberic.

He just smiled.

I looked him in the eye and frowned. "Will you get off me?"

His green eyes narrowed, and his lips curved into a tight smile. "I have a better idea." He dragged his firm and muscular body a little higher up my body. With his coat and waistcoat open, his silk shirt was all that separated his warm skin from my naked flesh.

Urgency flared white hot, and I gasped.

He lowered his head, lips parted and moist.

Time seemed to slow down while I watched in wide-eyed fascination.

His lips touched mine lightly, delicately, then his tongue swept past my parted lips.

Passion swept through me in a flood, as though straight from his mouth. Dazed, my tongue met his and stroked against him. He tasted of cool, misty moonlight and potent male.

He slanted his mouth to cover mine more fully and forayed more deeply, his tongue aggressive and hungry. With a shift of his hips, he settled between my thighs and pressed his trapped erection firmly against my unprotected cleft.

A throb of heat flared violently within my body. Dampness gathered and pooled in my lower regions. I moaned into his mouth.

His hand splayed warmly on the skin of my belly, then slid up.

I turned my head violently, breaking the kiss, and panted for breath. "I'm not so sure that this is a good idea."

His mouth made a hot, wet, shivery trail on her throat. "I think it's a *very* good idea." His warm hand covered my breast.

My nipple rose under his palm, tingling deliciously.

He circled his palm, rasping it against my sensitive flesh, then squeezed gently.

I bit down on my bottom lip to hold back a moan, but my hips lifted to push against his.

His open mouth traveled lower, licking and sucking lightly down my collarbone to the swell of my captured breast. He explored with his lips and tongue until he seized a nipple. He licked, then bit down, and sucked hard.

I gasped and my back arched.

He slid an arm under my bowed spine, around my waist to hold me against his tantalizing mouth. At the same time, his other hand slid down to work the buttons of his pants free.

It took more effort than I cared to admit to drag myself out from under the potent brew of overpowering desire and need to grab his hand. "No, really, I think we need to stop, right now."

He lifted his head to stare down at me, frustration and desire practically rolling off him in waves. He spoke in a voice deep and husky with passion. "Why? You want this as much as I do." His mouth lowered to mine.

He had a point; I wasn't exactly uninterested. Even so… I turned my head sharply. "Is this really the right time and place for this?"

His mouth skimmed my throat behind my ear, making me shiver. "I don't particularly care." He moved his fingers, opening yet another button on his pants.

I held onto his hand for dear life. "But…?"

"Julian…" He shifted his hips to slide his trapped erection directly against my exposed core.

I moaned. I just couldn't help myself.

"I can smell how wet you are, how much you want me inside you." His teeth closed on the lobe of my ear in a tender bite.

My body clenched hungrily, and a small whimper escaped. Gods above, I *did* want him.

Twenty-One

Alberic pushed up, kneeling between my spread thighs. With his half-closed gaze pinned to mine, Alberic pulled at his frock coat, tugging to get it off with near-frenzied haste. Not an easy task with the wings, even folded down. He practically ripped his waistcoat off, then yanked his shirt up over his head and tugged it free of his wings, exposing his pale, muscular body. He leaned over me to grip my wrists and pressed my hands against his chest, his gaze locked on mine.

Mesmerized, I slid my palms across his masculine nipples and felt them peak under my fingers. The scent of his skin, salty with sweat, and mouthwateringly rich, filled my nose.

The lids of his eyes lowered, and he sighed. "Yes, that's it." He leaned closer to kiss me, a brief touch of the lips. He then slid further down, leaving small, light kisses in his wake. His hand stroked along the curve of my waist to the flare of my hip, then over to cup the firm fullness of my ass. "Your body has become as pale as cream, and smooth as silk." He moved lower still, his gaze falling on the juncture of my thighs. "Hm… You've gone white there too."

I winced in mortification. "You don't need to go into detail!"

He grinned. "I happen to like the details." He lowered his head to press his lips against my feminine curls.

My flesh shuddered under his touch.

His palms pressed my legs apart and upward, then his hot, wet tongue swept against me to dance mercilessly on my damp and tender flesh. He licked and sucked every fold and crevice, then delved deeply into me.

I gasped and writhed, the waves of pleasure bringing forth uncontrollable shudders. The pulsing rise toward a swift climax made my body buck up into his mouth.

He lifted his head, releasing me, and licked his lips. "You taste like honey and fresh butter."

My cheeks heated with embarrassment, and all too physical frustration. "I didn't need to know that!"

With a sly smile, he slid back up my body and took my mouth, his tongue sweeping against mine.

I could taste the salty sweetness of myself on his tongue.

He broke the kiss to lick his lips again. "There, now you know even better."

"Gee, thanks." Even so, I licked my lips.

He smiled. "My pleasure." He leaned down to kiss me again, his lips gentle this time, his tongue gliding against mine slowly and gently. He drew my tongue into his mouth and began to suck it lightly.

Tingles cascaded deliciously through me. A moan escaped my lips. The twisting heat deep inside of my belly began to rise to something hotter, something more insistent, more desperate. My knees lifted, cradling his body against mine. My hands lifted to burrow into his golden hair, my fingers sifting through the silky strands to reach the warmth of his neck so I could pull him closer.

He moaned into my mouth and trembled. He pressed his mouth harder against mine, his tongue moving against mine strongly...hungrily. He lifted a hand to cup my breast, then broke the kiss with my lips to turn his head and kiss the taut nipple.

Erotic fire flashed straight down to the pearl at the apex of my feminine core. With a gasp, I arched up to press his mouth more firmly to me.

His mouth opened wide, and he sucked on the tight bud, his tongue lashing the sensitive flesh with enthusiasm.

I writhed under him, his weight, his *mouth*, sweet and exciting. Every tug on my nipple made something deep in my belly clench hungrily, and the pearl at the mouth of my body pulse.

His other hand slid between us. He groaned. Suddenly there was a hard, hot shaft pressing against my belly.

Despite rolling within a sensual fog of pleasure, I still knew full well that he'd drawn himself out, that it was his cock that pressed against me.

He lifted his head, freeing himself from my hands, and panting, clearly needing to catch his breath. His gaze was hooded, the pupils of his eyes wide and dark with only a slight ring of green around the midnight centers. His lips were red, plump, and wet. A string of saliva stretched to my wet nipple, then broke. He spoke in the barest of whispers. "Julian..." He looked downward and rose higher on one hand. His mouth tightened and his eyes closed with a soft groan.

Hot, rigid flesh brushed against the wet folds of my body's core.

I sucked in my breath sharply, and my heart fluttered.

He lifted his head to stare at me, his gaze still dark, his mouth and jaw tight. Then he rose over me, his knees pushing against the back of my uplifted thighs.

Firm flesh pushed into me, slowly, agonizingly slowly, making room for itself within me.

I set my heels on the mattress below us and slid my hands down his bare back, feeling the light sweat that had formed. I rocked my hips, rolling my belly, accepting the intrusion, the heat, the fullness, and the fulfillment it would bring.

Above me, he released a soft growl low in the back of his throat that bordered on a moan, his eyes closing. "If you move any more, I will lose myself right here and now."

Annoyed frustration sparked through me. I dug my nails into his back.

He winced, then grinned. "Is that impatience?"

I opened my mouth to say the one thing I thought would never come from my lips. "Shut up and fuck me."

His eyes opened wide, then he grinned broadly. "With pleasure." He lowered his head, pulled back just a little, and lunged forward and inward hard, sheathing himself completely.

I arched and gasped.

His mouth took mine aggressively, his tongue plunging in as though starving. He pulled back to thrust deeper, and harder, striking something deep inside.

A pang of pleasure went off in my belly, the sensation rippling through me like the deep knell of a temple bell. I arched and writhed to make it last.

He broke the kiss to pull back. Rolling his hips, he thrust again with greater depth and force, striking that delicious place inside me again, then again, and again...

I cried out with delight and lifted my legs to lock them around his hips, ankles crossed at the small of his back, pulling him tighter into my body, seeking more.

His hands came around me and slid down to cup my arse. Lifting me higher, he began to thrust more rapidly, increasing the tempo and power until he was slamming into me hard and fast.

My hips bucked into his thrusts in counterpoint, utterly out of my control.

The sounds of wet flesh striking wet flesh, moans, and gasps for breath filled the small tent. Lust, sweet and savory perfumed the air.

My gaze locked on the arch and flex of his body over me, moving inside me to strike that avaricious point within with frightening force.

Bright, fierce pleasure pulsed inside me, clenching and twisting tighter, and tighter. Finally, it reached the breaking point. I arched hard, rising up from the mattress of sweet grass, and gasped in a sharp breath, balancing on the edge. My nails dug into his back.

He pulled back to strike hard, and deep.

Release exploded deep within, my breath exploding out of me with a pained and rapturous cry. I shuddered and writhed, falling into a whirlpool of ecstasy, submerging under the rippling waves that flowed through me.

He choked, then released a hoarse gasp. His hands left my butt to grab onto my shoulders, pinning me to the mattress. He thrust hard, then again, then once more. Groaning deep and low, he buried his face in my shoulder then stilled. Inside me, his cock throbbed and pumped hot wetness.

He collapsed to sprawl heavily on top of me, his face beside mine, his panting breaths brushing against my shoulder, his golden hair clinging to his sweat damp back.

I worked my arms out from under his body to wrap them lightly around his shoulders, holding him against my heart while the aftershocks of our shared pleasure trembled through us both.

Alberic sighed, then rolled to the side a little, taking his weight off me. He propped himself up on one elbow and smiled lazily, his gaze heavy and dark with spent passion. "At last."

I frowned at him. "At last?"

He lifted his hand and swept a strand of damp hair from my brow, then leaned over to kiss me, a light press of the lips, a gentle sweep of the tongue.

Still drunk on passion, I returned his kiss without thought.

His green gaze locking on mine he spoke with a voice gone hoarse. "Do you have any idea how long I waited for you to come to me?"

I blinked, my mind still fogged with passing pleasure. "What are you talking about? I've been yours since childhood."

He cracked a sour smile. "Idiot... Do you have any idea how long I waited for you to be my lover?"

I frowned. "You already have lovers. Lots of them, in fact."

"But none of them were you." He leaned over me to press a quick kiss to my lips. "Only with you can I share all my secrets."

My heart gave a leap, but the rest of me was not so sanguine. "That's because you know mine, which gives you blackmail material."

He grinned broadly. "That too."

"By the way..." I folded my arms behind my head. "Any idea how we're getting home?"

Alberic sighed then dropped face-down alongside me. "I am tired unto death..." He threw an arm over me. "Sleep first. We can worry about getting home, later."

More than a little alarmed, I pushed to sit up. "You have no idea how we're getting home, do you?"

Alberic shoved me back down onto the mattress with his arm. "Do not worry. I will think of something."

I stared up at the ceiling of my tent. I wanted to insist that he find a way to get us home right then, but truthfully, I was dead tired, too. I threw an arm over my eyes and sighed.

"Are you sure doing it *that* way is a good idea?" Standing at the wooded edge of the palace gardens, surrounded by blooming tulips while in my plain gray leather traveling coat, black leather waistcoat, and gray leather breeches, I was well aware that I did not suit my surroundings. Even so, I eyed the newly crowned king with deep suspicion and tapped my black felt tricorn hat against my knee. "I have to cross an ocean, you know?"

Dressed rather casually in a lavender brocade frockcoat lavishly embroidered with white silk and a snowy white waistcoat, the king smiled. "I assure you, I have a fast ship at my disposal to carry the rest of your belongings, although it will be three weeks before they arrive. It's the least I can do for your assistance."

My prince, resplendent in an eggshell blue damask frockcoat and matching waistcoat, both heavily embroidered with gold thread, nodded firmly. "I accept."

"You *accept?*" Wide-eyed, I looked at my prince. "But this is across an *ocean!*"

The king sighed and combed his fingers through the fall of his snowy white curls. "Fawn, it does not matter what landscape exists here because the white forest is elsewhere." He tilted his head and looked away. "Or rather, else-*when.*" He shook his head, then stepped forward to set his hands on my shoulders. "All you need do is focus on your home and *run* until you arrive."

That sunset, I was back in my unicorn body with a saddle and saddlebags strapped to me. I looked over at my prince, my ears laid back. "The cinch is too tight!" It felt like it was squeezing me in half.

"The cinch is exactly as tight as it should be." Alberic stuck his foot in the stirrup and threw his leg over, to seat himself on my back. "Be glad I did not insist on a bridle too."

I snaked my head around on my long neck to bare my equine teeth at him. "If you even *attempt* to put a bridle on me, you will be taking the ship home with our trunks!"

Alberic folded his arms across his chest. "You are rather willful in this form."

The king chuckled and moved close to Alberic's side. "That's only to be expected. The fawn is royalty, after all."

Alberic turned sharply to stare at the king. "What did you say?"

The king smiled. "You didn't know? Our kind ruled this world long before any human stepped foot in it." He stepped away to stand by my head. "Do not forget, you are a creature of winter and shadow. Ice and snow are the heart of your power. Your power—*you*—will be weakest during the summer months, especially when the sun is high. Guard yourself during such times."

"Ice and snow?" My ears turned forward in alarm. "Are you serious?"

The king smiled sourly. "How else did you think the white forest came to be white?" He stepped back and frowned at Alberic. "Do not forget, Prince of Air, that you must not leave the saddle in the white forest, else you will fall into a sleep you will never awaken from."

Alberic's brows lifted. "White forest...?"

The king frowned sternly. "Yes. The white forest is especially dangerous for you, Prince of Air, as you are a creature of summer and light."

That did *not* sound good at all. I sidestepped nervously. "Maybe we should just take the ship?"

Alberic gripped my mane and dug his heels into my sides. "Absolutely not! I have a tinker to find. I will *not* have curses being sold in my kingdom!"

The king smiled. "Travel swiftly!" He swatted my butt

234

with the palm of his hand.

It actually stung. I leaped into the trees. I spotted the edge of the shadow forest and leaped into it. *Home… Home… I want to go home!* A few bounds later, the shadowy trunks of the trees turned white, with mist curling up from the unseen ground, the leaves overhead tinkling like crystal.

In my saddle, Alberic gasped. "Mother of All, it's cold!"

Cold? I didn't feel cold at all. In fact, I felt refreshed.

Alberic leaned over my neck, his gloved hands tucked under his arms. "Hurry! Before I freeze."

"Do you need me to stop so you can get a blanket from the saddlebags?"

Alberic shook his head. "No, no, just keep going."

I hurried, galloping as fast as my legs would allow.

After an eternity of running through the twilight-tinted forest of white, the white forest ended without warning.

One moment, I was bolting under crystal trees, and the next, I was moving through a forest made of shadows. I slowed to an easy canter, not sure when or where I should leave the shadow forest.

Alberic sucked in a deep breath. "Finally it's warm again." He shivered hard. "How you can bear it?"

I tilted an ear back toward Alberic. "It doesn't feel cold to me."

Alberic frowned. "Not at all?"

"No, not at all."

The scent of something…familiar floated on the wind.

I lifted my head and cantered toward the scent. The shadows abruptly melted into actually trees and bushes that had clearly once been carefully groomed. However, no gardener had tended to them in quite a long time. Grass as tall as my knees hid any walkways that might have existed. Wildflowers bloomed everywhere with abandon.

"This looks like a garden." One very overgrown, possibly

even utterly forgotten. I spotted the remains of a fountain and realized that it looked familiar.

Alberic stiffened. "Stop!"

I came to a halt. "Do you know where we are?"

Alberic dropped out of the saddle. "We are on the palace grounds."

We're home? I turned my head to look at him. "Are you sure?"

"Yes. I recognize that fountain." Alberic pulled off the saddlebags and tugged the cinch loose on the saddle. "You'd better return to your human form before one of the guards sees us." He pulled the saddle from my back.

I reared up and clothed myself in human skin. It tightened mercilessly around me, rendering me far smaller than my unicorn body, and knocking the breath from me. I groaned under the weight of being human but didn't quite collapse. I staggered to the saddlebags to pull out my clothes and began to get dressed.

Alberic sat on the rim of the disused fountain. "Hurry it up, peon, I want a bath, and to sleep among my own sheets before my royal father knows that I've returned." He looked away. "I still have yet to come up with what story to tell him."

"Yes, my prince." I dragged my clothes on with as much haste as possible. When finally dressed, I lifted the saddlebags to my shoulder, then reached for the heavy saddle.

"Leave the saddle. Get one of the stable hands to fetch it." Alberic rose from his seat on the edge of the fountain. "Let's go, peon. We have an appointment with my bath and my bed."

I stiffened. "We…?"

Alberic turned with a narrow-eyed smile. "Of course. Did you think I'd allow you to go back to sleeping in that closet?" He turned away and strode for the palace, hidden behind the overgrown trees. "Ah…! I can tell already that life is about to get far more interesting!"

I rolled my eyes. "And mine...far more complicated." I hurried after him.

About the Author

"For me, writing is more than a passion, it's an *obsession*."

Morgan Hawke has been writing erotic fiction since 1998. She has lived in seven states of the US and spent two years in England. She has been an auto mechanic, a security guard, a waitress, a groom in a horse stable, in the military, a copywriter, a magazine editor, a professional tarot reader, a belly dancer, and a stripper. Her personal area of expertise is the strange and unusual.

Ms. Hawke maintains a close and personal relationship with her computer and her cat.